PATRICIA H. RUSHFORD
HARRISON JAMES

SHE WHO WATCHES

INTEGRITY®
PUBLISHERS
Nashville

SHE WHO WATCHES

Published by Integrity Publishers, a division of Integrity Media, Inc.,
5250 Virginia Way, Suite 110, Brentwood, TN 37027.

HELPING PEOPLE WORLDWIDE EXPERIENCE *the* MANIFEST PRESENCE
of GOD.

Published in association with the literary agency of Alive Communications,
Inc., 7680 Goddard Street, Suite 200, Colorado Springs, CO 80920.

Cover Design: www.brandnavigation.com
Interior Design: Inside Out Design & Typesetting

ISBN 13: 978-1-5914-5437-3
ISBN 10: 1-59145-437-9

Details about *She Who Watches* obtained from the following sources:

Emory Strong, *Stone Age on the Columbia River* (Portland, Ore.: Binford &
Mort, 1959).
Jim Attwell, *Tahmahnaw: The Bridge of the Gods* (Chicago: Adams, 1973).

Printed in the United States of America
06 07 08 09 10 CHG 9 8 7 6 5 4 3 2 1

To the life and memory of a little girl with a big heart,
Marissa Kathleen Warstler,
called home by the Lord to help him take care of his horses.
To my loving parents, Joe and Deanna, and little sister Melissa—
I love you all.

HARRISON JAMES

To Miss Madelyn Marie, my first great-grandchild.
To my family, especially my husband Ron, who continues to
believe in and support my writing career.

PATRICIA H. RUSHFORD

And to our Lord and Savior, Jesus Christ, who leads and directs
and is with us always.

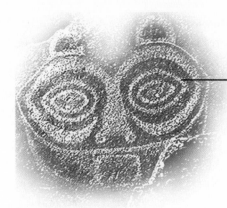

ONE

Sara Watson rushed out the door of her southwest Portland ad agency, expertly exchanging her high-heeled dress shoes for a pair of more comfortable slip-ons for the drive home. She had just enough time to run a couple of errands and pick up some groceries for this weekend's get-together before going to the day-care provider to pick up her toddler, Chloe.

Her cousin Claire, and Claire's ten-year-old daughter, Allysa, were finally coming down from Seattle for a long-awaited and much-anticipated visit. But company, no matter how welcome, cut deeply into Sara's already-packed schedule.

She stuffed the heels into her shoulder bag and fished around in the deep pockets for her car keys. Finding them, she unlocked the doors of her Audi coupe before removing the remote from her purse.

The car chirped its familiar signal. Sara rounded the back of the car, throwing her large bag in the trunk before approaching the driver's side. She stopped midstride when she noticed the broken driver side window. The glass had been shattered, leaving broken safety glass on the parking garage floor and the car's interior.

"Oh, no." Her shoulders drooped in exasperation. Her annoyance turned to concern as she realized the intruder might still be in the area. She dug around in her purse for the mace canister but couldn't find it.

"Great. That's just great." She rolled her eyes when she remembered she had left it at home after her early morning jog. Fortunately, she appeared to be alone in the parking structure. She should probably call the police, but that would take time—time she didn't have. Instead, she pulled out her cell phone and dialed her husband's office.

"Watson, Simons, and Keller, this is Jackie." The receptionist gave her usual perky greeting.

"Hi, Jackie, this is Sara."

"Oh, hi, Sara. How goes it?"

"Been better; my car was broken into at work."

"You're kidding."

"I wish. Is Scott around?"

"He is, but he's in a really important meeting with the finance group on the brewery remodel. I hate to interrupt him, but if you really need him . . ."

"Shoot." Sara sighed. Her husband's engineering firm was designing a multimillion-dollar renovation of an old brewery in downtown Portland into upscale condominiums. He'd be furious if she broke up the meeting for something like this. Something she really should be able to take care of herself. Sara looked around the parking lot again, then at her car.

"You want me to page him out of the meeting?" Jackie asked.

"No, don't do that, Jacks. I'm OK, and it looks like whoever did it is long gone." She peeked in through the window. "Except for the broken window, everything looks intact. They didn't take the radio or CD player. Just have Scott call my cell when he gets out of the meeting."

"Will do. Is there anything I can do for you?"

"No, thanks. I'm OK, just a little flustered. These things always seem to happen when you're up to your eyeballs in stuff to do. I still have some shopping to do, but I'll be fine. Thanks for delivering the message."

Sara snapped her phone shut and opened the passenger side door. She thought again about calling the police, but that would keep her here for another hour or two at best. And what good would reporting the vandalism do at this point? The odds of the police finding the culprit were less than the chances of winning the lottery.

After taking one more look around the parking lot, Sara leaned into the car and carefully brushed the glass chips off the passenger seat. Once the seat was clear, she climbed inside and checked the center console and the glove box to see if the thief had taken anything. The change they stashed for parking meters and such was still in the console, along with her expensive sunglasses and even an old cell phone that didn't work anymore—though the thief wouldn't know that. The remote for the garage was missing. Sara envisioned the thief gaining easy entry into their home. She sighed in relief when she realized it wasn't missing after all. She'd given it to Scott to replace the batteries over a week ago.

Sara pulled the owner's manual from the glove box. The plastic sleeve in which she kept her insurance card and car registration had been ripped off. Scott's emergency cash envelope, which contained one hundred dollars, and the roadside hazard card were missing as well. "Wonderful." The fear of identity theft crossed Sara's mind. She'd recently heard about thieves breaking into cars and houses to steal names and Social Security numbers.

In lieu of running errands, Sara opted to go straight home so she could notify the banks and credit bureaus, as well as the insurance company. On her way out of the parking structure, she dialed her day-care provider to let Lindsay know she'd be picking up Chloe at three. That gave her an hour to take care of this unexpected and unwelcome diversion.

As she aimed her car toward home, her mind churned with items on her to-do list. "Why now?" she whined. With the weekend coming, she had meals to make and a house to clean. Heaving a resigned sigh, she muttered, "Sorry, Lord. I know I shouldn't complain, but . . . Just help me get through this, OK?" She could be thankful for one thing: her car was drivable.

Sara turned down Salmonberry Road and into the Everwood Estates, where she and Scott had lived for only a year in their dream house. It had been built in the early 1900s, but they had completely remodeled it. After a few turns she reached Spruce Circle, a four-house cul-de-sac, and then headed down their wooded drive. Sara pulled into their circle driveway and stopped at the front door. She didn't plan on staying long, just long enough to get phone numbers and make some calls. Once she'd done that, she'd pick up Chloe and run her errands. Chloe would love that—she'd inherited the shopping gene from Sara and her mother and her mother before that. The thought made her smile and made the task at hand seem less formidable.

Sara ran upstairs and into the office she and Scott shared, and she yanked open the oak file cabinet. "Where are you?" she muttered as she fingered each of the tabs. "Here we go." She pulled a manila envelope out of a hanging folder and opened the file to make sure it held all her financial information.

Better cancel the Visa, MasterCard, American Express . . . what else? Sara tried to remember if there was, in fact, an emergency credit card with her roadside assistance membership. She decided to cancel all the cards to be on the safe side and have new plastic issued, leaving only her debit card valid to hold her over.

A master at multitasking, Sara picked up the cordless phone on the desk to dial the number for Visa while looking for the AAA file. No dial tone.

"Oh, Scott, not now, please." Sara jogged downstairs and into the kitchen. She must have told Scott a hundred times to put the phone back on the charger. She stopped ranting when she noticed the green light, indicating the phone was still charged. Sara glanced at the kitchen base unit, then at the empty wall plug. Someone had unplugged it, and the cord was nowhere in sight.

The hair on the back of her neck rose, and goose bumps shivered through her. Her mind conjured up a million scenarios, and none of them sounded good. Had the person who'd broken into her car broken into her house as well? They wouldn't have had to break in, she realized—she hadn't taken time to lock the front door.

A snap broke the silence. Fear tore through her. Sara instinctively reached for the small canister of mace she'd set on the counter after her run. Her hand struck it as the intruder whipped the phone cord over her head and pulled it tight around her neck. She heard the canister of mace roll off the counter and onto the floor.

The ligature tightened, turning her scream into a pathetic mew. Sara clawed at the cord and tried to pull away from her attacker. As she did, she caught sight of the man in the black microwave door but couldn't make out his features. He was big and strong, with a wide face and long, dark hair. She reached back and captured a handful of his hair. He pushed her to the unforgiving tile and drove a knee into her back.

Sara gasped for air, her open mouth frozen in desperation. She twisted, trying desperately to free herself and dig her fingers under the phone cord. *Oh God, help. Please help me.*

Sara glanced up to see the pictures of little Chloe and Scott on the refrigerator door. Chloe's handprints on a homemade Mother's Day card brought a cry of anguish. The thought of her baby growing up without her was as terrifying as death. She couldn't die. She just couldn't.

With her last bit of strength, Sara twisted to her left as she reached across her chest with her right hand to scratch her attacker's face. The man grimaced in pain and swore. He grabbed for his face with one hand, releasing the cord.

Sara broke away, scrambled to her feet, and ran for the door. Her attacker growled like some kind of wild animal. If she could make it to the door and get outside, she'd be safe. Maybe she could outrun him. He grabbed for her arm, and she jerked it away; but the movement caused her to stumble on the stair in the entry. Before she could right herself, he tackled her, grinding her face into the tile.

Fear had turned to anger, and Sara twisted around to face a man intent on killing her. Her strength was no match for his, but Sara Watson had no intention of making it easy for him.

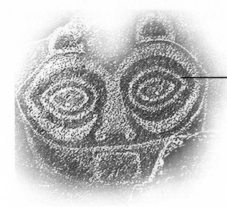

TWO

At 4:00 p.m., Claire Montgomery pulled her green Pontiac Bonneville into her cousin's driveway and pulled up behind Sara's Audi. "Looks like she's home." Claire tossed a smile at her ten-year-old daughter.

"Good. I hope Chloe's there." Allysa unbuckled her seat belt, stepped out of the car, and headed for the front door. "Look, Mom. The window in Sara's car is busted."

Claire had already seen it. "I wonder what happened?"

"We could ask." Allysa grinned, revealing a set of braces.

"Smarty." Claire pulled Allysa into a hug, planted a kiss on the top of her head, and ruffled her red hair.

Claire rang the bell several times, but no one answered. She peered through the glass panel.

"Maybe she's taking a shower." Allysa leaned forward and tried the door. It opened easily, and she moved forward with it.

Claire wasn't sure why, but she pulled Allysa back tight against her. Something wasn't right. The broken window on Sara's car, the front door unlocked and no one answering. Maybe Sara was taking a shower, but Claire doubted that. The Sara she knew would be ready and waiting for them. The coffee would be brewed and cookies or some decadent dessert set out on a plate.

"You're hurting my shoulders, Mom." Allysa tried to wriggle out of Claire's grasp.

"I'm sorry." She loosened her hold slightly but kept a firm grip.

"What's wrong?"

"I don't know." She turned Allysa to face her. "It's probably nothing, but I need you to wait in the car. OK?"

"Why?"

"Just stay in the car. I'll be right back." Claire watched her daughter reluctantly climb back into the car, and then she slowly turned and went inside. Leaving the door open, she called out, "Sara? Sara, are you here? Scott?"

The only response was an unnatural quiet. She moved ahead a few more steps and noticed several items lying on the kitchen floor. Pictures of Scott and Chloe, some refrigerator magnets, car keys, a canister of mace, and a phone. Fear coursed through her. Sara would never leave stuff lying around like that.

Stop it. Claire told herself in no uncertain terms that the mess was not an indication of foul play. A toddler in the house meant messes like this one. *The pictures, maybe, but not the phone.*

Being an avid *CSI* fan, her thoughts fled into scenarios she didn't want to consider. She knew better than to touch anything, but maybe she should have a look around in case Sara was hurt or . . . *Don't go there, Claire.* Wanting to give herself a fighting chance if she did encounter someone, Claire took a butcher knife out of the knife drawer and held it at the ready.

The walk-through was quick, with the main floor consisting of a tiled entry, kitchen, living room, laundry, guest room, and bathroom. Upstairs took a few minutes, as she checked the office, two bedrooms, bath, and the master suite. Everything was neat and clean, even the baby's room. Not touching the banister, Claire hurried downstairs. From her vantage point, she discovered the most damaging evidence so far. The tall vase in the entry, partially hidden by the front door, had been knocked over. Fragments of pottery and dry flowers littered the tile floor. Claire put the knife away, then carefully pulled the front door closed and hurried to her car.

"Isn't Sara home?" Allysa shifted in her seat.

"I don't think so."

"Where is she? I want to see Chloe. Sara said she'd be here when we came."

"I know. Maybe she's running late." Claire knew differently, but she couldn't bring herself to say it.

"What about her car?"

"Maybe she's using Scott's or a neighbor's. Maybe Grandy came to get her." Grandy was Allysa's nickname for her grandmother—Claire's mother and Sara's aunt.

Claire reached into the backseat for her purse and rooted around for her cell phone. "I'll call Sara's cell." She let it ring several times. When she didn't get an answer, Claire called information for Scott's work number.

"Watson, Simons, and Keller, this is Jackie," the receptionist answered.

"Jackie, this is Sara's cousin Claire. I'm at the house, but no one seems to be home. Is Scott there?"

"He isn't, but he should be home soon. He was going to pick up Chloe on his way. Sara was supposed to get her by three, but the day care called a few minutes ago to say she hadn't shown up."

Claire sighed. "OK. I'll wait here for him."

"Is everything all right?" Jackie asked.

"I'm not sure. Sara's car is here, and the window is broken."

"Oh, right. She called earlier to say it had been broken into at the garage where she parks. I offered to get Scott out of his meeting, but she insisted she could handle it herself." Jackie hesitated. "You don't suppose whoever broke into her car followed her home, do you? I've heard about stuff like that happening."

"I hope not." Claire managed to breathe through her tightening throat. "I went through the house, and she's not here."

"Good. That means she probably borrowed a car or maybe rented one so she could run her errands. She said she had to go shopping."

"But wasn't she supposed to pick up Chloe at three?"

"Look, Scott should be there in a few minutes. Maybe he'll have talked to her."

"Right."

"Claire, please call me when you learn anything. You have me worried. I'll never forgive myself if something has happened to her. I should have gotten Scott out of that meeting."

"I'll let you know. And don't blame yourself. Sounds like it was Sara's choice. Besides, it's too soon to panic."

While she waited, Claire called her parents, thinking Sara might have contacted them. "Dad." Claire released a long sigh and then told him about Sara. "I was hoping she'd talked to you or Mom."

"Hang on a second." Claire could hear him talking to her mom before answering. "Neither of us has heard from her. Have you talked to Scott?"

"He's on his way home now."

"Your mother and I will be there shortly. We were coming for dinner anyway; we'll just come early. And Claire, maybe you should call the police."

"It's too soon for that, isn't it? I'll see what Scott says."

"OK, but don't wait too long. There have been some threats against me, and—"

"Threats? What kind of threats?" Claire interrupted.

"It's a political thing. We'll talk more about that when we get there." Her father, known to his constituents as Senator Dale Wilde, hung up, leaving Claire feeling even more certain that something terrible had happened to her cousin.

Scott pulled in a few minutes later and used the remote to open the garage, waving to her as he drove in. Claire told Allysa to stay put and hurried into the garage behind him. "Please tell me you know where Sara is."

Scott climbed out of the car, looking none too pleased. "I have no idea. She was supposed to be here waiting for you. I haven't talked to her since this morning."

"Jackie said her car had been broken into."

"I didn't know about that until a few minutes ago." He ran a hand through his dark, wavy hair. "I've been in meetings all day."

Claire reached out for a hug, and Scott hugged her back. "It's good to see you, Claire."

"You too." She backed away.

"I don't understand this," Scott said as he shut the car door. "It isn't like Sara to just not show up."

"I know. I'm worried that something has happened to her. The front door was unlocked, and I checked through the house. She's not there, but I saw some things lying on the kitchen floor. I called Dad, but neither he nor Mom has heard from her. He said something about getting some threats against the family and thought we should call the police."

Scott groaned and drew his hand down his face. "Let's go inside." He rounded the car and pulled open the backseat to free Chloe from her car seat.

Claire hadn't seen the baby for six months, and the changes were phenomenal. Chloe stared at her, pressing back into her father's protective arms.

When he walked into the kitchen Scott pulled his cell phone out of his jacket pocket and dialed 911. Once he'd given the operator the information, Scott looked around at the items on the floor. "There's no way Sara would have done this. Someone was here." He pointed at the phone jack in the kitchen. "The phone is unplugged." His Adam's apple rose and fell as his dark eyes filled with fear.

"I'll get Allysa," Claire said. As she hurried back to the car she hollered over her shoulder, "I didn't touch anything just in case."

"Right."

Claire hurried back into the house. Scott hadn't moved; he just stood there, with the child in his arms, staring at the clutter on the kitchen floor. He avoided walking into the kitchen and joined Claire and Allysa in the family room. Chloe pointed toward Allysa, leaning forward to let her dad know she wanted down.

Scott set her down, his features drawn.

"Allysa," Claire said, "why don't you take Chloe up to her room and play with her?"

"Sure." Allysa held out her arms. "Come on, Chloe."

"Issa . . ." Chloe made a beeline for her older cousin.

"Scott." Claire searched for the right words. "It may be nothing. . . ."

He nodded. "I hope you're right."

"Jackie said Sara's car had been broken into. Maybe she called the police and had someone take her to the station."

He brightened then, but only for a moment. "She would have called the day care to let them know she'd be late." Still, he punched a number into the cell phone. "I'll call around—see if anyone's seen her."

THREE

"Y ou ready for tonight, Sarge?" Detective Mac (Antonio) McAllister asked when the aging sergeant, Frank Evans, strode into the detectives' office.

"Ready as I'll ever be." Frank glanced briefly into Mac's cubicle and continued walking on autopilot to his corner office—or what had been his office for the past two decades. Sergeant Frank Evans had worked the detective unit at the State Police office in Portland for nearly thirty years, having passed the retirement-eligible date years before. If it were up to Frank, he'd have stayed on many more years, but the public employee retirement system had undergone some reform earlier in the year, and he would have to retire by September 1 or start losing money on his investments.

In a way, Mac hated to see Sergeant Evans go. He was sad for Frank's somewhat forced retirement, but he also felt elated that his former partner, Kevin Bledsoe, would be taking the reins. Kevin was just as experienced an investigator as Frank, and very well qualified, but a little less intense. In fact, having been in the department for twenty-some years, Kevin Bledsoe was the perfect man for the job.

"You guys better not be doing anything to embarrass me tonight." Sergeant Evans directed his admonition to all of the detectives, but he looked at one in particular—Phil Johnson.

"Sorry, Sarge, no promises tonight," Dana Bennett, Mac's new partner, answered, grinning as she took a sip of her Starbucks iced coffee.

Detective Johnson, better known as Philly, stepped out of his office with an even bigger grin on his face.

"Philly," Frank said, "for old times' sake, just let me get my badge and plaque and be on my way. Don't do anything to embarrass me. My mother and both my kids will be there." The request seemed more like a plea than a threat. With his retirement party mere hours away, he had lost control of his troops and knew in all likelihood that Philly would do what Philly wanted—roast him unmercifully.

"Don't worry, Sarge." Kevin stepped out of his new office. "I'll make sure he does exactly what I tell him to."

Mac nearly choked on his coffee at the comment. No one told Philly what to do. While Mac didn't always agree with Philly's tactics, he had a deep respect for the man. Philly was a top-notch detective and a solid friend. When Kevin lost his hair to the chemo treatments, Philly had shaved his head to commiserate. The hair had grown back about an inch during the past few months, trimmed up around his ears and the back.

Philly approached the older man, his ample belly stretching the front buttons on his dress shirt. "I'm deeply hurt that you'd think me capable of causing you any embarrassment, Sergeant Evans." He placed his thick hands on the sergeant's shoulders and stood eye to eye with him. "Frank—I can call you Frank now, can't I?" The gleam in Philly's eyes told of the mischievous thoughts behind them. "Don't worry your pretty little head, my friend. I'm not going to let any of the dirt out of the bag in front of your family and friends. I promise." Philly pulled his left hand from behind his back to expose crossed fingers. He winked at Kevin and laughed. "This is going to be a fun night."

Sarge shook his head. "Don't forget, I'll still be around when you retire, Phil. And I bet I have a lot more dirt on you than you have on me."

Philly didn't seem the least bit intimidated.

"I can't believe I even invited you, Phil," Frank teased as he walked away.

Mac had been around these guys long enough to know that Frank wouldn't have it any other way. Even though Philly had been the office jokester for years, Frank trusted him with his life and considered him one of his closest friends. Frank knew full well that Philly would have it in for him tonight, but roasts were par for the course at police retirement parties. Mac could hardly wait. This would be his first retirement party as a homicide detective.

Frank and Kevin went back into Frank's old office and closed the door. Mac suspected that Sergeant Evans wanted to give Kevin some last-minute instructions before completely letting the reins go. Considering that Kevin had recently come out of surgery and chemo for prostate cancer, Frank had hung around longer than necessary, making sure Kevin could handle the load.

So far, Kevin was doing great. The bout with cancer surgery and chemo had left him bald, thin, and far weaker than he'd ever been, but none of those things seemed to affect his ability to lead.

"What are you wearing tonight?" Russ asked Philly. Russ was Philly's partner and his biggest fan.

"A thong and tube top. Why?" Philly answered, his features serious.

Russ looked embarrassed. "I was just curious. I haven't been to a fancy retirement party since I moved up here."

"If the Elks Club is your idea of a fancy retirement place . . ." Philly nudged Russ's shoulder and shook his head. "No wonder you're single! That, and the fact you ask other men what they're going to wear. I worry about you sometimes, Russ." Philly ducked into his office and shut the door.

"The invitation said 'casual,' Russ," Dana said, coming to his aid. "Slacks and a nice shirt will be fine."

"I'm wearing Dockers and a button-up shirt without a tie," Mac told him.

Dana offered Russ a smile. "You don't want Philly's advice on clothes. He'll be wearing something with high polyester content, so you wouldn't want to dress like him anyway."

Russ chuckled. "Thanks, guys. Nice to talk to someone normal for a change." Russell Meyers was a seven-year cop with four years as a detective, having transferred out of L.A. He was a nice-looking guy with brown hair and hazel eyes. He and Philly made a good pair, but Mac felt sorry for the guy. Philly's practical jokes could get a little tedious.

"Hey, I have a question for you guys. What are you going to call Kevin—I mean, his first name or sergeant? I've never had to work for someone who was promoted from my own peer group. I don't want to offend him either way."

"Good question," Mac said. "I've wondered the same thing. I think we better stick to Sergeant Bledsoe, at least when the brass is around. Sarge or Kevin is good for other times. I guess he'll let us know if he doesn't want us to use his first name. I've seen supervisors go both ways, so we'll wait and see."

"Well . . ." Russ cleared his throat. "I've got court in Clackamas County on a suppression hearing, so I'll see you guys down at the Milwaukie Elks tonight. Six thirty, right?"

"Right on. See you there." Mac pushed himself away from the wall and returned to his cubicle and mountain of work.

Shortly after Frank left, Kevin stepped out of his new office. "Mac, Dana!"

"Yeah, boss?" Mac eagerly looked up from the paperwork. "You got an assignment for us?"

"I do." Kevin stepped into Mac's cubicle.

"What's up?" Dana hustled into the small space still holding the iced Starbucks coffee Mac had brought her. He was buying her coffee for a month because of another stupid bet he'd lost with her. This made the second bet so far this year that he had lost to Dana, dipping into his pockets to buy her coffee for a month. But luck was bound to be on his side soon, Mac reasoned, eyeing the Starbucks logo on Dana's cup. Next time, he'd win the bet for sure.

"Come on into my office." The two younger detectives followed, and for a brief moment, Mac allowed himself a modicum of admiration for his partner. Dana Bennett was cute, blonde, shapely, and entirely off-limits. She was also a darn good cop, and he was lucky to have her for a partner. Not only that, she could outrun him, which was something he intended to rectify. He and Dana sat in the two chairs in front of Kevin's desk.

"We have a request from the governor's office to work a missing persons—a possible kidnapping case—with the FBI, and you two bought the ticket."

"I don't understand." Dana frowned. "I didn't think we did missing persons."

"Normally we let the FBI handle them, but this is a special case. Senator Wilde's niece, Sara Watson, is missing."

"And we do what?" Mac asked, his attention now solely on his boss. "The feds aren't going to like our coming in to investigate."

"They'll be the lead investigators. You and Dana will act as liaisons between the two agencies."

Mac didn't like the idea of playing politics but didn't voice his objection. He and Dana were the two newest detectives in the

Violent Offender Unit in the Oregon State Police, Portland office. It figured that they'd get stuck baby-sitting the feds.

"I know it doesn't sound like a plum job, but it's important." Kevin fingered the crease in his slacks. "You in?"

"Sure." Dana grinned, showing off her perfect teeth and deep dimples. "Sounds interesting, actually. I've never been in on a missing persons case."

Leave it to Dana to put a positive spin on things. "I'm in," Mac agreed, knowing Kevin had only asked as a formality. In a way, though, he had to admit, a missing persons case might be interesting, especially one as high profile as this one would be. "Senator Wilde's niece, huh?"

"Right. Her father was the senator's brother. He and his wife died years ago, and the senator and his wife practically raised her. She's married now and has a family of her own, but they are still close."

"She campaigned for the senator in the last election, Mac." Dana jotted some notes on her pad. "You probably saw her on television."

"The FBI agents are at the house, so you'll want to head out there right away." Kevin handed Mac a file. "This is all we have so far. Her cousin had plans to stay with the family for a few days. She found Sara's car in the driveway with a window busted out and the front door unlocked—nobody home. A mess on the kitchen floor. Husband was at work until the day-care provider called to tell him their little girl hadn't been picked up. Guess this is way out of character for Sara. One of our uniforms responded about an hour ago. Our CSI crew has been dispatched."

"OK, then." Mac stood up and snatched his jacket from the back of his chair.

"You ready, partner?"

"As soon as I get my briefcase." She stepped out of the office and leaned back in. "By the way, Kevin, um, I mean, Sarge. With you moving in here, who gets your old office?"

"You want it?"

"Yeah."

"It's yours."

"Wow. Thanks."

Mac frowned. "I thought it was a seniority thing." He wanted the office himself but thought it would go to Russ.

"Nope." Kevin chuckled. "Goes to whoever gets there first."

Dana stepped into the near-empty office and plunked her coffee cup on the desk. "I'm staking out my territory."

"Humph," Mac grumbled. "That's what I get for being a gentleman."

"You two can fight over the office later. Now git."

Mac put aside his annoyance with Dana for stealing the prized office space out from under him and grabbed his briefcase.

"You'll need to stay on the sidelines on this, kids." Kevin gave each of them a nod. "Just make sure you get all the details and keep abreast of the case. Be there if the feds need your assistance, and if you have any questions, call me."

"Not to worry, partner . . . er . . . Sarge," Mac assured him. Kevin was still getting used to his new job and tended to overstate his instructions.

Dana signed them out on the board near the door at 5:15 p.m., and the two detectives headed out.

"You want to drive, or should I?" Mac asked as they reached the parking lot.

"Go ahead. Your car is closest." Dana aimed for Mac's unmarked Crown Victoria.

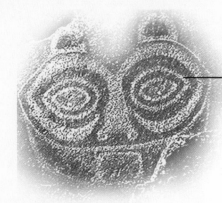

FOUR

While they drove, Dana read the preliminary report, restating Kevin's comments about the cousin's coming in from Seattle and the husband's coming home early and finding signs of a break-in and his wife missing.

Mac raised an eyebrow, wondering if the husband might somehow be involved in his wife's disappearance. It wouldn't be the first time. "Kevin said the husband was at work when the day care called. We'll have to verify that. What time did he call 911?"

"About four fifteen."

"No kidding. How'd the feds get involved that fast? Us, too, for that matter."

"I have no idea. According to this report, Sara had called him around two to let him know her car had been broken into."

"Hmm. That explains the broken window the cousin found."

"Right. He was in a meeting at that time, and Sara told his secretary not to bother him. He left work as soon as he got that message and the one from their day care. Sara was supposed to pick up their little girl at three, but she never showed up. The responding officers suspect kidnapping, but there hasn't been any contact regarding a ransom."

"Wonder how they determined kidnapping? Maybe the feds will have more information." Mac made a right and started up a steep hill.

The Watsons lived in a nice neighborhood in northwest Portland near the University of Portland, in an older but roomy Victorian-style home. The hills afforded lovely views, but the homes were too close together to suit Mac. There were a number of vehicles parked on the street, including two cruisers, a van from the OSP crime lab, a minivan, a green Pontiac, and a BMW convertible. They pulled into the wide circle driveway and stepped out. If he were buying a home, it would have to come with either an oversized yard or acreage.

"The two suits by the car in front of the door must be the FBI agents." Mac adjusted his tie and grabbed his suit jacket from the backseat.

"Must be." Dana looked apprehensive.

"Are you nervous?" Mac asked.

"A little. I haven't worked with the feds before." Dana straightened and grinned.

He didn't say so, but that dimpled smile of hers would have those guys melting all over her within minutes. "I haven't worked with them directly, but from what I hear, we're in for a treat."

"That doesn't sound like a compliment."

"Sorry. I've heard they can be a pain." Mac tried to rein in his preconceived notions about the feds. A lot of the guys he worked with had nothing good to say about them, but he needed to keep an open mind, especially if he was going to do the job Kevin expected of them. He and Dana showed their badges to the uniformed officer outside the crime scene, signed the sheet on his clipboard, and slipped under the crime-scene tape.

Dana opened her notebook, noting the time and weather conditions. *Warm evening, fading light, FBI and OSP crime lab on scene.*

"What do you make of it?" One of the two men in suits asked as he fingered some hard, white fragments on the floorboard of the car.

The second man leaned into the Audi. "Looks like some kind of shell or something."

"Probably a busted spark plug," Mac offered.

"A what?" The second guy, a heavyset man with a paunch, whipped around to face him.

"It's a piece of an automotive spark plug," Mac repeated as he pulled on his latex gloves.

Both men stepped away from the car, eyeing Mac and Dana as if they were onlookers rather than official investigators. Mac and Dana produced their badge wallets, displaying their credentials. Then with his hand extended, Mac said, "Detective McAllister with the Oregon State Police. This is my partner, Dana Bennett."

"I'm Agent Jim Miller." Miller, a well-proportioned man with a receding hairline, shook Mac's hand, then Dana's, and nodded to the larger man. "This is Agent Mel Lauden."

Once the introductions were made, Agent Miller cast a dubious eye on the two detectives. "What's the deal? You two with the crime lab or something?"

"Not the lab," Mac explained. "But we are OSP. We're assigned to the Violent Offender Unit out of our Portland office. We were dispatched at the request of the governor's office to act as a liaison between our agencies."

"I don't remember requesting OSP involvement, other than the crime lab. Ms. Watson is apparently a missing person, and so far there's every indication this is a kidnap investigation. You know that falls under our jurisdiction, not yours or the Portland Police Bureau."

"We are well aware of your authority," Mac said, annoyed by Miller's arrogance. "But we need to make you aware of some political ties that Ms. Watson has to a member of our state government. Sara is Senator Dale Wilde's niece. She's the only daughter of the senator's deceased brother. The senator is Oregon's state senate majority leader, and the governor requested we offer our full cooperation and assistance. So, if you have no objection, we would like to be involved."

"No objections here. Just so you know who's calling the shots." Agent Miller sounded more like a man making a personal challenge than an agent having a professional conversation with colleagues.

Mac swallowed back the urge to confront him. He didn't like playing a second-fiddle role in his own town, especially not to the "Famous But Incompetent," as Philly generally referred to the FBI. But then, Philly did tend to accentuate the negative. As much as Mac hated to admit it, the feds were the best when it came to kidnappings and ransom negotiations.

"So what was this about a spark plug?" Agent Lauden gestured to the white material on the floorboard.

Mac suspected the question was more to break up the awkward silence than to make an inquiry. He moved closer to the car, taking a moment to scan the interior before answering the question and before accepting a piece of the hard, white fragment from Agent Lauden. "It's an old auto thief trick." Mac rolled the tiny fragment in his gloved fingers. "Car clouts take a spark plug or shattered pieces of a plug and pack them for easy concealment for breaking into cars. The porcelain is dense in these plugs, designed to withstand some serious heat and friction. That makes the material a phenomenal tool for shattering glass. The thief throws a little piece of this, and the glass shatters like a bullet hit it. The beauty is that there's very little sound. Once the glass is broken, all the perp has to do is peck out the safety glass, and he has entry. The good ones will put duct tape on the glass before breaking it so they can lift the pieces away."

The agents glanced at each other, and Mel raised an eyebrow. He seemed impressed but didn't say so. Mac let the opportunity for some cockiness slide. FBI agents had their strengths, but they often lacked the street-crimes investigative skills that being in uniform and working the streets afforded. Mac noticed that these guys were at least wearing gloves and seemed to be preserving the crime scene.

"Can you bring us up to speed?" Mac asked.

Mel shrugged. "Sure. Looks like our victim was taken from the house. According to her husband's secretary, Mrs. Watson called to talk to her husband early this afternoon. Apparently her car had been broken into in the garage near her office. The secretary says that Mrs. Watson seemed OK and was planning to call the insurance company about arrangements to repair the car."

"She didn't call the police?" Dana asked.

Miller turned his gaze on Dana, his features softening. "There's no record that she did."

"And she came home to make the calls?" Dana frowned.

"That would be my guess. Your CSI technicians are inside right now. There may have been a struggle in the kitchen." He glanced over at the reporters who'd gathered at the scene and lowered his voice. "The vultures are here."

"As always," Mac mused. "The disappearance of a popular socialite with political ties would be impossible to keep from the press. I wouldn't be surprised if the senator himself briefed them." Not many politicians would be able to pass up a chance for this kind of exposure.

Miller shook his head. "Just makes the job harder."

"What makes you think we are dealing with a kidnapping?" Mac asked. "No disrespect, but I've never seen you guys get involved this quickly in the game without some hard evidence."

Agent Miller looked around behind him before answering. "So far, we've seen no obvious blood evidence or signs of trauma or anything that would give any indication she was killed inside the residence. We are well aware of Mrs. Watson's relationship to Senator Wilde. Word is that Senator Wilde has been receiving some threatening letters. He's afraid Sara's disappearance is related somehow to those threats, which is why we're here."

"Understood. Looks like we both received this assignment through political channels." Mac looked at Dana and thought about the stack of files on his desk, pending court cases, and personal plans that would need to be placed on hold so he could stand around with the FBI on a case that would more than likely never fall under their authority. On the other hand, the case could turn out to be a murder, which would land it in their laps. He hoped that wouldn't be the case. Regardless, Mac intended to stay on top of the investigation.

"Any leads on the abductor?" Dana asked. "Any witnesses or physical evidence?"

"No witnesses to the possible abduction that we know of. We have some uniformed officers checking at the victim's place of work to see if there were any witnesses or possibly a video surveillance of the original break-in. If we're dealing with pros here, I doubt they left anything behind. There doesn't appear to be anything obvious in the car other than what you'd expect for a break-in, but your lab people are having it towed to a garage to check for forensic evidence."

"Have you talked to the husband?" Mac leaned against one of the pillars holding up the wraparound porch.

"Yeah. He's inside with his little girl and the senator and his wife," Miller said. "There's a cousin in there too. Guess they were planning a big family get-together this weekend. We thought it best to give them some space for the time being."

Nice gesture, Mac thought. Maybe these guys wouldn't be so bad to work with after all. "What's his story?"

"Name's Lester Scott Watson, goes by his middle name," Agent Lauden read from his notebook. The husband is the one who reported her missing after coming home and finding the evidence of a struggle in the kitchen. The cousin was here a few minutes before that. She found the door unlocked and looked around but didn't find any signs of Sara. She's the one who called Senator Wilde."

"What's the cousin's name?" Dana asked.

"Claire Montgomery. She's the senator's daughter."

"What kind of mess are you talking about?" Mac peered past the open front door.

"A few items on the floor, nothing gory," Agent Miller responded. "No signs of forced entry, no evidence of a weapon or any obvious blood spatter noted on the floor or walls. The only thing out of place is the car break-in and the mess in the kitchen. The pictures that had been magnetically attached to the refrigerator door were all over the floor, along with some keys, a canister of mace, and a remote phone. The phone cord is missing on the kitchen base unit, and there's a broken vase near the entry. Unless the scene was staged, we think Sara fought with her attacker in the kitchen and in the entry area. No witnesses, no tire tracks or skid marks leaving the house, nothing to go on right now. We'll be checking with neighbors to see if they saw anything, though."

"You said no sign of forced entry. Any keys missing or theories about how the guy got in the house?" Mac asked.

"Nothing much to go on so far. All the keys were accounted for, and the victim's own set was among the items found on the kitchen floor. The husband said they often go into the house through the garage, but the victim's car was parked out front. We think the victim may have left the front door unlocked. Or, she may have used the remote keypad on the door, which makes it possible the suspect had the door code also."

"Is Sara's car remote for the garage door accounted for?" Dana asked. "A lot of these car clouters grab the car registration and remote control for the garage when they bust into a car."

"That's right," Mac said, appreciating Dana's thoroughness.

"The suspects get the address off the vehicle registration and burglarize the house while they know the victim is at work or school. We've had a number of local scumbags working that angle lately."

Agent Miller leaned inside the car, pulling down the driver side visor. "There's an indentation on the visor where a remote-control clip would have been. I bet you're right, Detective Bennett. Having the remote would allow our suspect easy entrance."

"Which may mean that Sara interrupted a burglary." Dana finished his thought.

"Possible," Agent Lauden said. "Unless the reason for stealing the remote was to gain access in order to pull off a kidnapping."

"Or a murder," Dana said. "That's why I never leave my remote in the car or give my entire set of keys to the repair shops when they have my car. Remember that rapist a few months ago who worked as a mechanic here in town, Mac?"

"Yeah." Mac remembered the case all too well.

The agents looked at them to elaborate, and Mac let Dana do the honors.

"We had a serial rapist/killer working the area, a few months back. It turned out he was a mechanic at a local car dealership. The guy would select his victims when they came in to have their cars serviced. He'd make a copy of their house keys on his break. The guy would then return the original set of keys to the customer and pay them a visit a few days later."

"How'd you catch him?"

"We didn't," Mac answered. "The guy picked the wrong victim. The woman who nailed him was a martial arts expert. She beat the guy within an inch of his life and called the police. Who knows how long the case might have dragged on without her? This guy was prolific and showed no signs of slowing down."

"I'd like to think we'd have found him anyway," Dana said.

"Eventually we'd have come up with the mechanic as being the common denominator."

"I hope that's not the case here," Agent Lauden grumbled. "Your guy is off the street, isn't he?"

"Yep, he's in the county lockup awaiting trial," Mac said. "That only leaves thirty-five hundred sex offenders here in the greater Portland metro area to eliminate."

"Wonderful."

MAC AND DANA SPENT THE NEXT HOUR looking over the scene and talking with their CSI techs, but they gained little more than what the FBI agents had told them. The techs found a couple of blood smears in the entry as well as a long, black hair. They would run DNA tests and call Mac and Dana with the results. They'd also determined that the garage door opener had not been stolen but was sitting in a drawer in the upstairs office. There was no sign of forced entry, so she may have known her abductor, or she'd been careless and left a door or window unlocked.

Before they left, Mac made it a point to introduce himself and Dana to the family: Scott Watson and his daughter, Chloe; Senator and Mrs. Wilde; Sara's cousin, Claire Montgomery; and her daughter, Allysa. While they were offering their condolences, Jackie Palmer, Watson's secretary, showed up. After the introductions, Jackie hugged Claire and Scott. From her apparent distress and the way she interacted with the family, Mac had the impression that she was a friend as well.

"If only I'd come home earlier," Scott told the senator. "Maybe . . ."

"It's not your fault, son." Senator Wilde patted the man's slumped shoulders.

Jackie dabbed at her eyes. "If anyone is to blame, it's me. I should have interrupted your meeting."

"It doesn't do any good to blame ourselves." Claire, who was holding Chloe, sat down beside Scott. Chloe immediately moved onto Scott's lap and snuggled into his arms. Mac nearly lost it when he thought about that little girl losing her mother. He swallowed back the lump in his throat and forced himself to look at the other child. Allysa, whom Mac guessed to be around ten, sat cross-legged on the floor in front of the television set playing a video game with the sound turned off.

Mac's gaze moved to each of them. His contact with them had been brief, but they seemed genuinely grief-stricken. He wanted to hang around longer and conduct the interviews himself, but with the feds in charge, that wasn't going to happen. Besides, they had a retirement party to go to.

The detectives left the scene at seven, making it to the Elks Lodge an hour late. Since the food service was just starting, all they had missed was happy hour. Russ signaled them, pointing to the two chairs between him and Philly. Mac glanced around, hoping to see Kristen, his sort-of girlfriend and the state's medical examiner. He spotted several people from the crime lab and finally saw her sitting with some of the deputy medical examiners and her indispensable assistant, Henry.

Mac sat down next to Russ and directed his attention to the front. Kevin stood at the podium, his now-thin frame evident under his sport coat. Kevin's bout with prostate cancer and chemo had not only stripped him of his hair, it seemed to have melted the muscles right off him. After asking everyone to take their seats, he waited until the noise subsided and led them in a prayer of thanks for their dinner.

The room was crammed full of Sergeant Evans's friends, co-workers, and family, with both retired and active officers scattered all over the room. The brass was there in full force, but Frank had asked Kevin to serve as the master of ceremonies. After dinner had been served and consumed, the hundreds of guests settled in for coffee and the awards presentation section of Sarge's retirement celebration.

Kevin read the usual list of letters from agency heads and commendation notes from Frank's career. He read a special letter to Frank's wife, Connie, thanking her for her service to the state and for sticking by her husband's side through it all. The letter was a small token for a spouse who had to endure hundreds of wake-up calls and cancelled personal plans through the years. Yet Connie didn't act like she minded one bit.

Mac couldn't help but think of his fiasco of an engagement to Linda, a woman who couldn't handle his crazy schedule—or lack of one. It took a special kind of woman to stay married to a cop for that many years. Frank had one of the best, and so did Kevin, as well as Mac's cousin, Eric O'Rourke, who'd moved from detective to lieutenant. Philly and Russ hadn't been so lucky in the love department. Both were divorced: Russ once and Philly—Mac couldn't remember—at least three times.

Thoughts of Linda, his ex-fiancée, brought back thoughts of the latest women in his life, Dana and Kristen. Not that he was dating both of them. Dana had declared herself off-limits. Kristen was . . . questionable. Would his tenuous relationship with the quirky medical examiner go anywhere? Right now they were trying to get together whenever their busy schedules allowed, which wasn't often.

Mac looked across the room and caught Kristen's gaze. She winked at him, indicating she'd see him later. Mac smiled back. With Kristen, he never knew what to expect. Tonight she had bleached blonde hair with black roots, the ends turned up in a style that looked like she'd been in a windstorm. She had on a black dress with a fragile-looking shawl draped over her shoulders. He dragged his gaze from her to the front of the room.

Kevin hugged Connie after providing the form letter to her from the governor's office. The time had come for the badge presentation, which was the one token all state troopers placed in high regard. Kevin presented Frank with his badge in a plaque shaped like the state of Oregon. Frank accepted the plaque with obvious gratitude, and he patiently posed for pictures.

Mac couldn't help but be sad, thinking of the hundreds of investigations the man had been involved with and the number of arrests he'd made. Frank had been in so many life-threatening situations, many of them worthy of a commendation. Now the memories would fade, and another officer would go his way after years of service. As he watched the proceedings, Mac thought about his own career, wondering about his own retirement someday. Would he even reach retirement? Would he have a wife to stand by him through the years and a family who loved him? He glanced across the room again, looking for Kristen, but her chair was empty. She'd probably been called out to a crime scene or to do an autopsy.

Disappointed, Mac tuned back into Frank's speech, where he thanked the department and his family. He joked about taking up golf and fly-fishing, but from the laughs he got, no one in the room could imagine Frank doing anything relaxing.

After Frank's speech, Kevin asked if anyone else in the room wanted to talk. A long cast of characters, mostly seasoned veterans, made their way to the microphone, telling childhood stories and funny memories. Finally, Philly ambled up to the front and took over the microphone. Russ, Mac, Kevin, and Dana groaned in mock protest.

"Thank you. Nice to see how much I'm appreciated around here." Philly summoned Frank to the podium.

"Get it over with, Phil." Frank rolled his eyes and crossed his arms, preparing himself for the king of roasts.

"Now, on the topic of Sergeant Frank Evans," Philly began, "we've heard a lot of funny stories tonight. I didn't want the evening to end without him hearing a thing or two from the detectives who worked with him every day." Philly grinned, and Frank groaned, obviously expecting the worst.

Philly cleared his throat and continued, "I just wanted to tell the family here tonight that we really depended on your husband and father to get us home safely each day. Frank is a man of integrity, a role model to me and the other guys in the back room. Guys . . . and gals." He glanced at Dana as he corrected himself. "Frank is a stern guy, but he's fair. He's a man of character and one of the finest detectives this outfit ever had. Frank, I just want you and your family to know how we feel about you. Please accept this gift certificate; the whole office chipped in." Philly handed Frank an envelope with a gift certificate to a local home improvement store and gave his boss and longtime friend a bear hug. They both got choked up, and Mac swallowed past the lump in his own throat. Mac wouldn't admit it, but he was a little disappointed that Philly had taken the high road.

"Thanks, Phil." Frank patted Philly on the back. "You better quit hugging me now, or my wife's going to get the wrong idea."

"You wish." Philly laughed and shook Frank's hand. "Good luck, you old badger. I'll be right behind you."

Frank remained at the podium while the crowd gave him a standing ovation. Then he turned to shake Kevin's hand before collecting his family and walking back into the crowd.

Kevin assumed his place behind the microphone once again to close the ceremony. "Thank you all for coming tonight. And on that note, Detectives McAllister and Bennett, please contact me ASAP."

"What's up?" Mac asked as he and Dana came forward. "Are we on cleanup detail?"

"You might say that." Kevin rubbed the back of his neck. "I was just wondering how your visit with the feds went."

Dana and Mac brought him up to speed while they gathered their jackets and headed for their cars. "I don't think those guys are too happy about our being involved," Mac said.

"I know they aren't. I got a call on the way over here from their supervisor. He wanted to know if our involvement was really necessary, and I told him it was. I offered our services, so be prepared to do some hands-on stuff."

"Such as?" Dana stopped at Mac's car, her hand on the passenger side door handle.

"The usual. They'll be in charge, but you'll be able to do some interviews, follow up on the sex offender list, check on other such crimes to see if they might be related. Whatever you can do to stay on top of it. Don't let these guys intimidate you. If this turns into a murder investigation, you'll take over."

"Whatever you say." Mac paused. "You doing OK, Kev? You're looking a little pale."

"I'm fine. Just tired. See you guys in the morning."

Mac dropped off Dana at the parking compound at the office and then headed home. He was a little tired himself and still wasn't too happy having to work under the feds, but he told himself it wouldn't be all that much different from being support investigators under Philly and Russ.

Mac shoved aside his concerns about the case and thought about the changes Frank's retirement would bring to the department. Dynamics would change. Someone would get the coveted office that Kevin was vacating. Probably Dana, since she asked him about it, but if he could get into the office early enough tomorrow morning, maybe he still had a chance. After all, wasn't possession nine-tenths of the law?

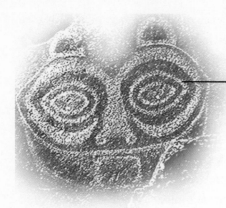

FIVE

Claire stayed in Portland for a long and excruciating week before heading home. She didn't want to leave, but she needed to pick up some items and take care of a few day-to-day details, like having her mail routed to Portland and her paper and garbage stopped. Though Scott insisted he'd be fine without her, she couldn't leave him alone with Chloe. Scott was a wonderful father, but he had a full-time job and little Chloe missed her mommy.

"I can stay, Scott, and it isn't a problem," she'd told him that morning over breakfast. She worked as a freelance editor and was between projects, so living in Portland for a while would not be a problem.

Scott had looked at her without really seeing, his eyes glazed over with exhaustion and worry. He didn't argue—probably knew it wouldn't do any good.

Claire couldn't bear the thought of leaving him and Chloe on their own. She couldn't bear the thought of being in Seattle when the investigation into Sara's disappearance was going on here in Portland. Her parents were supportive of her staying in Portland as well. So it was settled. Two hours ago, she left Allysa with her parents and headed north, promising to return the next day.

"What happened to you, Sara?" She spoke aloud, maybe to keep herself company, maybe because she needed to ask the question. "Are you still alive?" Part of her refused to believe otherwise, but another part knew the odds were slim. They hadn't received a ransom note. So if this was a kidnapping, like the police thought, why hadn't the kidnappers contacted them?

A week. An entire week had gone by, and they still had nothing. All the FBI agents had done was interview the family, casting suspicious looks at each of them as though one of them had instigated the kidnapping. *The agents have to rule us out,* she reminded herself. They seemed to have done that.

Now they were focusing on the threats. She knew very little about those. Her father had called them political in nature and doubted they were connected, but they had to be investigated. When she'd pressed him, he told her that the FBI insisted he not tell anyone about the threats, including her.

"But if threats had been made against the family, why did they choose Sara over me?" Again she put voice to her thoughts, and they crowded around her, stifling the air and making it hard to breathe.

A chill folded over her. Maybe because Sara lived in Portland. Whoever took Sara might not be finished. Maybe the plan was to pick off members of the senator's family one at a time.

Claire swallowed hard and, with the sleeve of her sweatshirt jacket, brushed unbidden tears from her eyes. *Allysa.*

She's safer with Mom and Dad than anywhere else. Dad had people around all the time. In fact, Grant Stokely, her father's chief of staff, rarely let him out of his sight. Since Sara's disappearance, her father had opted for extra security for all of them. Yet, now, she had none.

She nearly went through the roof when her cell phone jangled its tinny "Ode to Joy" tune.

"Hello?"

"Claire, where are you?" Dad asked.

"Just coming up on South Center."

"OK. I had Agent Miller contact the police up there. Should be an officer waiting for you at the house."

She rolled her eyes, on one hand annoyed at his interference and on the other relieved that she wouldn't have to go home to an empty house alone. "Honestly, Dad, you didn't have to do that."

"Yes, I did. Agent Miller agrees. Now you be careful."

"I will," she promised. "Anything new on the case?"

"Nothing."

They talked for a few minutes, ringing off with her dad telling her they were taking Allysa out for Asian food. Claire wished she were going with them. She hadn't lived close to her parents since high school and couldn't wait to get away once she'd graduated. She hated the limelight, the reporters—the kind of life that went with being a politician's daughter. Now she wished she had stayed closer. Her desire to leave home had driven her into the arms of a man ten years her senior. Just over eighteen and madly in love, she'd run away with him, gotten married in Vegas, and thought she'd live happily ever after. The marriage had gone sour after only a few months, when her husband started taking in strays of the two-legged variety.

Claire shook her head. Jeffrey was an idiot, thinking he could be unfaithful and get away with it. But that part of her life was over. Had been for a long time. The only good that had come out of her marriage was Allysa and the wisdom not to make the same mistake twice.

She had long envied Sara and the relationship she had with Scott. Sara had been the smart one, waiting to marry until she and Scott were both out of school. They'd waited two years after marrying to have Chloe.

Claire sighed, smiling at how much in love Sara and Scott were.

She couldn't imagine life without Sara. Claire had been eleven when Sara's parents died. She had welcomed her "little sister" with open arms. Claire's parents had become Mom and Dad to Sara in an almost seamless transition.

Her ruminating stopped when she pulled into the driveway. The house was dark, and she pressed the garage door opener, which raised the door and turned on the lights. A car pulled in behind her, and a man stepped out. Thinking it was the police officer Agent Miller had sent, she pulled into the garage and stepped out of the car.

But it wasn't a police car, and the man wasn't wearing a uniform.

"Mrs. Montgomery?" The husky voice came out of a dark-skinned face. He brushed his jacket aside, and she noticed the holstered gun.

Her heart pounded as she forced herself to remain calm. "Y-yes."

"I hope I didn't frighten you. I'm Agent Winslow. FBI."

Claire's knees buckled. She leaned against the car for support. "Thanks for coming," she managed to say.

The agent checked out the house before escorting her inside. "I'll be waiting in the car if you need any assistance."

She frowned. "All night?"

"Yes, ma'am."

She nodded. On one hand, she appreciated having the agent watch her house. On the other, Agent Winslow served as a stark reminder of just how much danger she and the rest of her family might be in.

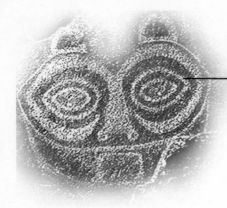

SIX

Russ paused to talk with Dana and Mac as he made his way to his cubicle. "How's that missing persons case coming along? The feds made any progress yet?"

Mac eyed Russ, wondering about his motivation for asking. Russ had been paying more attention to Dana than usual lately, and Mac had a feeling Detective Meyers was interested in more than the case.

"Nothing so far." Dana didn't seem to notice. "Not a lick of evidence or anything to indicate she's still alive or that she's gone off on her own. There's been no movement on any of her accounts, no attempt to contact family or friends. And there's been no attempt by a possible abductor to demand a ransom for her return."

"Not that we know of, anyway," Mac added. "I have a feeling the feds aren't telling us everything and that they are cutting us in on just enough to say they're cooperating."

"Wouldn't be surprised." Russ straightened his tie. "Anything ever develop on the Native American involvement the press reported on a while back?"

"I don't think so." Dana's gaze latched on to Russ's, and for a minute, Mac thought she might be interested in him too. He dismissed the thought, however. Dana wasn't about to get into a relationship with a cop. She'd made herself very clear on that point. If she changed her mind, he intended to be first in line.

Or did he? A month ago, he might have jumped at the chance. But things were changing. He and Kristen were closer, and he enjoyed being with her and her little boy. Mac didn't really want that relationship to end. In fact, he would be heading over there after work tonight for one of Kristen's gourmet dinners. If, that is, neither of them had to work late.

Russ cleared his throat. "Strange. The articles were pretty adamant about a link between the kidnapping and some threatening letters to Senator Wilde."

"Pure speculation on the reporter's part," Mac said. "At least, that's what the feds told us. Some of it was true, though. Senator Wilde is publicly opposed to the Confederated Tribes building a casino out near Hood River. There was some mention of threatening letters, but those allegations never panned out."

"What did the senator have to say about them?"

"Except for that first day, right after Sara disappeared, Dana and I never got a chance to speak with the senator. Only the feds had interviews with him, and I understand he was always with his aide and a room full of attorneys."

"That always makes it nice," Russ said. "So where did the paper get this thing about a tribal member supposedly kidnapping Senator Wilde's niece?"

"We'd like to know that too." Dana sighed. "But the paper wouldn't reveal their source."

"Humph." Russ shook his head. "I bet the source was a greedy editor who wanted to sell papers and had the writers fabricate the story."

Mac nodded, sharing Russ's distrust for the press. Practical experience had taught them that news publishers often used the police and the victims as pawns to sell papers or gain ratings.

"Is Kevin coming in today?" Russ asked.

"I'm already here." Sergeant Bledsoe stepped into Dana's old cubicle. "Did you need to see me, Russ?"

"Yeah. Philly and I are heading to Scappoose again this morning to follow up on that hit-and-run incident you sent us out on last night. We've got the crime lab on the scene and want to take a look at it in daylight."

"Good idea. Let me know what you find out. Where's Philly, by the way?"

"Ah, at home. I'm picking him up there. We were out pretty late last night." Mac noticed Russ's attempt to protect his partner.

"And Philly needed his beauty sleep," Kevin said, leveling his gaze on Russ.

Russ looked embarrassed. "Yeah. Um—Sarge, if you have a few minutes, there's something I need to talk to you about in private."

"Sure, Russ. Go on into my office. I'll be with you in a sec." Turning back to Mac and Dana, Kevin asked, "How are those reports coming?"

Mac shrugged. "Getting close." When he wasn't working on the Watson case, he was supposed to get the sex offender registration files up-to-date, and today was the deadline. "Did you know that thirty percent of those guys are out of compliance? They're not coming in for their yearly registration or making address notifications."

Dana frowned. "I knew they were pretty bad off, but how do they expect us to chase after these jokers if they keep cutting our positions?"

"Not only that, there's more of them all the time," Mac said.

"You gotta wonder where these perverts are coming from."

"You don't want to get me started on that," Kevin said. "My philosophy is that while we've always had our share of sex offenders, it's these perverted internet sites and the porn that multiplies them. What's worse is the media attention they're getting. You can't turn on the news anymore without hearing about some sexual predator."

Mac had to agree. It seemed like they were always arresting sex offenders with a history of deviant activities. "Yeah, it's pretty bad when half the newscast is dedicated to those guys."

"How's your job coming, Dana?" Kevin asked.

Dana had been plagued with interviewing local sex offenders who lived or worked in the vicinity of Sara's home and place of business. Mac didn't like the idea of her dealing with this kind of stuff, but Dana would deck him if he said anything. Being a cop meant doing the job—whether you were male or female.

"Another day should do it for me. I wish this Sara Watson case could be put to bed. I'd like to get onto something else. I'm not finding any connections to Sara with any of the local sex offenders. And I'll tell you, I hate interviewing these creeps."

"I know, and I'm sorry to put you through this detail, but it has to be done. We may have to cold case the investigation on Sara if something doesn't break soon. You two are up for the next investigation."

Dana nodded. "I wish we were lead on the case. Maybe we'd get somewhere."

Kevin gave them an imperceptible nod. Though he wouldn't outwardly agree, Mac suspected that he, too, thought his detectives might do a better job than the feds seemed to be doing. However, they still had a missing persons case, not a murder.

"I'd better get in and see what Russ needs."

When Kevin had gone, Mac followed Dana into her office. He looked around the small space, trying to tell himself that he hadn't really wanted it anyway. He liked his cubicle with its window and view. "What do you suppose Russ wants to talk to Kevin about?"

"I don't know, but whatever it is, he seemed concerned. Do you think it has something to do with Philly?"

"That would be my guess." Mac rubbed his chin, wondering whether or not to mention Russ's apparent interest in her.

"Did you need something else? I really have to get back to this stuff."

"No, just . . ."

"What?" She was getting annoyed.

"Maybe it's nothing, but I've noticed Russ looking at you a lot lately. I think he has a thing for you."

"Oh, come on, Mac. You're just jealous. He does not have a thing for me."

"Whatever you say. Maybe I am a little jealous, but I'm not mentioning it for that reason. I've noticed the way he looks at you and the way he's always going out of his way to talk to you."

Her cheeks flushed. "Russ likes anything in skirts. I know better than to take him seriously."

Mac poked his tongue in his cheek. "OK. Just an observation."

"Anyway, what do you care? I thought you and Kristen were an item."

"I guess. Sort of."

"Well, just for the record, I'm seeing someone too."

"Really? Who?"

"That, my friend, is none of your business." She grinned at Mac. "I'll tell you when I'm ready. Now get out of here so I can get these reports finished."

Mac shrugged and went back to his cubicle and back to the project he wished he could pawn off onto someone else. Unfortunately, paperwork was part of the job, and he had to do his share. Though for the past few weeks, he felt like he and Dana had done more than their share of paper pushing.

Two hours later, Mac aimed his Crown Vic toward his favorite medical examiner's house. He'd finished his project and felt like celebrating.

Pulling up in front of Kristen's place brought a wave of disappointment. Her silver Volvo wasn't parked in its usual spot. Mac got out of his own vehicle anyway and jogged up the walk. He rang the doorbell and knocked. No one answered. Mac dialed her number on the way back to his car.

When she didn't answer her cell phone, Mac called the morgue direct.

"Hey, Mac." The receptionist sounded entirely too cheerful for someone working in a morgue. "Dr. Thorpe had an emergency situation out of town. I'll have her call you when she checks in."

"Any idea when that will be?"

"No, sorry."

"OK, just tell her I called."

"Will do."

Mac wondered what Kristen had been called out on and checked with dispatch. They didn't have a record of her going to a crime scene. Annoyed that she hadn't called him, Mac headed home. On the way, he called his favorite Chinese restaurant for takeout, which was ready when he arrived. Back home, he fed his dog, Lucy, before gobbling down his dinner during the evening news. After the news, he changed into jeans and a sweater and settled into his recliner to watch reruns.

Mac didn't hear from Kristen until after seven. "Hi, Mac. Celia said you'd called earlier. What's up?"

"What's up?" Mac tried to keep the irritation out of his voice. "We had a dinner date tonight."

"Oops. I totally forgot about that. Listen, I'm sorry. I'll make it up to you. But not for a while. I'm in Florida, and . . ."

"Florida? What are you doing in Florida? Why didn't you call me?"

"I did—I mean, I am right now. You're mad at me, aren't you?"

"Yeah. I was really looking forward to seeing you."

"Oh, Mac."

He heard voices in the background. "What's going on?"

"Um—Brian, my ex-husband . . ."

"Wait," Mac interrupted. "What's he doing in Florida? You said that he lives in England."

"He does. . . . I mean, he did. . . ." Kristen stumbled over her words. "Look, apparently Brian has been living with his parents in Florida the past few months. And now he's been in a serious accident, so his parents called me. . . . It's a long story, and I really can't talk right now. But I'll explain everything later, I promise. In the meantime, say a prayer for Brian. The doctor says he may not live through the night."

"Sure." Mac hung up. A mixture of anger, disappointment, and jealousy stumbled around inside him. *What the heck is she doing with her ex-husband? And why would I pray for the guy?* According to Kristen, he was a loser. He'd left his wife and kid and hadn't come back. But maybe Brian meant more to Kristen than she let on. Obviously, if she'd drop everything and fly all the way to Florida to be with him, he meant something.

Mac dropped into his recliner and absently patted Lucy's head.

Had Kristen taken Andrew along? Mac had fallen for the little guy in a big way.

He'd even imagined himself as the kid's dad from time to time. What a fantasy that was. Andrew already had a father. And what about Kristen? He had to admit that being with her and Andrew had gotten him thinking about a wife and kids. They both wanted to take things slow; she didn't want commitment, and neither did he. Had she secretly been hoping to have Brian back in their lives?

Mac thought about calling Kristen's mother, who took care of Andrew when Kristen worked, but he couldn't remember her last name.

Kristen had asked him to pray, and he'd said he would. Rubbing his forehead, he lowered his head. "God, I'm not sure what I'm supposed to do here, but it would probably be a good thing if you saved this guy's life. Kevin says you know better than we do what we should pray for, so I'm just asking you to help Kristen and Andrew and do what's best for them."

His cell phone rang, and he frowned at it. Lucy sat at attention and cocked her head. Mac picked up.

"We have a body dump along the White River," Kevin said, sounding almost as gruff as their former sergeant. "I want you and Dana to head out there. Call dispatch on the way for details."

"Sure thing. Have you called Dana?"

"Not yet. Do you want to do the honors?"

"Be glad to."

Kevin thanked him and hung up. Mac phoned his partner and offered to pick her up, and she agreed. *Hallelujah!* When they'd first become partners, Dana wanted to make certain no one got the wrong idea about them, and refused to let him pick her up—even when it would have been more convenient. Now that she felt more secure in her job, she was loosening up a bit. She'd even come over to his place awhile back to watch a game with him and Kristen.

"Thanks for the lift," Dana said as she scooted into the passenger seat. "My work car is in the shop, and I've had to drive my POV for the last couple of days."

"I should have everything we'll need. Do you have your weapon?" Mac reached for his right pant leg. He pulled a small semiautomatic and ankle holster from its hiding spot. "Take my backup." Mac held out the weapon to Dana.

"Thanks, but I have my own." She patted her purse. "Never leave home without it."

He put his own weapon back. "If you need anything else, I can stop by the office.

"I'm good," Dana said. "You seem kind of moody today. Having PMS or something?"

Mac rolled his eyes. "I am not moody."

"Well, something's wrong."

He told her about his brief conversation with Kristen. "Doesn't it seem odd to you that she'd drop everything and rush to Florida to be by her ex's side?"

"Not really. She may not be in love with him anymore, but they were married once and that makes them family. And he is Andrew's dad. Maybe Brian wanted to see them."

"Humph." Mac didn't think much of the explanation.

"I'd better call dispatch." Dana picked up the phone, hitting the speed-dial button to the Oregon State Police regional communications center in Salem. She placed the phone back on the hands-free stand so they could both listen to the conversation on the car's speaker.

"State Police dispatch, is this an emergency?"

"Nope," Dana answered, accustomed to the question.

"Please hold," the call taker responded. Moments later, the male voice came back on the line. "Thanks for holding. How may I help you?"

"This is Detective Bennett out of station eleven; may I speak with the supervisor?"

"Sure, just a second."

The call was transferred to the floor supervisor, who held the call information for the more serious investigative crimes while the dispatchers on the floor dispatched the lower-priority calls to the uniformed contingent of the agency. Most detective calls were handled by phone, to avoid alerting the media or the general public who monitored police airwaves with their personal scanners.

"This is Patrick," the civilian supervisor answered.

The detectives could hear the hustle and bustle of the communications center, the dozens of police frequencies going at once as dispatchers spoke with troopers in the state's thirty-six counties. "Hi, Patrick, this is Detective Bennett out of Portland."

"Hey there, Detective, how's that plain-clothes gig going?"

"So far so good. I hear you have some work for us. Sergeant Bledsoe said to give you a call on a twelve-forty-nine on the east side of Mount Hood."

"Got the info right here, Dana; you ready to copy?"

"Yeah, go for it," Dana poised the pen above her pad.

"We received the call around nineteen hundred hours from Warm Springs P.D. The caller was camping along the White River, just south of Highway 216. He found a body and called it into Wasco County. The initial directions put the body on the Warm Springs Indian Reservation, but we're being told now it may be just outside."

"Hey, Patrick. This is McAllister. Has that information been confirmed yet?"

"Hi, Mac. We've got a tribal officer on scene. I'm hearing conflicting stories. They're talking ancient burial grounds, but I also heard the body dump was fairly recent, so I don't know what's going on."

"They've activated the FBI, per their tribal protocol, and the State Department of Indian Affairs to proceed with the excavation. The agents responding, Miller and Lauden, requested you two be notified; they said you would know why."

Mac looked at Dana, who was giving him a questioning look. "Patrick, tell Warm Springs we are coming up from Portland. Even in this summer light, we'll be pushing dark before we make it up there. Where does 216 come in off of Highway 26?"

"Once you get over Mount Hood at Government Camp, you're looking at another twenty or thirty to the Wamic/White River junction on Highway 216."

"Thanks. We're on our way." Mac pressed his foot into the accelerator.

"There's only one reason Miller and Lauden would bring us in." Dana put away the phone. "They must think the victim is Sara Watson."

"That would be my guess."

"Then what's with the ancient burial grounds bit?"

Mac shrugged. "Guess we'll find out soon enough."

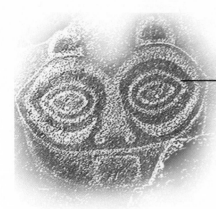

SEVEN

Dana shot Mac an odd look.

"What?" He glanced at her and then focused back on the road.

"I hope it isn't Sara."

"Me too." Even though they hadn't been able to work the case in more than a support role, it was hard not to be affected emotionally.

"Better not to speculate. Like Patrick said, one report said the remains could be from an old burial ground."

"Well, one way or the other, they have my attention." Dana made a couple of notes on her pad. "Shouldn't we get the lab techs on the way?"

"Probably not if they think we're dealing with ancient remains." The reservation was located about an hour and a half from Portland, between the state's most populated metro area and the central Oregon town of Bend. Neither CSI lab would be called until their services were needed. And they didn't respond to ancient remains, which was fairly common with the tribes and Oregon Trail graves.

Mac forced himself to think about their destination rather than the body waiting for them at the end of the line.

Warm Springs was the largest Native American reservation in the state, a sovereign nation located in central Oregon about ninety miles southeast of Portland. The high desert location was home to thousands of members of the Warm Springs Confederated Tribes. They employed their own police force, and due to their status as a sovereign nation, Mac and Dana had no police authority on the reservation. The only Oregon State Police presence allowed was on the state highways that ran through or around the reservation. The real estate off the highways was treated the same as a foreign country for the troopers. The only non-tribal enforcement that was permitted on the reservation was that of the FBI, who nationally have police and investigative authority on Native American lands.

Mac's cell phone rang while en route. He answered, surprised to hear Kevin's voice. After speaking for a few minutes, he snapped the phone shut.

"That the boss?" Dana asked.

"Yep, more complications. Did you see the news report about a forest fire on the reservation?"

Dana nodded.

"Well, it's moving toward our destination. Kevin wanted to let us know the fire is only about twenty miles away from the body dump and is still burning out of control."

"Oh, great. That fire has already eaten up about ten thousand acres."

"Close to fifteen now. It merged with another fire, and they don't have any sides contained yet."

Dana let out a low whistle. "Let's hope the wind blows it in the other direction. Or at least that we get the evidence we need before the body is destroyed."

"You ready to make some time?" Mac asked as they hit Highway 26 south of Gresham.

"Let her rip." Dana flipped on the red-and-blue strobes and the wigwag headlights.

Mac crushed the gas pedal and pointed the car toward Mount Hood. Nothing was more beautiful than the mountain at sunset with the year-round snow reflecting the glimmering red, gold, and purple of the sky. And tonight the sky and the mountain were glorious.

Mac and Dana crested the summit of the Government Camp pass on Mount Hood at sunset. The pink reflection of the sun was fading on the snowy peak, while the crest of clouds to the east reflected something dark and sinister. The Simnasho wildfire was burning hot and fast, painting a wide brush of red, gold, and black across the high desert landscape.

Centuries ago, an ancient eruption from the then-active volcano had left the eastern half of the landscape a barren wasteland. Even today, you could see the demarcation leaving the west side lush with dense forests of Douglas firs.

Dana looked over at the digital clock on the dash, then back to her own watch to compare the time. "Looks like we'll be working this gig in the dark. I was hoping for a little light."

Mac took a left onto Highway 216, starting toward the town of Maupin and the milky-looking White River. "We might have cell coverage now. Why don't you hit dispatch, and we'll see if there are any updates. The fire looks closer than I thought."

Dana phoned their dispatch in Salem, again speaking with the floor supervisor. "Hi, Mac, Dana. Not too much more I can tell you except that it's definitely a recent body dump."

"You're sure?"

"We got the verification from Officer Webb with the Warm Springs P.D. A deputy medical examiner from Wasco County is just arriving at the scene."

"What about our CSI people?"

"They've been requested, but it'll be at least another two hours before someone from Portland could get out there, and the fire is blocking the folks from Bend."

"Do we have anyone from the Bureau of Indian Affairs?" Dana asked.

"Negative. They have their hands full dealing with the fire. Word is they're going to wait for the medical examiner's report."

Mac tipped his head down to get a better look at the sky. "We may not be able to wait for the crime lab. We'll have to grid the site ourselves if the fire pushes any closer."

"Have you done that before?" Dana asked, a hint of hesitation in her voice.

"Once, but I've seen it done several times. I have plenty of twine and stakes in the trunk." Mac turned right into the White River campground.

"This must be the place." Dana motioned to a green Chevy pickup with the yellow Warm Springs Police Department logo printed across the door.

Mac checked out on the radio, requesting the ODOT crews out of the Bear Springs station to bring some light standards to the scene in preparation for having to work in the dark. He would rather hold the scene processing until morning, but with the fire bearing down on them, he couldn't chance it.

They parked next to the green truck, noting the medical examiner's white van on the other side of the wooded campsite, and prepared to process the scene.

Special Agents Miller and Lauden pulled in less than ten minutes later, just as Mac and Dana had finished taping rubber covers over their shoes to prevent scene contamination.

"Hey, Jimmy." Dana smiled as the lead agent exited his car. The agent nodded back, mumbling something to his partner as they approached the detectives.

Jimmy? When had Dana gotten to a nickname basis with the guy? He pushed the thought from his mind. He had to stop obsessing over Dana and her relationship or nonrelationship with other guys.

"Is it Sara?" Miller cut to the chase. Agent Lauden looked a little uncomfortable with his partner's abruptness.

Mac motioned to the yellow crime-scene tape and the vehicles in the campsite. "No idea. We just pulled in and were readying our gear so we can approach the scene."

"If you haven't seen the body, why would you think it was Sara?" Dana asked.

Miller folded his arms. "We can talk about that later."

"We were just about to log in," Dana told them. "I just hope the fire stays on that side of the river."

"No kidding." Agent Lauden looked up at the crimson sky. "Looks threatening. How far out is it?"

"According to dispatch, flareups are as close as seven miles away and moving fast." Mac ducked into the trunk, pulling a hammer from his tool kit. "Since we don't have time to wait for the crime lab, we'll have to process the scene ourselves. Our Portland lab techs are hooked up on another assignment."

"You don't have anyone closer?"

"We have a CSI unit in Bend, but they're not available either. Statewide budget cuts and too many crimes have made for a backlog. Besides, they're cut off by the fire."

"That for the stakes?" Dana pointed at his tool kit.

"Yep. Hope you brought your muscles," Mac said. "This ground looks pretty rocky."

"Oh, please."

Mac approached the crime-scene tape, making eye contact with the uniformed tribal officer. The slender, muscular man of medium build lowered his clipboard to his side as he approached the yellow tape from the opposite side.

"Howdy." The officer held his hand out over the crime-scene tape. "Nathan Webb from Warm Springs P.D."

Mac shook his proffered hand and introduced Dana and the two agents.

"I know these two turkeys," Nathan teased as he shook hands with the federal agents.

"Hey, Nate." Agent Lauden nodded. The FBI agents, stationed in Portland and Bend, were regulars on the reservation and were often called to assist with complex investigations.

"Are we on the reservation?" Mac directed his question to Officer Webb.

"Nope." He pointed to the river, meandering about forty yards away. "Once we cross over that river from the reservation, we're back in the Oregon Territory."

Good, a sense of humor. Mac grinned.

"Huh?" Dana frowned, obviously not getting the innuendo.

Nate laughed. "An inside joke. The reservation is inside Oregon, but being that it is a sovereign nation, it is not Oregon. We're kind of like a doughnut hole in the state."

Mac pointed toward the body dump. "What do we have, Nathan? Can you give us a rundown?"

"Please, call me Nate." His smile was warm and genuine. "From what I understand, the body was discovered by a camper, Mitch Foster. He and his family have been camping out here for the last few days. Their little boy, Nick, was walking his dog along the river trail."

Dana winced. "Don't tell me the kid found the body."

"Fortunately not. Like I said before, the reservation ends at the river, and this area is still part of the state park." Nate pointed toward the improved campsites. "Anyway, this little guy was walking his dog, and the pooch leaves the trail and starts off on his own."

"I take it this trail we're standing on is the one you're talking about," Mac interjected, wanting to get his bearings.

"Yes, it wraps around down by the river and has access to nearly all the campsites at one spot or another. At any rate, the dog took off and started digging. The kid called his dog, but it wouldn't come. He started to pull the collar and saw that the dog was chewing on something. The boy pulled it out of his mouth. Turns out, it's a piece of beaded leather." Nate produced a plastic bag from his pocket with a torn-off piece of brown leather, decorated with intricate beadwork.

"What is it?" Agent Miller asked.

"Hard to tell. It may be from a bag of some sort or a necklace. A talisman, maybe. I think we only have a small part of it, though. I can't tell right now what the significance is. I'd have to ask one of the tribal elders. I don't know if it is an artifact or not. My wife and several other members of the tribe do beadwork like this and sell it at powwows and such."

Dana admired the piece. "It's beautiful. That beadwork is something else." When they'd each gotten a look, Nate started to slip the piece back into his shirt pocket.

"I'll need to take that to the lab, Nate," Mac said. "We can get photos for you, though."

"OK. Sounds good."

"How did we get from the dog finding that piece of leather to the body?" Mac asked.

The officer nodded. "The kid took the leather piece to his dad, who returned to the spot where the dog had been digging. Mitch thought the dog might have inadvertently uncovered an ancient Indian burial ground. Instead of finding more artifacts, he found a body buried in a shallow grave. He immediately drove into Maupin to notify the cops."

"We heard there were some conflicting stories," Mac said. "Are we looking at an ancient burial ground or a recent body dump?"

"I've been called out to dozens of so-called ancient burial grounds only to find 'Made in China' labels or deer bones that some hunter tossed out of his truck after butchering his kill. I'm pretty sure this one is human, and it is definitely not ancient. I didn't dig around—wanted to preserve the scene as much as possible, but I can see some matted hair and the side of what appears to be a female's face and left arm sticking out of the dirt.

"Unless we determine that the victim is a tribal member, this is your case. I'd be obliged if we worked together, though. The beaded leather may or may not be related to the body—in which case, we may have a murder case as well as an archeological find."

"Always glad to share the wealth." Mac checked his watch. "Ready to take a look, Dana?"

"I am." Turning to Nate, she asked, "Have you started a crime-scene log yet?"

He raised his clipboard. "Right here."

A set of headlights highlighted the scene as Mac and Dana introduced themselves to Steve Whitman, the deputy medical examiner for the county. Mac hoped Whitman would be half as good as Kristen Thorpe. As the head medical examiner for the state, Dr. Thorpe often made field visits, and though Mac sometimes thought she'd like to, she couldn't respond to all thirty-six counties herself. For this reason, each county employed deputy medical examiners who were trained in the field of death investigation. All unnatural deaths were routed to Dr. Thorpe's office in Portland if the deputy examiners determined they would require an autopsy to determine the cause of death or for identification.

"What's ODOT doing here?" Nate asked as the vehicle with the lights pulled up to them. The orange color of the truck indicated that it was an Oregon Department of Transportation vehicle—the one Mac had requested to bring up the lights.

"I invited them," Mac answered. "They're bringing some halogen lights for us to use while we process the scene. I figured we'd be working through the night with that fire looming over us."

"Good call." Nate looked across the river, toward the direction of the fire. "We have our entire department on the fire; I'm afraid I'm the only resource we could spare at the moment with the road closures and evacuations. Your troopers out of Madras and The Dalles are helping out on the east side, but we could use even more help."

"We'll make do." Mac motioned toward the ODOT guys and told them where he wanted the lights. "Let's get going. With the fire bearing down on us, this scene isn't going to hold until morning." Mac set his box on the ground and pulled out a digital camera. He photographed the scene, taking several pictures of the earth around the body in the event the camera could capture a footprint that his eyes were missing in the poor light. The smell of smoke partially masked the sour odor of rotting flesh, making the job easier than usual.

Dana sketched the area, dictating notes onto her tape recorder as they approached the body. "Any idea on how long she's been here?" Dana asked the medical examiner.

"Not really," the heavyset man replied. "I can't give a guesstimate until we get her out of the hole."

"I have enough pictures," Mac said, going back to his box. "Dana, I need you to help me grid the scene."

Dana knelt next to Mac and pulled out a stack of wood stakes and some twine.

Mac gestured toward the two FBI agents, who were standing nearby. "They're a big help, aren't they?"

Dana shrugged. "Guess they figure it's not their case either way now. If our victim turns out to be Sara, it's our ticket. If she's a tribal member or anyone else, it will probably still be ours. Besides, do we really want them mucking up our crime scene?"

"Good point."

Dana cleared her throat, apparently affected by the condition of the remains. "They probably just want some closure, Mac. It must be tough seeing your hopes of finding someone crushed like that."

"We don't know it's Sara yet." Mac stood up and took the stakes from Dana. "Let me take those. I'll hammer the stakes if you document the evidence; you have better handwriting than I do."

"Deal." She picked up her clipboard and legal pad as Mac walked toward the body.

A mass of thick, dark hair and rigid cheekbone were visible above the soft dirt. The eye socket was beneath the surface with the rest of the face. "The hair length looks like Sara's, only the color seems a bit lighter," Dana noted.

"It could be the dust." Mac approached the body. "Let's lay out a twelve-by-twelve grid with square-foot grid markers."

Mac pounded the stakes into the ground, one after another, until he had a chessboard grid set up around the body. He'd used heavy stakes at the perimeter and thin wire standards closer to the body to support the twine and hopefully not destroy any evidence. They would process the scene the same way in which an archeologist would process an ancient tomb or preservation site. Because of the fire, however, they'd have to move much more quickly.

Mac photographed and processed each square of the grid around the body. After a cursory search of each square foot for evidence, he shoveled the dirt from the squares into a plastic bag and labeled each bag with an evidence tag.

"What's he going to do with that?" Nate asked Dana, who was documenting each bag on the department evidence form.

"We'll sift the dirt once we get to a controlled environment, to make sure we aren't missing some evidence, like a bullet or something that was dropped or passed through the body."

"Check."

Nate seemed truly interested in the process, and Mac appreciated that. He painstakingly processed the area, and it was well after midnight when he indicated that they could began to exhume the body.

"The body is nude," he told Dana, "and seems to be covered with a white powder. Lime, I'll bet." Mac scratched his chin with his wrist to avoid touching himself with his latex-gloved hand. He secured some of the powder and dropped it into an evidence bag.

"Lime?" Nate hunkered down beside him.

"To decompose the body and throw off time of death. The lime works great if it's wet and decomposes the body. The lime here probably didn't do much because there hasn't been much rainfall. My thinking is that whoever buried this gal wanted the body to decompose quickly. But he forgot to do his homework on the conditions needed to make the lime work. We'll have to let the crime lab verify that, though." He handed the bag to Dana, who added it to her evidence roster.

"One thing for sure." Mac grinned up at Nate and lifted the dead woman's left hand out of the shallow grave. "This isn't an ancient site. Not unless your ancestors wore wristwatches."

"Humph. I concur with your findings, Detective." Nate raised an eyebrow at Mac's attempt at humor. "But we still have that piece of beaded leather."

The medical examiner assisted in cleaning the dirt from the body, every particle going into an evidence bag. The body was lying on its right side in the hole. There was no evidence of restraints or clothing. "She can't have been here too long. The high desert only gets around six to eight inches of rain a year," the M.E. said. "Most bodies found out here look like mummies, with the skin stretched over bone and tendon. This woman hasn't even begun to mummify. I'm guessing maybe four to five weeks."

"That's how long Sara's been missing," Dana said.

Preparing to pull the body clear of the shallow grave, the medical examiner nodded at Mac. "You ready for this?"

"Just a sec." Mac looked for and found a better handhold. "OK, let's get her out. I hate doing it this way; we should take more time. But it looks as though Mother Nature has other plans for us."

Mac and Steve pulled on the body, sliding it out of the shallow grave and setting it down about four feet away. The hair was long and black. "Any of your people unaccounted for, Nate?" Mac asked.

Nate shook his head. "Nope—not that I know of, anyway."

Mac dusted off the face and then stood and backed away from the body. Without looking at the agents, Mac asked, "You guys have a picture of Sara?"

"Yeah. Hang on a sec." Miller went back to his car and hurried back to where Mac was standing. He handed over a large black-and-white photo of their missing person. Mac scrutinized the photo, focusing on Sara's beautiful features. He placed the photo on the ground beside their victim's face. Sara had high cheekbones and a small mole on her cheek. So did the corpse.

"We'll need the doc here to tell us for sure," Mac said, "but I'm guessing this is Sara Watson."

EIGHT

Mac and Dana secured an evidence tag over the zipper of the body bag after Sara's body was loaded in the back of the medical examiner's truck.

"Looks like the investigation is yours now, Detectives." Agent Lauden rubbed his forehead. "I hate to see a case end like this."

Dana nodded, offering empathy. "We were all hoping for a better outcome."

"She was probably killed within a few hours after the abduction." Miller pursed his lips. "We'll meet up with you guys Monday morning to brief you and turn over our files."

"Thanks," Mac said. "Appreciate the offer."

"I'm taking the remains into Portland," the M.E. told them. "We won't be able to get to the autopsy until late morning."

They would need the official report from the medical examiner's office, of course, but it looked as though all the rumors and speculation of Sara's whereabouts had come to an end with a dog's find in a shallow grave. Mac watched the M.E.'s taillights move into the darkness outside of the bright halogen lights. Tires crunched on rocks and pavement as Steve pulled out of the campground, en route to the state medical examiner's office.

He looked up at the red sky, the peaceful glow of the sunset long since replaced by the forest fire's ominous presence. Ash fell like snow over the White River and the empty campground behind him. *Why, God?* Sara's sweet little girl would grow up without a mother.

"The fire's getting close." The voice startled him. He turned to see Nate standing beside him.

"Sure looks that way. I hope our scene is still intact later. I'd like to see it in the daylight. Any reports from the fire line?"

"Burning hot, still heading north, northeast." Nate pulled off his green ball cap and wiped his brow with a once-white handkerchief. "My wife and kids are going to Madras to stay with her sister, just to be on the safe side."

"Do you live on the . . ." Mac stopped midsentence, not knowing the acceptable term for the Indian reservation. Although listed on the map as a reservation, the word sounded a little harsh to Mac, and he didn't want to offend Nate.

"On the rez?" Nate smiled. "Yeah, I have a house on Warm Springs tribal land and have some pasture land in Jefferson County."

Mac nodded. "Sorry, I didn't know the proper name."

"No worries. The reservation or rez is fine. I'm proud of my heritage and my home. I left Warm Springs for a few years, but my heart and my spirit longed to come back."

"You moved away for work?" Mac asked.

"Actually, I moved away for eight years after high school—four years in the army and four years at Oregon State University. My wife and I moved back to the reservation after college to farm, raise horses, and have a family. Things were a little tight a couple of years back, so I took a job as a police reserve at the sheriff's office. One thing led to another, and I ended up taking a full-time officer assignment at Warm Springs. I like this line of work more than I

thought I would. The Spirit led me to this profession for a reason—
if nothing else, to give back to my people. Many of them are not as
fortunate as myself. Alcoholism still runs rampant on the reservation, and many of our people have lost focus."

"The Spirit?" Mac asked, thinking Nate would spin an interesting yarn of Native American beliefs.

"The Holy Spirit." Nate turned to look at the red glow of the
fire. He slapped the cap back on his head. "Do you believe in God,
Mac?"

Nate's directness startled him. A few years ago, the question
might have been met with a sneer and a flippant answer from Mac.
Maybe having Kevin as a partner had changed him—made him less
cynical and more at ease with the idea of God. He remembered
when Kevin had asked the same question of him in the early days of
their friendship. His response had been much different then. He'd
answered more out of embarrassment than a true reflection of his
personal beliefs.

"Yeah, Nate, I do." Although he didn't understand many things
in today's world, Mac's faith had grown over the past year to the
point he could answer the question with little hesitation. "Are you
interested in working this case with us, Nate?" he asked.

"You mean it?" Nate smiled.

"Of course," Mac said.

"You bet I am." Nate couldn't keep from grinning.

"Not that you'd have much choice." Dana, who'd been talking to
Miller and Lauden, joined them. "Having the body dumped this
close to your jurisdiction, I'm sure we're going to have some follow-
up that would require your expertise."

"Ever been to an autopsy?" Mac asked.

"A couple of times, both on natural deaths."

"Why don't you plan on coming to the post with us?" Mac
offered. "That is, if you can get away."

"I'll try. Since there may be some tribal ties to the case, I doubt the police chief will have a problem with my attending. I'll tell him I'm in for the experience. He's pretty progressive with our training. Where should we meet?"

"How about our OSP office in southeast Portland at around ten? We'll shoot for a post time of eleven or so. Is that too early for you with the drive time built in?"

"Let's see. My workday starts around three a.m. to take care of the farm and horses before I go to work. I may be able to drag myself out of bed on a Saturday by seven o'clock to make your schedule." Nate grinned and slapped Mac on the shoulder.

"I'm not getting up any earlier than I have to. I guess I wouldn't make a very good farmer." Mac glanced at his watch. Almost one thirty. Even with a late start in the morning, they wouldn't get much sleep.

"Tell you what, Mac. There's nothing better than working the earth with your own hands. I'll make a deal with you. I help you solve this case, keeping in mind I don't get paid overtime on my days off like you city slickers, and you help me on the farm for a weekend. Deal?"

A broad smile inched across Mac's face. "Do I get to drive a tractor?"

"Sure."

"Then it's a deal." Mac offered his hand.

Nate looked over Mac's proffered hand before shaking it. "Looks to me like you could use some work that puts a few calluses on those hands, though."

"If you two are done bonding, would you mind if we wrap this up?" Dana yawned.

"I'm ready," Mac answered. "Let's get those bags of soil loaded up, and we're out of here." Looking over at Nate, he said, "Why don't you go on home? I'm sure you have things to do—like making sure that fire isn't encroaching on your property."

"You're right, thanks. I'm pretty sure my place is going to be fine, but I would like to get home and check my livestock. It's the smoke I'm worried about now. You better take all you need from here tonight. With this southern wind blowing fuel into the fire, this place will be history."

"Hopefully, we have all we'll need. I went down over a foot under the body in soil collection, and I have plenty of photographs of the scene to look over if need be. It's not ideal, but we'll make do if we have to."

"You calling it a night after you leave here?" Nate helped them load the bags into Mac's trunk.

"Unfortunately not." Dana sighed. "We have to log all this evidence into the Portland office before we can even think about going home. We both live across the river in Washington, so we are a good three hours from hitting the pillow."

"Oh, are you two . . .?" Nate pointed a finger at both of them, asking if they were a couple.

"Oh, no, no." Dana was quick to respond. "We just live in the same town. Not the same house."

"You don't have to make it sound like the idea is totally repulsive, partner." Mac tried to look insulted. "I feel you owe me an apology."

"Oh, please." Dana slapped her hands together to brush off the ash and dust. "I'll see you later, Nathan."

"See you, pal." Mac scanned the parking lot, the gravity of his mission returning to him. He took one last look at the body dump and the glowing red sky before loading the remainder of the soil sacks into the back seat. Dana had placed a yellow plastic emergency blanket out across the back seat to afford the seats some protection from the dusty plastic sacks.

She secured the beaded leather piece she'd gotten from Nate inside a second evidence bag before writing a case number and date on the outer bag. Then she placed it in her briefcase.

With their work complete, the detectives started westward. The initial excitement of the call had long since worn off and turned to exhaustion.

"You think we ought to contact Scott Watson right away, let him know we think we found his wife?" Dana asked.

"Let's hold off until we can confirm the identity at the post tomorrow. We can at least give him one more night of rest before we make the call."

"I don't think I'd be resting much if my spouse was missing. I think I'd like to know," Dana countered.

"I agree, but I think the best call is to confirm her identity though the M.E. and meet with the hubby tomorrow. If it turns out to be Sara, which I'm ninety-nine percent sure it is, then we're going to have to be prepared for a comprehensive interview with her husband after making the notification. Who knows? This guy could be dirty."

"Your call, Mac. Don't know if I agree with you, though. I just think the decent thing to do is let the guy know, that's all."

The decent thing wouldn't be to dump your wife in a shallow grave. Mac kept the thought to himself. More often than not, murder victims were killed by someone they knew, and female victims were most often preyed upon by a male counterpart. Dana knew that, so what was her problem?

"I'd rather do it by the book, Dana. I'm sure that's what Sarge would want us to do. Another half day won't matter."

"Like I said, Mac, it's your call." Dana crossed her arms and stared out the window.

Mac shook his head and gripped the steering wheel with both hands. He knew better than to argue with Dana when she was tired. Besides, if she was upset with him, it might be something he did hours or days ago that came to a head over a discussion on the death notification. Or she could simply be a little tired and grumpy, a danger for everyone in their line of work from time to time.

He would cut her some slack and give her some space. Mac was a quick study if nothing else.

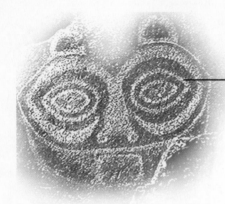

NINE

Claire Montgomery couldn't sleep. She hadn't slept most of the night. The newscaster on the Channel 8 news had reported on a body find in central Oregon. There was little reason for Claire to think it might be Sara, but she couldn't help but wonder. For the past five weeks, any mention of a body being discovered captured her attention and didn't let go until the police made a positive identification. Although the police weren't releasing information, a camper was describing the gruesome find to the local media after alerting authorities. The red numbers on the clock radio told her it was only 6:00 a.m. Saturday. She could have stayed in bed for at least another hour. Probably should have, but there might be new information. Being careful not to wake Allysa, with whom she shared the guest bedroom, Claire eased out of bed and dragged on her bathrobe.

Downstairs, she plucked the *Oregonian* off the front porch and perused the headlines. The body, a woman, found near the Warm Springs Indian reservation, had not been identified. The medical examiner and police were not available for comment. That didn't keep the reporters from speculating on the preliminary information from the man whose dog found the body. The reporter had listed several local women and reiterated the circumstances surrounding their disappearances. A college girl from Eugene, a middle-aged woman from The Dalles. And Sara. Tears blurred the page, and the familiar heartache settled into her chest.

She brushed aside the tears and put on the coffee, then settled into a chair at the table in the breakfast nook, where the sun was already brightening the predawn sky. Soon she'd make breakfast for the four of them as she always did. During these past few weeks, they'd settled into a routine—like family, yet not like family. With Sara still missing, they were more like robots carrying on, doing what needed to be done and little more. Normally, she spent her days caring for Chloe and Allysa, cooking and cleaning, comforting and encouraging Scott and the others, and working when she could slip in a few hours alone.

She didn't want the body to be Sara's. She wanted Sara to come home. More and more, these past few weeks of hearing nothing had led to a number of speculations. The most likely scenario was that she had been abducted and murdered. Others, primarily those who didn't know her well, thought she might have run away to start a new life.

"You're up early." Scott's deep voice startled her and, at the same time, brought comfort.

"Couldn't sleep. So I got up to read the morning paper, and . . ." Her throat caught and she nodded toward the paper. "They found another body. A woman."

He stood behind her for a moment and then went to the cupboard, pulled out two mugs, and filled them with coffee. Setting one in front of her, he lowered himself into the chair beside her. "Do they think it's Sara?"

"There isn't enough information. Just this sinking feeling in the pit of my stomach. I want her to be alive, but. . . ."

"Not much chance of that." His gaze focused on the paper, but he wasn't reading. "I know this sounds callous, but I just want it to be over. I want to know what happened once and for all."

"It's not callous." She placed a hand on his arm. "I want the same thing. So do the others. Waiting is the hardest part." She moved her hand and reached for her coffee. "I'll call the FBI agents again this morning. Maybe they know something the papers don't."

Scott's gaze drifted up to hers. "Thanks."

"For what?"

"For being here. Picking up the slack." He set down his cup and, elbows on the table, dropped his face into his hands. "I don't know what we would have done without you."

Claire settled an arm around his shoulders. "It'll be all right, Scott. No matter what happens, we'll be OK."

The words had a hollow ring to them. How could things ever be right again? After a few moments, she got up and took her coffee into the kitchen. She'd made baked oatmeal the night before, and all she had to do this morning was heat it and cook some sausage. Taking care of Scott and Chloe was the least she could do for Sara.

TEN

Mac yawned as he rolled out of bed and focused blurry eyes on his alarm clock. Eight o'clock in the morning, and he could still use several hours of sleep. He'd had only three hours of restless sack time. It seemed he had the most trouble falling asleep when he needed it the most. Though analyzing the cases often complicated his sleep, it was the way Dana had acted on the ride home that had troubled him the most.

Was she jealous of his relationship with Kristen? Or maybe she was stewing over some guy. Mac thought back to a recent date that had turned into a fiasco. Maybe the guy was bothering her again. If the opportunity arose, he'd ask her about it. Of course, she could have been reacting to Nate's assumption that they were an item. He'd teased her about being hurt, but her reaction had affected him more than he cared to admit.

Lucy, Mac's golden retriever, ambled into the room, looking for some affection. The dog's thick tail thumped the wall as Mac rubbed her head and ears. "I'll be back later for a walk, old girl, I promise. I have to work again today, but the overtime is nice. We like the overtime, don't we?" Mac smiled at the dog, who seemed to understand what he was saying.

Mac showered, put on a pair of gray slacks and navy blue blazer, and grabbed a tie for the road. He wouldn't need it for the autopsy, but he might need it for the follow-up and death notification. Mac locked Lucy in her kennel and left a message for his neighbor, Carl, to pick her up, which was standard practice with his schedule. His widowed neighbor and Lucy both enjoyed each other's company, a little too much sometimes. Mac couldn't help feeling a little jealous when Lucy seemed to enjoy seeing Carl as much as or more than she liked seeing him.

They'd managed to get the autopsy scheduled for eleven that morning. Thoughts of the morgue reminded him of Kristen's unexpected trip to Florida and put him in a sour mood. He really wanted her to perform the autopsy. Besides her being the best, he liked working with her. He liked her banter and her sense of humor and her cooking and the way she kissed him.

Mac groaned. He had to stop thinking about Kristen. From the way she sounded the other day, their relationship, like much of Oregon, had gone up in smoke.

He left his Vancouver apartment and drove south to Portland, crossing the wide, ambling Columbia River that served as a boundary between Oregon and Washington. Many of the troopers assigned to work in Mac's office lived on the Washington side to avoid paying Oregon's property taxes. Mac lived there to be close to his grandmother, who resided in a retirement community not far away from his home. On the way, he stopped at a Starbucks for a coffee to go. He almost got one for Dana but decided against it. After the way she'd treated him on the way home from Warm Springs, he opted not to. On top of that, she had refused his offer to pick her up this morning.

Mac punched the gate code and drove into the back lot, parking his Crown Vic next to Dana's Pontiac. He walked through the patrol side of the building, greeting a few of the uniformed troopers on his way to the back room where the plain-clothes detectives worked. The door to the detectives' office was already open. Apparently, he and Dana were not the only ones pulling overtime today. Weekends were generally days off for the detectives, but it looked like the entire crew had come in. The narcotics guys had served a warrant the previous day and had to act quickly on their arrests if they wanted to move up the drug-dealing food chain to the supplier.

Philly and Russ, the other pair of detectives assigned to the Violent Offender Unit with Mac and Dana, were working a murder investigation out of Clackamas County. They were pulling together a search warrant affidavit on an outlaw biker clubhouse, which would require the department SWAT team to assist them. The murder suspect, a dope dealer accused of killing a junkie, was in custody and looking to make a deal by ratting out some buddies at the clubhouse. He claimed to have witnessed a large weapons cache at the clubhouse, along with a substantial supply of crystal meth.

"You look lovely this morning." Philly met Mac in the doorway. "How come Dana beat you to work, and she doesn't look like she slept in her car?" He took a sip of coffee from his dingy yellow cup.

"How come you look like a train wreck every day?" Mac countered. He took the last sip out of his own coffee before throwing the empty container into the garbage.

"Well, I never." Philly shrugged and walked back into his office, where Russ was typing an affidavit for a search warrant application. Philly loved a good insult exchange, but thankfully, he knew when not to press a tired detective who'd only had one cup of coffee. He'd withdrawn for now, but Mac had no doubt that he'd find time to exchange barbs later.

"Morning, Dana." Mac poked his head into her new office

before going to his cubicle. Once there, he powered up his computer and began checking phone messages.

Dana came in and set a paper sack and a cup of coffee on Mac's desk.

"What's this?" Mac asked.

"Coffee and a scone, the fattening pumpkin one you like with all the icing. Sorry about last night—or this morning, actually. I wasn't mad at you; things just came out wrong."

"No problem. I'd forgotten all about it," Mac fibbed. "Thanks for the coffee, though." Mac felt guilty. He wished he'd taken the high road and purchased his partner a treat too.

"Any messages from Nate?" Dana asked.

"No, you?"

"Nothing, so I assume he's still coming."

"Yep. He's married, you know," Mac teased.

"Yes, I know." Dana flashed him a smile. "Too bad, though. He's pretty cute. The good ones are always taken."

I'm not. Mac ignored the jab or tried to.

"Any word on the fire?" she asked.

"I haven't heard. I'll call RDC and see if they have something." Mac dialed dispatch to get an update. He spoke with the floor supervisor for less than a minute. He'd expected the fire to do damage, but hearing it firsthand left him feeling disappointed and angry. He hung up with a little more force than necessary. "You want the bad news or the bad news first?"

"Oh, how about the bad news?" Dana leaned against his desk.

"The fire jumped containment lines to the east and crossed the Deschutes River and is burning toward Maupin. Sounds like a U.S. Forest Service employee was hurt by a falling tree about the time we were on the scene."

"Oh, no. How bad?"

"They didn't know for sure, but I'm sure having a tree fall on you would do some serious damage. That's the first part; ready for the second?"

Dana nodded.

"The fire jumped the White River, and our body dumpsite is ablaze. With the fire burning the earth several inches down from the surface, that land will be sterile for months. On top of that, we'll probably have fire retardant and who knows what else dumped all over the place. It's a good thing we processed the scene and took what we did last night."

"I guess so. I hope we didn't miss anything." Dana sipped her iced coffee through a straw in the plastic lid. "We should tell Kevin."

"I was just going to call him at home and update him."

"Good. I'll let you do that while I get back to my paperwork."

After calling Kevin to brief him on their progress, Mac worked on writing his reports and documenting their actions from the crime-scene evidence processing.

NATHAN ARRIVED AT THEIR OFFICE shortly after ten and was led to the detectives' office by a uniformed trooper who'd seen him drive into the lot.

"Hey, Nate." Mac shook his hand.

"Good morning, Mac. Hey, Dana," Nate said as she emerged from her office.

"Find the place OK?" Mac asked.

"Yeah, I found the place just fine. Good directions once I got into town, although I had to drive into The Dalles and come in on I-84 due to the fire. Highway 26 is closed right now. Did you know the fire ate up the White River campground about three hours ago?"

"We heard." Mac sighed. "Are you sure it went over the body dumpsite?"

"Positive. I was in contact with the smoke jumpers who flew the area. It's a half mile from the White River now, so that's well past our crime scene."

"I can't believe we were just there," Dana said.

"Look on the bright side," Nate offered. "If that kid's dog hadn't unearthed that piece of leather, we might have never found the body."

"I guess that's one way of looking at it," Mac replied. "How's your family?"

"Doing good. They're safe and sound in Madras this morning. They'll be heading back to the farm later today. The fire is staying well away from us. I keep a pretty clean place, so there wasn't a lot of fuel for the fire to eat on. I was mainly concerned about the smoke and how it would affect our livestock. We have a new paint colt that's only a week old, so I didn't want her getting a lungful of smoke. She's doing great, though."

"That's a relief. You sure you're OK to be gone today?"

"No problem. The chief said he couldn't pay overtime, but he's going to let me trade days and take another day off."

"No pay? Now that's dedication." Dana smiled.

"What can I say?" Nate turned to look at Mac. "If we solve this, you're still working the place with me."

"I know, but I'm bringing Dana. She's my partner, and we stick together, through thick and thin."

"That would be the *thin*, partner," Dana laughed. "And you're on your own with this one. You shouldn't write checks you can't cash."

"Well, Dana." Nate chuckled. "If you change your mind, we'd love to have you visit."

Mac introduced Nate to Philly and Russ before showing him around the station house and giving him a key to the building so he could access the office during the time they were working together.

While Mac briefed Nate, Dana finished logging in the evidence, primarily the soil samples taken from the dumpsite. She kept the leather scrap with the beadwork out for the post, in the event the medical examiner wanted to see the evidence. She also made arrangements with the State Police forensics lab to process the soil evidence for additional trace items that could lead them to their killer. The soils would have to be sifted, with any small items analyzed under the microscope.

"You ready, Dana?" Mac asked when he and Nate returned to the detectives' office.

"All set, guys. We're lined up with the crime lab to process our soil. Angela will give us a call when and if she can send some techs out to the office. She made it pretty clear that sifting through the dirt was not a job for CSI unless we located some trace evidence. I guess she figures we could handle the task."

Mac didn't especially like the idea of sifting through all that dirt, but they had no choice. "All right, then. Let's head to the post and see if the M.E. can put an official name to our victim and tell us how she died."

ELEVEN

Mac walked down the hall and through the squad room with Nate and Dana, wading through the crowd of SWAT team members who were making preparations to serve the warrant with Russ and Philly. The officers were assigned all over the state, most working uniform patrol when not involved in tactical team duties.

"Hey, Mac." One of the troopers in the black-and-gray camouflage utility uniforms looked up from his automatic MP-5 rifle.

"Danny? Daniel Revman?" Mac peered into the face covered in ash-colored paint.

"In the flesh." The young trooper shook hands with Mac. "Hey, Mac. I haven't seen you since the academy. Looks like you're doing pretty good for yourself." Daniel eyed Mac's sport coat. "You look like the brass."

"Not hardly. Been working detectives for some time now. I just moved to violent offenders crimes about a year ago. You still working the road?"

"That's right; don't plan on leaving it either. I'm down in Medford, and I've been on the SWAT team for about four months."

Daniel motioned around the room at his stonefaced peers. "You married, Mac? Any family?"

"Not yet. Working on it, though." *Now why had he said that?* He glanced up, relieved to see Dana and Nate walk out the door.

Daniel grinned. "The family or the wife?"

"Both, actually," Mac admitted, though he wasn't sure why. Wishful thinking, Mac decided. Was he still seeing Kristen or had he made a mistake getting close to her too? "The woman I'm seeing has a little boy. How about you?"

"Been married for four years now, and we have one in the oven. I'll be a daddy in about two months. A little girl."

"Congratulations." Mac shook Daniel's hand again. "So are you and the team hitting that biker house this afternoon?"

Daniel nodded. "We're waiting on the paperwork and the detective briefing."

"OK, people, let's get started," the barrel-chested SWAT sergeant barked from the front of the room. "Get your weapons and equipment check going."

"We already checked, Sarge," a trooper yelled from the back of the room.

"Then check it again!" the sergeant yelled back.

Daniel gave Mac a nod and fell in line with his squad. Mac handed him a business card. "Give me a call when you get a chance so we can catch up."

"Will do." Daniel placed the card in his breast pocket while keeping a close eye on the sergeant.

By the time Mac got to the door, Dana had pulled her car around, which was now back in service, and Nate was sitting in the backseat.

"You don't have to sit in back, Nate," Mac offered. "I could have jumped back there."

"No, I'm good. Besides, you're taller. I fit back here just fine." Nate smiled. "And I wouldn't want to break up the team."

Mac folded himself in and snapped on the seat belt. "Sorry I kept you waiting. Ran into an old friend I went through the academy with. We ended up working a few hundred miles apart, and I lost track of him. He's on the tactical team now, has a baby on the way."

"That's nice." Dana feigned interest. She didn't have much to do with the guys on the SWAT team. Those guys were the jet pilots of the outfit, enjoying the fast pace of their assignment. Dana found them to be a little too fast for her liking, having been the object of taunts and inappropriate jokes while she was in their company. They were pretty good one-on-one, but together they could be a little over the edge with their frat house antics.

When they arrived at the M.E.'s office, Dana grabbed her plastic evidence tub from the back of the car and handed her camera equipment to Mac.

Nate offered to carry the evidence kit for Dana.

"Finally, a gentleman in the bunch." Dana grinned at both men, softening her insult.

"Don't get used to it," Mac teased.

He turned toward the brick building and noticed Kristen's silver Volvo in the parking lot. Had she come home, or had she just left her car there? The thought of seeing Kristen brought a measure of excitement pulsing through his veins. The idea of seeing her shouldn't have him reacting like a teenager with raging hormones. *Careful,* he told himself. *She just went to Florida to see her ex. She might not even be interested anymore. Besides, she's not your type.* Mac had been telling himself that for months, but it didn't wash. Appearances aside, she was very much his type. He just hoped she hadn't opted out of their tenuous relationship.

The three signed in at the back of the morgue, setting their supplies on the exam room floor and evidence shelf. The two-table autopsy room was warm and humid—probably from all the hot water running through the exam tables to wash the stainless steel equipment. Condensation clung to the small outside windows, evidence the room had been used earlier this morning for autopsies.

"You ready for Doc Thorpe?" Henry asked, poking his head inside the room. Henry, a medical assistant at the morgue, had worked there for years and was one of the best.

"You bet, Henry. We're the only ones coming," Dana answered.

Mac wanted to ask Henry about Kristen, but he didn't trust himself to speak just yet. Too many emotions had his heart rate doing double-time.

"All right, then; I'll get our customer. Doc Thorpe is on her way down." Henry entered the cooler and, seconds later, wheeled the gurney with their victim on it to the examination room. The body was still covered with the rubber and plastic body bag that they'd enclosed it in last night, the red body tag giving evidence that the zipper had not been tampered with.

Mac made note of this formality in his notes, in the event a defense attorney tried to claim the body had been accessed and evidence planted. The tag was clipped around the special zipper with metal tabs to ensure the body would not be disturbed until the post. He snipped off the tag and secured it for evidence. As he was bagging the item, Dr. Kristen Thorpe entered the room. His stomach lurched.

"Hello, gang." She gave each of them a friendly smile, her gaze skimming from one to another without meeting Mac's eyes.

"I thought you were in Florida," Mac said, ignoring Dana's questioning look.

"I was." Without elaborating, Kristen grabbed her rubber apron from a hook on the wall and tested her dictating system.

Mac's stomach felt as though it had been filled with lead. She clearly didn't want to talk about her trip, and she didn't seem pleased to see him. Mac wouldn't press it. Not here, and certainly not now.

With none of her usual gallows humor, Kristen pressed the

metal foot pedal on the floor and gave a test count into the microphone hanging from the ceiling. Once she was satisfied it was in working order, she jotted the time and date on the grease board to use for a reference while dictating her autopsy. As she progressed, she would add elements to the board: height, weight, age, and eventually the weight and mass of the organs she removed from the body.

"Who might you be?" Kristen turned to Nate, offering a wooden smile.

"Sorry. I should have introduced you," Mac answered as Kristen moved in to shake Nate's hand. "This is Officer Nathan Webb from the Warm Springs Police Department. He's working the murder with us. Nate, meet the infamous Dr. Kristen Thorpe."

"It's a pleasure."

"I'm pleased to meet you, Nathan." Instead of regaling them with a grin, she turned back to the body bag. "Is this a tribal member?"

"We don't think so," Dana answered. "We have a visual identification, such as it is, and believe our victim is Sara Watson, Senator Wilde's niece."

"Oh. Sorry to hear that."

"Us too," Dana sighed. "We recovered her body up by the Warm Springs Reservation, and due to the proximity of the body dump to the tribal lands and in case there is a tribal connection, Nate has agreed to help us out."

Kristen nodded and unzipped the body bag to reveal the corpse, still coated with dirt and apparent lime residue. She collected several samples of the soil from the victim and from within the body bag before requesting Henry's help in hoisting the body onto the examination table.

Dana and Mac secured the possible evidence items as Kristen handed them over, while Nate photographed the autopsy. Kristen somberly dictated her findings, or lack of them, into the microphone. Sara's case had been in the paper for some time now, and it always made it a little more difficult on all of them when they knew something about the victim and the family. She made note of the caesarean scar on the victim's abdomen, consistent with what she expected to find on Sara from childbirthing. Kristen also documented a substantial scar on the left knee from a previous surgery. Mac confirmed from the reports that Sara had knee surgery after a skiing accident.

After the initial examination of the feet, legs, and torso, Kristen turned her attention to the head and neck area. She noted some purple and blue striations on the neck, making a verbal note into her dictation device that she needed to check the esophagus for evidence of ligature strangulation.

"See these marks?" Kristen pointed, stopping her dictation. "Looks like there was something wrapped around her neck and face. Grab my blue light, Henry."

Henry shut off the lights and handed Kristen a simple-looking light with a special blue bulb on the end, covered by a red plastic shield on one side. Kristen waived the wand over the body, finding nothing other than soil until the special lighting reached the head and neck area. The striations took form now, showing wide, structured patterns on the neck. She shut off the light after taking measurements and recording the information on the Dictaphone. Henry turned the lights back on while Kristen stood back from the table and thought for a moment.

"What do you think?" Mac asked, knowing the look on Kristen's face.

"Duct tape would be my guess, something that was tightly wrapped around her face and neck. You guys better take some scrapings from her face, hair, and wrists. I wouldn't be surprised if we found evidence of some type of resin or glue on her."

Kristen examined the hands of the victim more closely, this time with a magnifying glass. "Her nails are trimmed down to the pad under the nail. They are cut right into the dermis. No woman would keep her nails like this." Kristen raised the right hand for Dana to view.

"You're right. First of all, it would be too painful. Look how uneven they are; I'm surprised they aren't bloody in spots," Dana added.

"Probably because she was dead when they were cut," Kristen noted. "No heartbeat, no blood pumping. Her killer apparently took great care to remove the bindings and trim the fingernails, along with all the clothing. Too bad. We might have found forensic evidence on her clothes. This creep put quite a bit of thought into it." Her jaw clenched. "He knew exactly what he was doing."

Kristen moved up to examine the eyes and the nose, noting some hemorrhaging characteristics on the whites of the eyes that evidenced lack of oxygen. "I can't say for sure if she was choked or strangled, gang, but there is evidence of oxygen deprivation."

Doc Thorpe put her left hand on the victim's forehead and her right palm on the chin, forcing open the jaw with a crack. "We have something inside the mouth. Give me some light here, Henry." She held the mouth open while Nate photographed the object and moved aside so Kristen could remove it. "It's some kind of leather pouch or something."

Kristen set the object on the table, turning over the small brown leather object to reveal the same kind of intricate beadwork they'd found on the object they'd recovered near the body.

Dana told her about the find. "The leather and bead coloring look like a match. What do you guys think?"

Nate took several more photos. "Hard to tell. But I'd say it's a good guess."

"I have the piece we found so we can compare." Mac retrieved the evidence bag. The beaded leather piece the dog had unearthed looked like it had been a flap over the pouch and had been torn away. Mac pulled the item from the evidence bag, smoothing the wrinkled leather with his gloved hands. He examined that piece alongside the larger section that Kristen had pulled from the victim's mouth, comparing the beadwork and leather. "It's a match, all right."

"There's something inside the pouch." Kristen pulled open the leather string and withdrew a small round stone, which she set on the examination table. "There's something I haven't seen before." Kristen stepped back so Nate could photograph it.

Mac moved in for a closer look. Carved into the face of the stone was a crude image of a catlike face or possibly an image of a raccoon.

"Tsagagalal." Nate peered down at the image. He looked back up at the others, stunned and obviously disturbed. "The leather pouch is a talisman of some sort. According to Native American tradition, it has many uses. The image on the stone is that of Tsagagalal."

"Which, in English, means what?" Mac asked.

"She Who Watches. It's one of the Indian stone idols."

"Do you know this for sure, Nathan?" Kristen bent down to examine the object.

"Yes, I'm sure." He stepped back. "There is a well-known legend behind the image. I don't know if it has anything to do with the case or not."

"Spill it." Kristen smiled, and this time it was genuine. "I love this stuff."

"I would have to go to an elder for the entire story, but I can tell you what I know. This is the story told by the Wishram people.

"A woman had a house where the village of Nixluidix was later built. She was chief of all who lived in the region. That was a long time before Coyote came up the river and changed things and people were not yet real people. After a time, Coyote in his travels came to this place and asked the inhabitants if they were living well or ill. They sent him to their chief, who lived up on the rocks, where she could look down on the village and know what was going on.

"Coyote climbed up to the house on the rocks and asked, 'What kind of living do you give these people? Do you treat them well or are you one of those evil women?'

"'I am teaching them to live well and build good houses,' she replied.

"'Soon the world will change,' said Coyote, 'and women will no longer be chiefs.' Then he changed her into a rock with the command, 'You shall stay here and watch over the people who live here.'

"All the people know that Tsagagalal sees all things, for whenever they are looking at her, those large eyes are watching them."

"Fascinating," Kristen said.

"Yes." Nate smiled. "She Who Watches has also been called the stone Owl Woman Who Watches. Indian women sometimes go to the stone and kneel before it. They say something like, 'You who watch, please look into me and see my problem and help me to solve it.' A ray of light comes down to shine on the stone face then. After the woman goes to her teepee to sleep, a dream comes, telling her how to deal with the problem. That woman may go again to the stone, and the ray of light comes down again on the stone, and the next dream gives her even more details as to how to solve the problem."

"Wow. So the original stone is still around?" Dana asked.

"Yes," said Nate. "The original stone is ten thousand years old, and it is sacred to our people."

"Where is it?" Mac asked.

"On the Washington side of the river across from The Dalles. It's both petroglyph and pictograph, which means it is both carved and painted. I've actually been there with my grandfather. It's amazing. The image of She Who Watches is a symbol of protection for many of our people and for neighboring tribes in the Northwest.

I could only guess what meaning it has here. I'll take some photos back to our tribal elders so they can confirm my initial impression, but I'm ninety-nine percent sure that's the correct image. I'd also like their opinion on the authenticity of the piece, see if they have an opinion on the artist."

"That is wild." Kristen looked back at the body. "How does a professional woman like Sara Watson get tangled up in a mess that ends up with this type of ritualistic message, whatever that message is?"

"That's what we're going to have to find out, I guess." Dana's gaze moved back to the beaded pouch.

"I have an idea," Mac said.

"Let's hear it," Dana and Kristen said in unison.

"Sara is Senator Wilde's niece. He's the majority leader who could swing the vote on the Native American casino in the gorge."

"That's right." Dana's eyes lighted up. "There was some speculation that the tribe was behind Sara's disappearance. Maybe those articles weren't as bogus as the federal agents led us to believe."

"You think one of my people killed this girl to put pressure on her uncle to vote for a casino?" Nate asked, sounding insulted.

"Maybe they didn't intend to kill her," Dana replied. "Maybe it started out as a kidnapping to scare the senator into doing what they wanted."

"No offense intended," Mac added. "You have to admit that finding her with that pouch in her mouth is highly suspicious. It's an idea that bears checking out."

"You'd think the feds would have told us if they thought there was anything to the articles suggesting Native American involvement." Dana eyed the pouch and stone again.

"Would they? You and I both thought they were holding out on us."

"I don't know, Mac." Dana bit her lip. "They saw that torn piece of beaded leather out at the body dumpsite. You'd think they would have said something then."

"We better pay a visit to our agent friends when we're done with the post. I want to see if anyone's holding out information, so we don't put our foot in anything we aren't supposed to."

"Don't you think we'd better contact the husband first?" Dana asked.

Remembering last night's argument, Mac agreed. He was getting ahead of himself. A visit to Scott Watson was in order for a number of reasons. "You're right," Mac said. "We'll head over from here and take a black-and-white photo with us for ID."

Kristen completed the autopsy in less than two hours, finding little of value in the internal examination of the body. She extracted body fluids to forward to the OSP lab for toxicology screens, in the event Sara had been poisoned. Though there was bruising on her throat, and some ligature marks, Sara's windpipe was intact, lending no physical evidence to point to strangulation as the cause of death.

Kristen had no comprehensive evidence to make her call, which was often the case. She finally gave them a tentative cause. "I'm going to rule the death a homicide due to asphyxiation, guys. The probable evidence of the duct tape remnants and the airway obstruction are pretty compelling items. I'll wait for the crime lab results before typing out the death certificate, but this is enough to give you a start."

"Thanks, Kristen," Mac said.

"Sure." The tone was decidedly cool.

Mac hung behind the others, hoping for a chance to talk to Kristen alone. She, however, showed no indication she wanted to talk to him. With Henry still in the room, he decided not to wait around. Maybe he'd call her later. He wanted to know where he stood with her. On the other hand, maybe he didn't. "Women," he muttered under his breath and headed outside.

TWELVE

Nate opted to return home after the post, so they dropped him off at the station before taking the evidence to the lab and getting their photos developed. The OSP lab in Portland was in the same building as the Portland Police analysis units, often sharing specialized equipment, though the State Police scientists completed all the forensic work. On the way, Mac tried to reach the FBI agents but hit a dead end. Both men were unavailable until Monday. They dropped Nate off at their office parking compound and agreed to meet on Monday morning so they could all go over their case files with the feds.

"It must be nice to have the weekend off," Dana commented as she pulled out into the street.

"Hmm. Looks like we're in for the long haul." They'd be working the entire weekend doing background investigation and lining up potential players.

"Want to grab a bite to eat before we take care of the evidence and photos?" Dana asked.

"Thought you'd never ask."

"Wendy's OK? I like their salads."

Before he could answer, she pulled into a Wendy's parking lot. "Let's go inside. We need to talk."

Mac didn't like the sound of that. Had she noticed Kristen's frosty attitude toward him? He didn't want to discuss Kristen. Then again, maybe Dana wanted to talk about her own troubles. That he could handle. Maybe.

Once they'd ordered and taken their seats, Dana fidgeted with her napkin and poured dressing on her salad. "So what's the deal with Kristen?"

Mac held up a hand. "All I know is what she told me. Her ex was in an accident and not expected to live—she flew back to Florida. I was surprised to see her back here so soon. That's it."

"Hmm. She must be exhausted. I guess that could explain her somber mood. But she sure was acting strange toward you."

Mac shrugged. "I thought I'd call her later."

Dana nodded. "What I really wanted to talk to you about was my attitude last night. I get cranky when I'm tired."

Mac grinned. "No kidding."

She kicked him under the table. "There's something else too. I've been getting strange calls."

Mac sat up straighter. "Strange, like how?"

"It's annoying more than anything. The caller doesn't say anything and then hangs up."

"You're sure it isn't a telemarketer?"

"Yeah." She dug a fork into the greens.

"How often?" Mac bit into his hamburger.

"Every night. It's probably some kids fooling around."

Or maybe a stalker, Mac thought. "Any ideas on who it might be?"

"Not a clue. I've been around long enough to make a few enemies, but. . . ."

"What about that guy you went out with a while back? The one you tagged as a potential DUI."

"Brian Henderson? I've thought about him. It may be nothing, and I'm probably being paranoid. After working on all those sex offenders, a person can get a little gun-shy."

"Have you reported the calls?"

"To the Vancouver police? No." She moved the greens around on her plate. "The caller hasn't done anything so far except to disturb my sleep."

So far. Mac didn't like it. "You're concerned, and so am I. Call the police and file a report. Maybe they can beef up patrol in your area."

"I will. I don't want you to worry about it. Just wanted you to know why I've been a little short-tempered lately."

"Thanks for letting me know. You'll tell me if anything else happens, right?"

"Of course." Her dimples deepened as she flashed a dazzling smile at him.

He focused on his hamburger. He wanted to ask Dana about a number of things—like why she'd called Agent Lauden "Jimmy" and if there was something going on between her and Russ, but he thought better of it.

"Is everything OK between you and Kristen?" Dana asked.

He didn't want to talk about Kristen anymore and had no idea what the woman was thinking. "I don't know. Why do you ask?"

"I keep thinking about how distant she seemed today."

"As far as I know, we're still seeing each other. What about you?"

She ducked her head and speared some greens. "The only guys I seem to attract are cops and jerks."

"Are you saying one is synonymous with the other?"

She chuckled. "Maybe I just need to get out more. Or lower my standards."

"You could give up on your determination not to date a cop."

"Actually, I almost did. Jim Lauden asked me out, and we met for coffee. He's nice."

"But?"

She pushed her half-empty plate to the center of the table. Resting her arms on the table, she said, "Mac, if I were going to date a cop, you'd be the first in line. But I'm not, so. . . ." She leaned back. "Do you have any normal single friends?"

"What happened to the attorney you told me about?"

She shrugged. "He's OK. Just . . . no sparks. Actually, that's not entirely true. I had to break several dates. Haven't heard from him in a while, so I figure he's given up on me."

Mac thought about Kristen and how she'd asked him if he was really over Dana. He hadn't been able to answer and still couldn't. If Dana asked, he'd be there for her. So what did that say about him? He really needed to get past the Dana thing if he ever expected to move on in his relationship with Kristen. On the other hand, did he really want to pursue his relationship with Kristen? She apparently had issues with her ex-husband. Mac finished his fries and crumpled the napkin a little harder than he needed to.

THEY ARRIVED AT THE WATSON HOME at nearly three in the afternoon after visiting the lab and getting the photos. Dana pulled the black-and-white photo Kristen had taken at the post out of the envelope and placed it in her briefcase in a manila folder. This was the one they'd show Scott Watson for identification. She slid the rest of the photos into a separate envelope.

"Think we should've called first?" Dana asked.

"No. These things are better done this way. Kevin taught me to study the reaction to a death notification, but not to put too much into the response. Everyone reacts differently."

Dana pulled into the circular drive and checked out with dispatch before she and Mac made their way up to the front door. Mac rang the doorbell, peering through the partial glass door. Scott Watson, looking leaner than he had a few weeks ago, met them at the door. He was barefoot and dressed in jeans and a stained T-shirt. His dark hair was matted on one side, looking like he may have been taking a nap before they'd arrived. He leaned against the doorjamb. On their first visit, he'd been clean shaven and wearing a suit. Of course, this was Saturday.

"Can I help you?" Scott looked like he'd fall over if forced to stand on his own.

Mac and Dana held up their badge wallets. "We're with the State Police." Mac answered. "I'm Detective McAllister, and this is Detective Bennett. You may not remember us, Mr. Watson, but we met a few weeks ago, the day Sara disappeared."

"Oh, yeah, I remember you now. Is this about Sara?" He made no move to allow them entry.

"I'm afraid so, Mr. Watson. Is it OK if we come in and speak with you?" Mac asked.

Scott rubbed the back of his neck. "Did you find her? Is she OK?"

Mac wondered if Scott had read the morning paper or seen the news. "We'd like to come inside and talk, if that's OK." Mac glanced over at the neighbor's home. He really didn't want to deliver a death message on the front porch.

"Sure." Scott opened the door all the way and backed up. "Come on in."

They followed Scott into the living room, more than a little concerned about his demeanor. Scott flopped on the couch, bent forward and elbows resting on his knees. "What's going on?"

"We've been working on your wife's disappearance with the FBI."

"I know." Scott sat motionless, his gaze shifting from Mac to Dana. "Did you find her?" Tears seeped into his eyes. As so often happened, Scott knew what they had come to tell him. Still, it didn't make the telling or the receiving any easier.

Mac nodded. "I'm sorry to be the one to tell you this, but we've recovered an adult female body on the east side of Mount Hood and have reason to believe it may be Sara."

Scott's shoulders sagged. He started to stand but then sat back down and shook his head. "You're sure it's Sara? I mean, how do you know?"

"Well, sir," Mac answered, "we have a visual likeness and several distinguishing marks and scars that are consistent with Sara's. We have a black-and-white photograph we'd like you to take a look at and verify that it's your wife." Dana pulled the eight-by-ten from her briefcase. "This can be pretty rough. Is there anyone home that you'd like to come sit with you? We could call a friend if you want."

He shook his head. "Chloe's upstairs sleeping, and Claire should be back from the mall pretty soon. Claire is Sara's cousin; I think you met her the day Sara disappeared. Anyway, she's staying here for a while to help me with Chloe. I'd rather just take a look and get it over with." Scott held out a trembling hand.

Dana glanced at the black-and-white picture. Sara had been so beautiful in life, and now. . . . The face was fairly intact, the eyes wrinkled and sunken, her hair wet and combed straight back. The black-and-white film softened the cadaver image and lessened the impact of the gray-tinted skin. Kristen had combed back her hair with water after cleaning her up. If not for the barely visible striations apparent at the post, Sara almost looked as though she was resting after a shower.

Dana walked around to sit next to Scott and held up the photo for him to see.

He glanced at it for a moment and then looked away. "That's her." He covered his eyes and leaned forward.

Dana settled a hand on his shoulder. "I'm sorry for your loss, Mr. Watson."

Mac teared in empathy at the man's response. He swallowed hard and blew a puff of air into his eyes to dry them—a self-taught trick he'd used countless times to maintain his composure at times like this. Mac wasn't much for tears, but he never got used to other people's suffering and at times found their crying contagious.

"Are you sure we can't call someone?" Mac asked.

"I'm OK," Scott looked at the picture again. "I'll have to let her aunt and uncle know." Looking up at them, he said, "Please, before you go. It was supposed to be a kidnapping, and now. . . . How did this happen?"

At that moment, Claire came in, talking with Allysa about spending the night with her grandparents. She stopped when she saw Mac and Dana. Then turning to her daughter, said, "Allysa— why don't you run upstairs and check on Chloe, okay?" She waited until Allysa was out of sight before acknowledging them.

"You . . . you're the detectives who were here when Sara first disappeared."

Her gaze slipped from the detectives to Scott and to the photo. She dropped the bags she'd brought in and covered her mouth. "It was Sara? The body you found last night?"

Dana hurried to Claire's side. "Why don't you come in and sit down." Claire glanced at the bags and then let Dana lead her into the living room. "We were just about to tell Scott about our findings," Dana told her.

Claire dropped to the sofa next to Scott, her arms going around him, his around her.

Dana searched for and found a box of tissues for them.

Interesting, Mac thought. The husband and cousin seemed pretty close. Something he intended to find out about. They waited for a few minutes while Claire and Scott pulled themselves together, then Mac and Dana spent the better part of an hour attempting to answer their questions without giving away investigative leads.

They both knew they would have to eliminate Scott as a suspect, and possibly the cousin, but they wanted to be sensitive to their grief right now. Once the questions had been answered, Mac and Dana sat through several heart-wrenching phone calls to friends and family members, while Scott broke the news to them one by one and Claire busied herself in the kitchen preparing dinner.

Mac made a mental note of who Scott was calling, as these were people they might want to interview at a later date. Mac also kept a watchful eye on Scott, noting his reactions and facial expressions. He'd called Anne, the senator's wife; his parents; Jackie, his secretary; and a family friend. Mac recognized the names from the list he'd compiled that first day.

They had no real leads at this point, only speculation. They would let the family grieve for a couple of days before delving into the details of Scott's and Sara's lives.

Mac wasn't looking forward to that. They would have to ask uncomfortable questions about her work and home life, in addition to any other issues that may be known or unknown to her husband. These investigations too often revealed awkward practices by suspects or the deceased, which could hinder or obscure the investigation. Mac knew firsthand how people could obstruct key evidence if it might embarrass them or put them in a poor light.

He'd worked a death investigation in a rest area once where homosexual men frequented the area at night. The victim, found strangled wearing women's underwear and a dog collar, was an upstanding member of the community with a wife and children. It took Mac months to locate witnesses and discover that the death was an accident. The delays came only because the other men at the scene were businessmen with families, and many were not openly gay. The risk of embarrassment was too much for them, and the case almost went unsolved.

Anne Wilde, the senator's wife, arrived just as Mac and Dana were about to leave. Scott's secretary pulled up right behind her, and then came Scott's mother, who introduced herself as Judith Watson. The women were all crying, and Mac couldn't imagine having to deal with the four of them at once. Mrs. Watson joined Scott on the couch. With one hand she fumbled with a tissue, trying to stop the flow of tears; the other hand lightly massaged Scott's shoulder. None of the women seemed shocked at the news, though they, like Scott, had questions.

"How long has she been dead?" Judith asked. She must have been around sixty, stocky, with reddish hair. She wore no makeup and had on slacks with a loose short-sleeved shirt and sandals.

"We suspect she was killed around the time she disappeared," Dana answered.

"The senator and I saw on the news that a body had been found," Anne Wilde said. Her silver hair was pulled back in a severe chignon. She wore a gray pantsuit with a fuchsia blouse. "My first thought was that it might be Sara. When we heard the location, we felt sure of it."

"Why is that?" Mac asked.

"Well, there had been some talk about the Warm Springs casino—that one of them may have kidnapped her. That's the first place I'd look."

"We'll do that." Mac wondered how she'd come by that information and made a note to talk to the senator's wife later. Of course, there had been reference to the casino in the news. Maybe there was more to it than what the feds had told them.

Anne excused herself to go into the kitchen to make coffee for the others.

"I can't imagine anyone killing Sara." Jackie sat on the edge of her chair, her hands tightly clasped. The secretary seemed more a family friend than an employee, but he'd noticed that during their earlier visit. She was a brunette with wide blue eyes, attractive. As Mac recalled, she'd blamed herself for not alerting Scott to Sara's initial phone call after the robbery. If her facial expression had any merit, the guilt feelings were still there, only magnified now that Sara was dead.

Mac and Dana excused themselves, agreeing to call on Monday to set an interview time with Scott and Claire. They both left business cards in the event Scott had any questions for them over the weekend.

They sat in the car for a while to gather their thoughts and share impressions.

"His grief seemed genuine, don't you think?" Dana asked.

"Yeah," Mac had to agree. "Either that, or he's a darn good actor."

"I'm glad Scott has family with him. I have no doubt they'll take good care of him."

Mac nodded. "I wonder how long the cousin has been staying there."

Dana shrugged. "You caught that too? She and Scott seemed a little too intimate for my blood."

"Yeah. The wife is kidnapped, and the cousin moves in. You gotta wonder if something wasn't going on before Sara disappeared. Maybe the two of them decided to eliminate the third part of the triangle."

"I don't know, Mac. The information we got before indicated that Sara and Claire were like sisters. Maybe she felt obligated."

"I'd be interested in Lauden's and Miller's take on it."

Mac left a message for agent Miller with the FBI to confirm the identity of the body and hopefully set up a meet time for Monday.

He would have liked to talk to the FBI agents immediately, but that wasn't going to happen. He also called Kristen's office, hoping she'd had time to officially attach a name to the body. She had.

Mac was turning down the police radio on the way back to the office so he could speak on the phone with their agency public information officer, or PIO, as they referred to them. "What's going on here?" Mac slapped the phone shut. "The PIO had to get off the phone. His pager was going nuts."

Dana noticed the green light on the police radio flashing on and off, indicating there were several transmissions going out over the radio. She turned up the volume to hear the troopers giving out locations and asking for updates. "Sounds like some sort of emergency." She instinctively picked up speed.

The sirens and frantic talk on the radio set Mac on edge, shoving his adrenaline into high gear. "Something big is going down. Can you tell where they're going?" Mac listened intently, trying to make out the destination and nature and to sort through the commotion.

"Sounds like Clackamas County; all the locations are on Highways 212 and 224."

Impatient, Mac dialed dispatch to get the scoop. After being placed on hold for several minutes, he finally got the dispatcher. "Oh, no." Mac could almost feel the color drain out of his face.

"What's wrong?"

Mac snapped the phone shut. "We have an officer down." Mac nearly choked on the words. "At the search warrant location where Russ and Philly are serving the warrant in Eagle Creek."

Dana activated her lights and sirens and headed for Eagle Creek.

Mac clenched his fists. If Kevin had been there, he'd have prayed. Mac stared at the road and offered up a silent prayer of his own.

"God, please let our guy be OK," Dana said aloud, echoing his thoughts. "Please."

THIRTEEN

They arrived at the outlaw biker clubhouse in record time. Due to the number of police cars and other emergency vehicles that were lining the street to the rural home, they could only get within a block of the house. They ran toward the front of the house, where they found Sergeant Bledsoe.

With a cell phone to his ear, Kevin held up a finger to indicate he wanted them to wait with him. He was obviously briefing a more senior command staff member, most likely from the superintendent's office. The look in Kevin's eyes said it all—one of the OSP troopers had gone down.

"I hate not knowing what's going on." Mac said as they waited in breathless anticipation for news on who had been injured. He scanned the strobes and flashing lights for a glimpse of Philly or Russ, praying the two of them would come walking out at any second.

"Me too." Dana shivered and folded her arms.

Kevin stuffed the cell into the pocket of his blue raid jacket and reached over to clasp Mac's shoulder. His grip was firm and solid, and Mac felt as though his former partner needed the physical contact to reassure himself that two of his detectives were OK. He did the same to Dana and then turned his attention to an ambulance emerging from the back of the house. With sirens on and lights strobing, the vehicle screamed by them.

"Who is it, Sarge?" Mac asked. "Do you know?"

"Yeah. A SWAT entry guy. Trooper Revman from District Three."

Mac's knees buckled, and the side of Frank's unmarked car was the only thing holding him up. Only hours ago, he and Daniel had made plans to meet.

Dana touched his arm. "Oh, Mac. I'm sorry."

"You know him, Mac?" Kevin asked.

Mac nodded. "We came on together, and I just hooked up with him again today. He told me his wife was expecting their first child."

"Why do they always have pregnant wives or young children?" Kevin mumbled.

"What happened?" Mac asked.

"Philly had a warrant on the place. You know the history?"

"I know the basics. What happened to Daniel?" Mac needed to know.

"We hit the door with the team, and everything went down as planned. SWAT had five in custody and called for us to come to the door and start the interviews and search the place while they backed out." Kevin blew out a long breath. "Then we heard this loud explosion at the back of the clubhouse. It took awhile to figure out what went down, but it looks like Trooper Revman got caught in a booby trap. We think he turned on a light bulb that was injected with gasoline and BB shot. It took off most of his face, Mac." He shook his head. "It doesn't look good."

"Oh, man." Mac rubbed a hand across his forehead.

"Where's the ambulance heading?" Dana asked.

"Emanuel Hospital in North Portland."

"Shoot." Mac moved away from the car. "Dana and I just came from Portland. We were ten minutes away from Emanuel."

Kevin looked back at the house. "I'd head up there, but I've got a bomb tech en route. We need to make sure there are no more improvised explosive devices in the house. The fire department is going to wet the scene, but we'll have to hand-comb the dwelling before we can secure. I have a detective team coming from Salem to investigate the injury to our guy." He gripped Mac's shoulder again and looked from Dana to Mac. "Just pray he pulls through, kids."

"We're ahead of you there, Sarge," Dana assured him.

"Would you mind if we head up to the hospital?" Mac asked.

"Not at all. In fact, I'd appreciate it. Give me an update once you hear anything."

"Will do." Mac could hardly talk let alone make his way back to the vehicle.

They started the trip back to Portland, hardly sharing a word between them. Dana pulled into the emergency room parking lot, which was overrun with dozens of police cars from various agencies. Vehicles littered all of the designated spaces, curbs, and even the grass. She found a spot not far from the door and parked. "Looks like the gang's all here."

Mac didn't answer. An injured officer brought nearly every available officer to the hospital. They were like family in that way, waiting to hear the news, praying, worrying.

Having been there dozens of times for crashes, stabbings, and shooting follow-ups, Mac punched in the security code to the emergency door. Emanuel Hospital was Oregon's premier level one trauma center, playing host to the worst of the worst injuries.

It was also one of the finest burn centers in the country. When Mac worked patrol, he had "Emanuel Hospital Only, O positive" written on his ballistic vest to indicate his blood type and his choice of destinations in the event he was injured and unable to communicate. Police officers often drafted last-minute instructions on their ballistic vests, like a soldier's dog tags, for paramedics or doctors to read. Some also sketched prayers or symbols on their vests for "extra protection" from the forces that they might encounter.

Daniel's injuries could have been prevented. This was an age-old booby trap that they were all trained to look for in these dope houses. The bad guys would drill a small hole in a standard light bulb and then inject gasoline into the reservoir with a syringe. Sometimes they added projectiles, which was apparently the case here. When an unwitting officer, dope thief, or other intruder turned on the light, the electrical charge would ignite the gas and burn the victim or hurtle glass and metal projectiles at them. Daniel had had special training on the SWAT team, so he had to know about these things. It had to have been a moment of carelessness. A tragic mistake.

Dana kept a watchful eye on Mac. She'd only seen him like this once, and that was when she herself had been hit. Fortunately, her vest had kept the bullet from blowing out her chest. Mac seemed lost now. Dazed. Her arm looped through his, she led him through the maze of city officers, county deputies, and state troopers who crowded the emergency room waiting area.

Their faces mirrored Mac's, hit by the reality of how vulnerable they all were. Any one of them could have been in Daniel's place. All they could do was wait and find a modicum of comfort in their comrades. A small crowd of officers gathered in one section for prayer, the men in different-colored uniforms bowing their heads—some kneeling, some standing, their hands folded.

"Do you want to join them?" Dana asked when Mac looked toward the group.

"Not yet. I want some answers first." He glanced at his watch. "Someone will be bringing Daniel's wife in. They're probably en route." He'd been at the hospital with injured officers before, but for some reason this time felt so much worse. Daniel had been a good friend back in basic training.

Mac introduced himself to a charge nurse and told her he was an OSP detective and friend of the injured trooper. The nurse made a call to someone and, when she hung up said, "You can wait in the room with the family if you'd like."

"I would."

"Wait by the security doors, and I'll buzz you in."

"You want to come with me?" he asked Dana.

"Sure." She wasn't about to leave Mac's side.

Half a dozen SWAT members were already inside. Mac recognized the sergeant he'd seen earlier at the office. Mac gave him a nod and sat down in one of the chairs.

"Want some coffee?" Dana asked.

"Yeah." He watched as she made her way around the officers to the coffee service area. She brought back two steaming cups and sat down next to him. "Thanks." After taking a sip, he grimaced. "Not as good as Starbucks, but not bad."

She leaned back and crossed her legs. "I remember Daniel," she said in a hushed voice. "I didn't realize it was him until you mentioned his name in the car. He was in one of my classes in college."

Mac nodded. "We both went right from school into police training. That's when we hooked up. I got to know him pretty well."

Dana picked up an old *Newsweek* magazine, and Mac stared straight ahead. The minutes dragged by as they waited for news. Daniel's wife, Jennifer, came in after they'd been there for an hour. She was obviously in late-term pregnancy and physical discomfort in addition to the emotional trauma. From what Mac could decipher, she'd been flown into PDX in a department aircraft. A good call, since Medford was near the California border.

She took a chair next to Dana, the only other woman there. With her experience in grief counseling, Dana fell into the role of support person and counselor, offering tissues and comfort. Mac introduced himself as a classmate of Daniel's, and they talked for a while about earlier times.

Another forty minutes passed before the trauma doctor in soiled blue scrubs walked into the waiting room. "Mrs. Revman?"

"Yes." She awkwardly got to her feet.

"Mrs. Revman." He took hold of her hand, and Mac knew. They all did.

Jennifer began to cry. "No. Please, no!"

"I'm sorry. Daniel was a fighter, and we did all we could for him. But his wounds were too severe, and he lost too much blood."

Jennifer held a hand over her mouth and sank back into the chair.

One by one, the men offered Jennifer their condolences and filed out of the room. Some angry, some stonefaced, some tearful.

Mac held himself together, but just barely. His stomach ached, and his head felt like it would explode. Somehow he managed to speak his condolences to Jennifer and get out of the room and out to the car.

Once they were buckled in, Dana called Sergeant Bledsoe.

"Thanks for the call, Dana. I just heard. How's Mac taking it?"

She glanced over at Mac, wishing he'd just cry and get it over with. "Not great."

"OK. You two go home. Take tomorrow off."

She hung up and turned to Mac. "Kevin said to go home. We can take tomorrow off."

Mac sighed. "Sounds like a good plan. But let's talk in the morning—see how we feel."

Mac's emotions were a study in chaos. He hadn't seen Daniel for years and didn't know Jennifer at all, yet he felt as though he'd lost his best friend.

"Mac." Dana looked over at him. "Um—I know this has hit you pretty hard. Maybe you shouldn't be alone. Do you want to hang out at my place tonight? I have a guest bedroom. We could go right there, and I can bring you over to the office to get your car tomorrow."

Mac rubbed his eyes. "Are you sure? I wouldn't want anyone getting the wrong idea."

"You need a friend."

"Yeah. Thanks."

Mac wondered what Kristen would think about him spending the night at Dana's. Oddly enough, he found himself wanting to be with the eccentric medical examiner, holding her and crying on her shoulder. He took a deep breath and closed his eyes, much too weary to worry about his relationship with Kristen or Dana or anyone else.

FOURTEEN

Mac awoke Sunday morning to the smell of bacon and the brightness of sunlight streaming through blinds. Groggy and disoriented, he lay in the daybed for several minutes while events from the evening before settled back into his brain like particles of dust.

He and Dana had stayed up for two hours once they'd gotten to her apartment. They'd talked a lot and cried together, then ordered in pizza and gorged themselves on food, soda, and talk. He felt better this morning. Funny how a little friendship could help. Of course, the sadness of Daniel's death and his young widow would be with him a long time, but he felt like he could at least function.

He pulled his slacks over his boxers and went into the adjoining bathroom to brush his teeth and use the facilities, using the comb and toothbrush Dana had supplied. He needed a shower, but that could wait until he got home. He pulled his dress shirt on over his T-shirt but didn't button it. Barefoot, he shuffled out to the living room/dining/kitchen area where Dana was plating bacon, eggs, and hash browns.

She'd already showered and dressed and was wearing a soft

pink angora sweater and plaid pants. Her hair was still damp and clipped at the back. The scene should have had him salivating, but his hormones seemed to have gone by the wayside, replaced, no doubt, by grief. This morning Dana was just Dana, his partner and friend.

In the corner of the counter, a television set flashed scenes of police cars. The on-scene reporter talked about the drug bust and how Trooper Daniel Revman had lost his life. Mac couldn't help but feel disdain for the press, who were quick to second-guess police officers' actions on a year-round basis and then showed the face of remorse when an officer was killed. "How can you stand to watch that stuff?"

"Good morning to you too." Dana set two plates on the table, then reached over with a remote and snapped off the TV. "I turned it on for the company. Ready to eat?"

"After all that food last night, I shouldn't be hungry; but I'm starved."

Dana pulled a carton of orange juice from the refrigerator and filled two long-stemmed glasses, then set them on the table.

"I'm hungry too," she gestured toward the plates, "which is why I made breakfast. I usually just grab a yogurt and granola."

Mac eased into one of four wooden chairs in the small alcove. "Thanks for letting me crash here last night."

"Don't mention it." She pulled out a chair opposite him. "I'm glad you were here."

They ate in relative silence, finding comfort in the sunny spot, the good food, and each other's company.

Dana drained her juice and said, "I'm going to church this morning. Want to come?"

He raised an eyebrow. "I didn't know you went to church."

"I do when I have Sundays off."

He sighed. Church seemed like a good place to be this morning. "I'd like that, but I need to get home and shower. I'm thinking I should go in to the office. Start working on the Watson case."

"I thought you might. We could go to church first and then head over there. I need to drive you there anyway to get your car."

"True." *Church.* He hadn't been to a church since the funeral he'd attended for Megan Tyson. Megan's murder had been his first assignment as a homicide detective. "Sure, why not? Only you'll have to take me by my place so I can shower and change."

CHURCH TURNED OUT TO BE A PLEASANT SURPRISE. The minister, a soft-spoken man, talked about Daniel Revman and how he'd lost his life in the process of making the community a better place. Mac appreciated that.

They were filing out of the church when a familiar voice called out his name. "Antonio?"

He whipped around. "Nana?" A grin spread across his face. Glancing at Dana, he said, "Did you know she was coming to church here?"

"Um—yeah, I did. She's the one who invited me. At Eric's barbeque last spring."

"Huh." Turning back to the older woman with white hair, he gave her a hug. "I didn't know you came to this church!"

"Well, you would if you'd come with me. How many times have I asked? And it's always, 'I'm working.'" Her gaze flashed to Dana. "How did you get him to come?"

Dana smiled. "Long story."

Nana nodded, knowingly. "So are you two dating?"

Mac flushed. Nana never minced words.

Dana, as usual, was quick to dispute the allegation. "We're just friends, Nana."

She clicked her tongue. "Too bad. Can you come by my place, Antonio? Have lunch with me. It's been too long."

"Just last week." He tried to stop by at least once a week, but for her it was never enough.

"I know, but it seems longer."

He bent down to kiss her wrinkled cheek. "Later, Nana. When I get off work. I promise. Right now, Dana and I need to get to the office. We're working on an important case."

"You work too hard. Both of you." She heaved a resigned sigh. "Be careful."

MAC AND DANA STOPPED FOR A QUICK LUNCH and coffee before going in to the office. Once there, Dana went on ahead while Mac lingered in the squad room. His gaze roamed over the spot where he had last seen Daniel, and he gripped the back of the chair Daniel had been sitting in. He small-talked with the troopers who were passing on rumors and speculating about how the trooper had died and what would become of the suspects who'd been arrested during the raid.

A sergeant with Fish and Wildlife entered the squad room and tossed a small manila envelope on one of the tables. Several small black cloth bands spilled out of the package. "We were out of these, so I had them shuttled up from the stockroom in Salem," the sergeant told them.

The contents of the package needed no explanation. They were black mourning bands to be worn over their badges. Mac picked up one of the bands and slipped it over his silver five-point badge, then clipped the badge back on his belt. He grabbed a half-dozen more for the detectives in the back room, took a drink of his coffee, then swirled the contents in the paper cup before taking one more and tossing the cup in the garbage.

Dana, Philly, Russ, and Sergeant Bledsoe were all in the break room when Mac walked in. Philly looked especially shaken, and

Mac suspected he carried a big helping of guilt since he and Russ were lead detectives and had initiated the bust. His eyes were bloodshot, and he was taking slow, shallow breaths, his appearance confirming some of Mac's suspicions. Philly was a recovering alcoholic, and was obviously drinking again.

A glance at Dana told him she was thinking the same thing. Russ had made an effort to cover for his partner's tardiness, but Philly was making it difficult to conceal his problem. If this kept up, it wouldn't be long before Philly got called on the carpet. He wondered if Russ had confronted him. Maybe they all should. If peer pressure couldn't bring Philly around, then he would be referred for a fitness-for-duty evaluation and lose his gun and badge until recovery.

"I heard Revman was a friend of yours, Mac," Philly said. "Can't tell you how bad I feel."

"There was nothing any of us could have done, Philly." Kevin slapped the big man on the back. To Mac, he said, "We'd just gotten inside when the blast went off, and there were no intelligence reports to indicate booby traps."

"I can't imagine what Daniel was thinking," Mac mused. "You come to expect those things in an outlaw biker clubhouse." On the other hand, Daniel hadn't been with the SWAT team all that long.

"Did you find any other devices at the house last night?" Dana asked.

Kevin nodded. "Bomb techs found a spring-loaded shotgun in an attic access. They almost missed it. It was set up with a rat trap attached to the trigger by a string, set to go off if someone sprang the trap door without depressing this special rigging they had set up."

"Any more IEDs like the one that took out Daniel?" Mac wanted to know.

"That was the only one. It was set on a pull chain, which is why he was so close to the blast.

"We found lots of guns and dope. They were dealing pretty heavily out of the house," Philly added. "Pieces of filth. A good man dies so they can protect their dope from other thieves. Crooks worried about crooks—a never-ending circle." Philly tossed the rest of his coffee in the small sink and leaned against the counter. He shook his head in disgust and then let out a long string of profanities aimed at the bikers who lived and dealt out their poison.

"Come on, partner." Russ patted him on the back. "We've got paperwork to do."

"Phil, I need to speak with you before you take off," Kevin said.

Mac had no doubt as to the topic of the conversation. Russ apparently knew what was up as well and excused himself, mumbling something about getting started on the reports.

Philly nodded and straightened. "I figured you would." His look was one of embarrassment rather than fear.

Mac felt bad for Philly and Russ. It was their warrant that had brought the SWAT team to the house, and nothing anyone could say would ease their guilt. Even though the bad guys had planted the explosive device that cost Daniel his life, the officers present would be caught in the blame game. The brass and even the media would scrutinize the information the detectives had prior to serving the warrant. Mac hated the politics of it all. Even though it was not their fault, the uniformed contingent of the department would likely be critical of the detectives' planning and preparation.

The situation created a ton of extra work. Kevin would have to coordinate the investigation with an outside detective team, while Russ and Philly coped with their guilt the best way they could. They would put together their original case and hand it off to a new detective team from Salem, who would put together an aggravated murder case on the bikers.

One good thing would come out of it. Because a police officer was killed, the case would automatically be a qualifier for the death penalty if the Clackamas County district attorney sought the reso-lution. The citizens of the rural county and the state's police officers wouldn't be happy with anything less.

Mac gave them the black bands he'd picked up and mumbled something about getting to work. Minutes later, sitting at his desk, he pored over dozens of e-mails and listened to his voice-mail messages. He had a subpoena for a suppression hearing on a Columbia County murder he and Dana had worked earlier in the year. The suspect in this case was attacking some statements he'd made at the time of arrest. Attorneys drove him nuts.

He heard Philly come out of Kevin's office and go into his own, making some inane comment to Russ about not having the paper-work done yet. He closed the door, and Mac didn't hear Russ's comment.

Half an hour later, restless and unable to concentrate, Mac went around the partition to Dana's office. "Hey."

"Hey, yourself." Dana tipped her head. "You OK?"

"Yeah. Just having trouble concentrating."

"Me too."

"What say we sift through the soil we recovered around Sara's body? It probably won't yield much, but it's something physical to do."

"Sounds like a plan."

Mac borrowed the temporary evidence key from Sergeant Bledsoe to remove their soil sacks from the evidence room. When officers logged evidence in the temporary compound, they secured their items with large padlocks that only the supervisors had keys for. Once they were processed, they would be logged into a perma-nent evidence facility, which only a few select individuals could access. Because it was homicide evidence, their policy required that the evidence be maintained for one hundred years. This would weather all the appeals, court hearings, and claims of innocence by those convicted of the crimes.

It wasn't uncommon for the appeals process in the liberal state of Oregon to exceed detectives' careers and, in some cases, their lives. The average death penalty appeal took fifteen years, so the detective may have retired or died before the case was resolved or set for a new trial. In that case, they had to rely on the evidence and the written report. The physical evidence had to be maintained in the event the officers were no longer around to testify to its importance.

Mac walked out to the boat sheds in the back of the patrol office, where the wildlife officers kept their boats and other paraphernalia, looking through a storeroom of odds and ends for the sifter boxes. After wading through old tires, floor jacks, and old patrol car parts, he found the two sifter boxes. The sifters, wood-framed boxes lined with a fine wire mesh, stood on two legs made of wood and metal. Mac set out large tarps in the shade outside the boat sheds, so they could gather the sifted soil and return it to the large black evidence bags when they were finished.

He helped Dana carry out the sacks of soil, placing the bags alongside the first sifter box with the larger mesh. They would sift the soil through the first box, removing all the large rocks and sticks, then through the second sifter that had even smaller mesh that should remove everything but the bare soil. After the process took the refinement down to the sifted soil, he and Dana would have to use fine hand sifters to look through the samples. The pans with a fine mesh resembled something early miners used to locate flakes of precious metal.

"You want to do the dumping or the sifting?" Mac snapped the second latex glove around his wrist.

"I'll do the dumping." She grinned. "It takes a little more upper body strength to do the other, and let's face it: you are physically stronger than I am."

"Wow. I never thought I'd hear you admit something like that."

"And you probably never will again." Dana picked up a garbage sack as Mac grabbed the corners of the sifter box. She dumped in several pounds of dirt and rock, with Mac starting to rock the sifter back and forth until all the soil was worked through the mesh. After working all the bags through the first sifter, Mac dumped the final tray of contents that were too big to go through the mesh onto a tarp. The collection was mostly rocks, but they did manage to bag and tag some broken glass and an old beer bottle cap that looked like it had been there for years.

When all the rocks and sticks had been set aside, Mac brought over the second sifter with the smaller mesh, and they went through the entire process again. This time, it took the better part of an hour to sift through the dirt, even the finest pebbles and soil holding up in the quarter-inch squares in the wire mesh. After sifting, they had to then dump the remaining items from the tray back on the plastic tarp and go through the items piece by piece to locate any additional evidence. Their backbreaking effort yielded small pieces of glass, probably from the beer bottle the cap had been attached to. Although the items were most likely not connected to the crime, they bagged them. If they didn't seize them, a defense attorney could accuse them of not doing a thorough job at a later date.

"Now comes the fun part," Mac said sarcastically. "We have to hand-search the entire soil pile with those hand plates there. This is going to take awhile, but anything that goes through that fine mesh is going to stay hidden." He tossed a plate to Dana and pointed to the side of the pile. They sat down on the tarp and began the tedious process of sifting pound after pound of the soil. They worked late into the afternoon, making small talk about the case and last night's tragedy.

"Does Daniel's death make you think about your shooting, Dana?" Mac asked.

"For sure. I think about it every day, but I thought about it a lot last night and this morning." Dana smiled and blew a lock of hair out of her eyes.

The average remaining tenure for a police officer who had been involved in a deadly force incident was less than five years. Many quit their jobs and found other lines of work. The jury was still out on Dana; it had been only a few months since she'd taken a round in the chest. Dana still struggled with some issues, but she showed every indication that she would survive the incident professionally.

"Still having nightmares?" Mac wanted to know.

"Not so much anymore."

Mac leaned back and rubbed the sore muscles in his back. They looked like seasoned archeologists rather than homicide detectives.

"Oh." Dana glanced up at him. "I think I found something." Dana picked up the small object and held it up to the fading sunlight.

"What is it?" Mac squinted to see the small object, barely protruding from Dana's gloved hands.

"Come look at it and tell me what you think." Dana moved the small object to the palm of her left hand.

Mac stepped over to where Dana was seated and peered down at her find.

"What does that look like to you?" she asked.

Mac squinted. "A fingernail maybe. At least part of one."

"That's exactly what I was thinking." Dana grinned. "This could belong to our victim."

"Or the killer. Either way, we just might get us some DNA."

FIFTEEN

Hoping to find more evidence, and concerned they may have missed something, the detectives sifted the dirt by hand a second time.

"I hate for us to get our hopes up with this one find, but it's hard not to," Mac said.

"I know," Dana responded. "Cutting her nails off like that makes me wonder if her killer is a professional."

Mac nodded. "That's possible, or maybe he watches those *CSI* shows. Too many killers these days know too much about the evidence-gathering process."

"Do you watch the cop shows?" Dana grinned at him.

He ducked his head. "Guilty as charged. How about you?"

"I like them. The only thing is, in real life we can't always afford to do those kinds of tests. And the time frame is crazy. They get their results back way too soon. Like the CSI techs are going to drop everything for us."

"Well, sometimes they do." Mac chuckled. "You just have to know how to talk to them."

"Right."

Before going home for the evening, he and Dana submitted the information they had to the HITS unit, or the Homicide Information Tracking System, at their headquarters. The information on the apparent cause of death, age of the victim, and the unusual items found in Sara's mouth were included in the packet they submitted to the specialized unit. The analysts assigned to HITS would enter the data into a special computer system that would compare and share the data with unsolved homicide cases across the country. Detectives could compare similarities and explore the possibility they were working the same suspect in separate crimes.

Investigators were often able to solve cold cases this way, sometimes making the grim discovery that they had a serial killer working across multiple jurisdictions. Detectives across the country also submitted information to the national HITS system after making an arrest for a homicide that involved unusual characteristics, primarily stranger-to-stranger crimes. Although this was a tool to solve connecting crimes, it primarily served as resource for forensic profilers, whose job it was to give approximate ages and motives to detectives investigating apparently random homicides.

"I'm heading for the gym," Dana announced as they walked out the back door.

"Where do you get your energy? All I want to do is go home and play couch potato."

"Me too, actually, but exercising will get my blood pumping and give me some energy—at least for a while. It helps with the emotional stress too."

"If you say so." He thought about going with her but opted not to. What appealed to him more was not going home but talking to Kristen. He really wanted to find out where he stood with her and what was going on in her life. On the way home, he called her.

"Mac. It's good to hear from you. How's the Watson case coming?"

"Not making much headway, but we may have located one of her fingernails."

"Cool."

"Um—are you interested in having dinner with me tonight?"

She hesitated. "I'm not sure I'd be very good company, but hey, we both need to eat, right?"

"You don't sound very enthusiastic."

"Sorry, Mac. It's not you. Come on over. I'll whip something together."

"I was thinking we'd go out. Someplace nice."

"Sure. When?"

"I have to drop over to visit Nana for an hour or so. What say I pick you up at seven thirty?"

"I'll be ready."

Feeling gritty from working in the dirt, Mac went home to shower and change before heading over to the Retirement Inn where his grandmother lived. He talked with her about Daniel's death and life in general.

"Are you still seeing Kristen?" Nana asked out of the blue.

"I'm taking her out to dinner tonight."

She nodded. "I like her, but I like Dana too. You like them both, don't you?"

He leaned forward, elbows resting on his knees, hands clasped. "You don't miss much, do you?"

"You're very easy to read, Antonio. Always were."

"So, do you have a preference?"

She tilted her head to one side. "My sweet boy, I can't tell you which one to go with. Only your heart can do that."

He sighed. "Well, my heart bounces around a lot."

She smiled. "It's your brain that does the bouncing, not your heart. You need to listen to your heart for a change. Why do men find that so difficult?"

He told her about Kristen's sudden interest in her ex and the trip to Florida and Dana's aversion to cops. "I probably won't end up with either one of them."

"And if that is God's will?"

The question pulled him up short. "Then I guess I'll have to live with it."

"Don't worry, Antonio. If not Dana or Kristen, God will bring you just the right woman. But I hope he hurries. I'm getting old, and I want to meet my great-grandchildren before I die."

Mac didn't comment. He wanted that too.

Nana yawned. "Didn't you say you had a dinner date with Kristen?"

Mac glanced at his watch. It was already seven fifteen. "I'd better go." He stood up and bent down to kiss her cheek.

Her fragile hand patted his cheek. "I will be praying for you, Antonio."

"I need it," he muttered.

FROM THE RETIREMENT INN, he headed back over the river to Kristen's place, a cute older-style house in southwest Portland. Her Volvo was sitting out front, and he sat in his car for a few minutes before dragging himself to her front door. He hated not knowing where he stood. But he didn't like the idea of finding out the truth either.

He rang the doorbell and waited for what seemed like five minutes before she finally opened the door. "Hi, Mac. Come on in and sit down. I'm on the phone."

She picked up the receiver. "I'm back. That was Mac. He's taking me out to eat."

She smiled. "No, not pizza. I miss you, too, honey."

Honey? She must be talking to Andrew. It was then that Mac realized how empty the house felt. Had she left Andrew in Florida? That had to mean she was going back.

"Maybe. I'll ask him." She crooked her finger for Mac to join her. "It's Andrew. He wants to talk to you."

Mac took the phone. "Hey, buddy. How's it going?"

"Good. I'm in Florida with my new gamma and gampa. They're taking me to Disney World tomorrow. Can you come?"

Mac smiled despite his concerns. "I'm afraid not. I have to work."

"Oh." Silence. Seconds later, a much older person said, "Hello? Kristen, is that you?"

"No. I'll get her." Mac handed the phone back to Kristen. She and the other woman talked for a while. Mac tried not to listen, focusing instead on the curves of her cream-colored top and matching slacks. She had a great figure, and she looked different somehow from the last time they'd been together.

"I know, but I'll be there on Tuesday. I need to clear some things off my desk and get a new schedule worked out." She glanced at Mac. "I told you I would. OK, thanks. Give Andrew a hug and kiss from me." She hung up and stared at the phone for a moment before turning back to Mac. "I'm sorry. Andrew needed to say good-night to me."

"Isn't it past his bedtime? It's three hours later in Florida."

"Yes, but he isn't used to Brian's parents. He was missing me and wouldn't stop crying. His grandmother finally enticed him with a trip to Disney World."

"So I heard." He frowned. *What's going on? Why did you leave him? Are you going back for good?* They were all questions he wanted to ask but wouldn't. At least not yet. Kristen would tell him in her own time.

"I'm glad you called, Mac. Truth is, I didn't feel much like cooking."

He held her coat. "If you don't mind a bit of a drive, I know of a great place to eat."

"I don't mind in the least."

Once they'd settled into the car, Kristen leaned her head against the seat.

"Tired?"

"Exhausted. I haven't slept well in two days."

Mac reached into the back of his car for a small neck pillow and handed it to her. "Why don't you nap while we drive?"

"Thanks." She closed her eyes, and Mac worked hard at being patient. He wanted to talk and he wanted answers, but first things first. He looked over at her profile, thinking she was much more normal looking than the last time he'd seen her. Her hair was a kind of dishwater blonde, and it wasn't sticking out all over her head. She wasn't wearing earrings either. She seemed depressed. He could identify.

Mac drove down I-84 east and cut over to the Washington side at Cascade Locks, then on up to the Skamania Lodge located near the small town of Stevenson. He parked on the hill above the lodge, and after turning off the car, leaned over to kiss Kristen awake.

"Mmm." Her arms went around his neck, and she returned the kiss.

After a few heart-pounding moments, Mac moved away.

"What was that for?" she asked.

He shrugged. "Just couldn't resist. You look great tonight."

"Are you saying I don't look great all the time?" Kristen teased.

"No." He cleared his throat, not sure how to respond. "Um—we should go in."

When she figured out where they were, she seemed elated. "I've always wanted to come here, but I never seem to have the time."

"Me too."

The lodge was warm and inviting, and its large fireplace and wood floors gave it a log-cabin look. Mac guided her to the dining room, where they were seated right away.

Kristen raised her eyebrows at the prices. "Mac, are you sure you can afford this?"

"Not every day, but I figure you're worth it once every year or two."

She raised an eyebrow. "Hmm."

Now what did she mean by that?

The waiter came by, and they placed their orders. Roasted leg of lamb for Mac and salmon for Kristen. The place had a definite Northwest flair.

"I was surprised to see you in the morgue yesterday." Mac said.

"I didn't really want to come back, but I left things in a mess and had some scheduling problems."

"I heard you say you were going back to Florida on Tuesday."

"Right."

"So, how is Brian?"

"He's still alive." She pinched the bridge of her nose. "Barely."

"You seem pretty shook up about it. I mean. . . ."

"I know what you mean. I thought everything was over and finished between us. I'm surprised at the depth of feelings I have for him and his family." She sighed. "Watching him lying there in that hospital bed about broke my heart."

And you're breaking mine. Mac didn't say the words—only felt them slice through him. "I'm sorry."

She reached over and placed a hand on Mac's. "Let's not talk about all that. It's just too hard. One good thing: Brian's parents are thrilled to have Andrew with them."

Mac nodded. "He seemed pretty happy to be there."

"He is." She pulled her hand away. "So tell me about the guy who was killed last night."

Mac didn't want to talk about Daniel, but it was better than the alternative. He could feel Kristen slipping away, much like Dana had, and he didn't like it one bit. Maybe he should break it off with her right now, save himself the embarrassment and pain of her rejection. His gaze lifted to hers, and his mouth went dry. He took a sip of water.

"Mac, are you OK? If you don't want to talk about the trooper, that's fine." She offered a wan smile. "We're a fun pair tonight, aren't we?"

"I guess so. I don't mind talking about Daniel. He was an old friend, and his death hit me harder than I expected. I keep thinking, what if it had been me? And then I think, why did it have to be him?"

"I heard on the news he had a wife and a baby on the way."

"That makes it even harder." He sighed. "I know things like that come with the territory, but. . . ."

"That doesn't make it any easier."

"No. It doesn't."

Their food came and with it a shift in the conversation to safer topics. Kristen talked about the autopsies she'd had that day and how she had to rearrange everyone's schedule so she could take more time off.

"How long will you be gone?" Mac asked.

"A few days."

Mac nodded. *Why are you going? What about us?* He wanted to ask those questions and more, but he didn't want to sound selfish.

The drive home felt awkward and the conversation stilted, as though both of them wanted to stay away from the subject of their relationship and whether or not they had a future together.

Mac pulled up to the curb in front of her house at ten thirty. He walked her to the door, but she didn't invite him in. Her kiss was sweet but reserved.

"I probably won't see you again before I go," she said.

"So I guess this is good-bye."

Without answering, she kissed his cheek and went inside, closing the door softly behind her. Mac stood there for several long seconds. He hated not knowing what the deal was with her. If she didn't want to see him again, why not come right out and tell him? He envisioned himself ringing the doorbell and pushing his way inside, demanding to know if she was in love with her ex. Kristen would step back, surprised at his sudden assertion. "I . . . I don't know," she'd say.

He'd stand there, hands on his hips, and say, "Well, when you figure it out, let me know, OK? And one more thing. I love you and Andrew, and I don't want to lose you." Then he'd pull her into his arms and. . . .

He got so far as to put his hand on the doorknob, then he stopped, turned around, and walked to his car. He could hardly believe he'd even considered confronting her like that. He wasn't ready to make a commitment, and she definitely needed some space. He had imagined telling her that he loved her, but did he really? He thought about what Nana had said about following his heart. He felt certain there was a place for Kristen and Andrew in there.

Mac considered going to her and telling her how he felt, but when he looked back at the house, the lights were out.

SIXTEEN

Mac came into the office early Monday morning, now better able to focus on what needed to be done. The murder investigation forced him to think about something other than Daniel Revman's death and his own relationships—or lack of them.

It was only 7:00 a.m., and all four homicide detectives along with Sergeant Bledsoe were busy at work in the small detectives' office.

Daniel's death had been hard on all of them, but none more than Philly, who felt personally responsible. It brought all Mac's fears to the surface, knowing it could just as easily have been him. This morning Philly looked like he'd slept in his clothes, if he had slept at all. He knew how fragile life was, better than most of the population, having worked hundreds of homicides in his career. Mac thought about the talk Kevin had with Philly the day before when Phil had come to work with a hangover. He'd worried from time to time about Philly's lifestyle and wondered how much trouble the big guy was in. With the age difference, Mac felt uncomfortable offering Philly advice or help. And what advice could he give? Stop drinking? Philly already knew that.

Cops had as many personal struggles as any one else, if not more. Unfortunately, they were often the last ones to ask for help. Maybe that's why people in his profession committed suicide at three times the rate of the general population.

Mac heaved a heavy sigh and, elbows on his desk, pressed the heels of his hands against his eyes. He hated seeing Philly like this. Philly's drinking problem brought back memories of his own father and the drunken stupors he'd fall into. His dad had been a cop, and Mac had always hated him for what he'd done to their family. Seeing Philly gave him an understanding of his dad he'd never had before. Jamie McAllister had seen his share of ugliness as well. Not that drinking was an excuse—it never would be—but Mac could see how a guy could use alcohol to numb the pain.

Philly could use some lessons on dealing with problems in a healthy way, and Kevin was just the person for the job. Kevin had worked the back room as long as Philly, and he had seen his share of horrors as well. Yet the sergeant always remained grounded in his family and moral convictions. The difference couldn't have been more obvious. Kevin had told Mac more than once that his faith had kept him on an even keel. Looking at Kevin and Philly, he had no doubt as to which man he wanted to emulate—but could he?

Considering the male role models he'd had growing up, Mac feared his genetic makeup might have more power than his own determination. He wanted to be a devoted husband and father like Kevin and like his cousin Eric, now lieutenant over the entire Portland OSP operations. He heaved another heavy sigh. How was he supposed to make plans for the future when he might not have one past today?

"You can't do it alone, Mac," Kevin often told him. *"You need God."* Mac agreed. Something the pastor had said during his sermon on Sunday morning found its way into Mac's thoughts. *"When tragedy strikes, and it will, the question we need to ask ourselves is not why,*

because we'll never be able to answer that completely. What we need to ask is this: is God with me? The answer to that will always be yes."

He took a huge gulp of lukewarm coffee to rid himself of his random thoughts and forced himself to concentrate. Maybe he could at least read his e-mails. Some of the messages were from his academy classmates, running a message tree to discuss a get-together after the funeral. The funeral date hadn't been set, but it would be by the end of the week.

Mac saw Nathan Webb's pickup go by the office window. Time to go to work.

"Nate's here." Dana came into his cubicle.

"Yeah, I saw him pull in." Mac closed down his e-mail program.

"And," Dana said, "maybe there will be some forensic evidence in the soil that we couldn't find with our hand search. I'm excited that we actually found something in that pile of dirt. I never realized how much fun sifting through the dirt could be. Maybe I ought to become an archeologist. I could be exploring pyramids or something."

Mac smiled at her enthusiasm and was about to offer a rebuttal when Nate came around the corner.

"Hi, you two. I'm surprised to see you here so early." Nate grinned.

"Same here." Dana reached out to shake his hand. "You must have gotten up with the chickens."

Nate laughed at the comment. "Way before that. And the saying is 'up with the rooster,' not the chickens."

"We appreciate your coming." Mac shook his hand as well. "That's quite a drive."

"Just three hours. Things are a bit different on our side of the mountain. Nothing is ever close-by—well, almost nothing. We don't have coffee shops and grocery stores five minutes away like you guys in the valley." Nate leaned against Mac's desk. "Ever notice that you city slickers measure distance by time instead of miles?"

"What?" Mac had no idea what he was talking about.

"No, really. You ask someone from the country how far something is from a certain place and they'll say ten miles or fifty miles, something like that. You ask someone from the city how far something is, and they'll say ten minutes or thirty minutes away. Why is that?"

"Maybe because something that may be five miles away can take you thirty minutes to get there, depending on the time of the day. We have little obstacles like rush hours and traffic jams, something I doubt you miss much, living on your side of the mountain."

"You've got that right. Just an observation. I don't envy you in the least. Traffic coming into town was horrendous." Nate cleared his throat. "Hey, before we get started, I just want to say how sorry I am to hear about the loss of the trooper the other day. I didn't hear about it until yesterday. Was he from this office?"

"Thanks. He was from down south, just up here as a member of the SWAT team. His name was Daniel Revman. We came on together. Daniel got hold of a booby trap during a warrant at a biker hangout." Mac glanced at Dana, looking to change the subject.

Dana must have felt the same way. "So, how's your family and your farm?"

"Great. We came out unscathed—a little blackened acreage, but no lost crops or livestock. Mama and the little ones are back home now; looks like the fire is continuing to move to the northeast. We were lucky to recover that body when we did."

The wording of the statement caught Mac's attention.

"Did you hear what we found yesterday?" Dana smiled.

"What *she* found," Mac added.

"Yeah, what I found."

"No. I haven't heard a thing."

"Oh, sorry, Nate," Mac said. "I should have called you."

"That's OK; you had a few things on your mind." Nate's gaze moved back to Dana. "What did you find?"

"Well, you know at the post how Sara's fingernails were cut off?"

"Yeah. Looked like the guy knew what he was doing."

"We sifted through all that dirt we recovered from around the body and found a single fingernail. We'll take it to the lab this morning."

"We'll take the soil down to the lab too," Mac added. "Have the pros go through the whole batch again—make sure we didn't miss anything. Good thing Dana is a woman, or we might have missed it."

"What does being a woman have to do with anything?" Dana huffed.

"Women notice stuff like that. You probably missed two bullets and a knife tip, just spotting the fingernail." Mac laughed at his attempt at humor.

"Good thing Nate's here, or you'd be in serious trouble." Dana's dimpled grin diminished her warning. "Although . . . speaking of nails, it's about time I had mine done." Dana examined her fingers.

"See what I mean?" Mac eased past Nate and Dana. "You guys ready to head out?"

"Lead the way." Nate followed behind Mac, who stopped by Kevin's office to let him know they were heading for the crime lab.

"Be careful." Kevin always said that, but he always sounded genuinely concerned.

"I hope you're still OK with my tagging along," Nate said from the backseat. "I don't get in on the nuts and bolts of murder investigations all that often."

"Glad to have you, Nate, especially this morning." Mac eyed him in the rearview mirror. "You can help us lug all those sacks of dirt up to the crime lab."

Nate smiled. "I knew there had to be strings attached."

When they arrived at the Justice Center, they divided the bags between them and, after passing through security, hauled them into the elevator and up to the twelfth floor. Mac logged in the soil, along with the leather beaded pouch and the stone that carried the image of She Who Watches.

After the crime lab secretary logged those in, Dana turned in the various tissue and fluid samples from the autopsy. "We'll need a full workup on the samples for a DNA standard and test for toxic substances in the blood."

"I'll get someone on it as soon as I can." The lab secretary placed the items in a bin. "Is there anything else?"

"Just one more thing." Dana handed over the possible fingernail sample. It was secured in a paper fold, sealed inside a small manila evidence envelope with red evidence tape. The signature across the brittle red tape would be a quality-control element for the forensic scientist, who may have to testify one day that the sample was not tampered with prior to his or her analysis.

"When will you get the results back?" Nate asked.

"Hard to tell," Mac answered. "Since we're not trying to tie it to a suspect, prepare for court, or draft a warrant, the evidence has to take a back burner to other cases that have priority. The lab processes hundreds of thousands of cases each year, most of them drug related."

"Can't we put a rush on it? It is a murder case."

"I'd like to," Mac said, "but we can't justify the extra pressure on the scientists at this point. We have no suspects, and we have dozens of interviews to do before we can come up with a list of possibles."

"The DNA process alone takes about a week, unless an offender or victim sample is on file for review," Dana explained to Nate. "The extraction of the DNA material is a painstaking and laborious process of typing and comparing samples."

Mac grinned. "But that doesn't mean we can't get things done in a hurry."

"We've made some good friends here in the department," Dana added as they stepped into the elevator.

"Don't let her fool you, Nate. All Dana has to do is walk into the lab, and the guys will work through their lunch hours."

Dana rewarded Mac's compliment with a punch in the arm.

They walked to the federal building, which was only a few blocks away, to make their nine o'clock appointment with Special Agents Miller and Lauden at the FBI office.

Mac had the feeling the agents, up until now, hadn't been totally honest in the spirit of sharing information, but to what extent, he didn't know. Hopefully, they'd put everything on the table now that the case was no longer in their hands.

Dana pressed the buzzer in the lobby of the FBI office, and the security officer admitted them into the reception room. Mac studied the office furnishings while they waited for the agents. The oak desks and elaborate decorations were a stark reminder of how federal and state funding differed. OSP had to make do with surplus furnishings in their office, and many of the desks and chairs were older than Kevin. It bugged him that the feds seemed to have such deep pockets while, at the state level, they had to make do with hand-me-downs and second-rate equipment. Mac reminded himself that he couldn't control what the various agencies did or didn't have. He was there to take over a murder investigation.

"Good morning, Detectives." Agent Mel Lauden appeared in the reception area with his hand extended.

"Morning, Mel." Mac shook his hand. "Thanks for meeting with us this morning."

Agent Lauden led Mac, Dana, and Nate into a conference room with a large mahogany table in the center surrounded by matching chairs. Grease boards lined the walls, and several three-legged easels held writing pads. The agents had apparently mapped out Sara Watson's disappearance, complete with possible suspects and leads, on the board.

Mac scanned the notes, not recognizing many of the names of

people who were apparent players in the case. He clenched his jaw, wondering just how much information the FBI had withheld from the OSP.

Agent Lauden checked his watch. "Can I get you some coffee or juice? Jimmy is on the phone with an unrelated case; he'll be in to give the briefing in a minute."

Mac and Nate agreed to a cup of coffee while Dana took a small can of apple juice. While they waited, Dana transferred the notes on the board to the pad. Mac made a few notes as well. Ten minutes later, Agent Miller entered the room.

"Sorry to keep you waiting." Miller sat down at the table and loosened his tie after greeting them. "I've been on the phone with my supervisor in Seattle. We have an Amber Alert on a kid out of Spokane, may have some abduction ties here in Oregon."

"Anything we can help with?"

"Not at this time. Appreciate it, though." Miller smiled. "Now to the Watson case. The FBI is not prepared to totally relinquish this case as yet, but we do recognize that the local governments have a vested role in the investigation. We are dedicated to total information sharing at this point and are prepared to assume a subordinate role in the investigation."

He produced a case file stamped CONFIDENTIAL and tossed it on the table. "Before we hand over our findings, there are a few details of a sensitive nature that we need to discuss with you."

SEVENTEEN

What kind of sensitive details?" Mac pulled the thick file toward him.

Agent Miller paused, as if searching for the right words. "We've listed two Native American individuals as persons of interest. Both are still under investigation."

"What about all these other names on the grease boards?" Mac motioned around the room.

"Individuals who meet the profiler's description. They're mainly registered sex offenders and other losers who were in the Portland area when Sara disappeared. None of them panned out, or we would have told you about them."

Mac nodded.

"This has been our strategic planning room since day one," Miller continued. "Many of the men listed are in prison or dead, so you can see they didn't require much follow-up."

"Who are the Native American suspects?" Nate asked.

Miller frowned at Nate and then shifted his gaze to Mac. "I'm sure you understand, Mac, but I don't want this lead going outside OSP."

Mac cleared his throat. "Officer Webb is working the investigation with us. He needs to be in the loop every step of the way."

"Can we count on you to maintain confidentiality?" Miller asked Nate.

"Of course."

"All right then." Agent Miller flipped open the file to reveal some surveillance photographs of an older man, probably in his late fifties. "This is Therman Post, resident of the Warm Springs Reservation. He's a political activist and has been a very vocal advocate for the placement of the Native American casino in the Columbia River Gorge."

"You think Therman Post killed Sara Watson?" Nate sounded surprised. "What would be his motive? Sure, he wants the casino, but he's not a killer."

"You know this guy?" Agent Miller asked.

"Of course I know him; he lives in my community. He's done a great deal for our people. Therman is the main proponent for the new tribal interpretive center in Warm Springs. He can be a pain sometimes, but kidnapping and murder? I don't know about that." Nate glanced over at Mac. "He's a good man."

"I appreciate your input, Nate." Mac knew better than to draw conclusions early on, but he felt obligated to accept Nate's opinion—at least for now. "Is Therman a suspect or a person of interest? I heard both terms thrown out here."

"Person of interest right now," Miller answered. "He's been rather persistent in a letter-writing campaign to Senator Wilde, threatening repercussions if the senator didn't approve the planning and placement of the casino. As you know, Senator Wilde is Sara Watson's uncle."

"Not an easy thing to forget." Mac took a closer look at the photo.

"The letters from Therman were well documented and reviewed by the senator's security delegation and chief of staff," Miller went on.

"We should have been apprised of this," Mac said. "We read about the connection between Sara's disappearance and the casino in the papers, but we figured it was media hype. Apparently, they knew more than we did."

"We suspect someone from the senator's office may have leaked the information to the press. The articles were pure speculation, and I can assure you, they didn't get anything from us. As to not informing you, the senator gets thousands of letters every year, and a lot of them contain threats."

"And these threats aren't taken seriously?" Dana asked. "Didn't the senator make the connection between Sara's disappearance and these threats?"

"Yes, he did. That's why the FBI and the OSP were brought in so quickly. The senator rarely reads the mail that comes into his office. Most mail is read and replied to by his administrative staff. I guess they thought he should see the ones that came from Mr. Post. He didn't take them seriously until Sara went missing."

"So you've had these from the onset." Mac still couldn't believe the FBI agents had kept this information from them.

"We were directed by our supervisors not to disclose the information. There were political directives that I wouldn't be at liberty to discuss, even if I knew exactly what they were." Miller seemed apologetic. "We followed up on them ourselves. The guy wasn't too cooperative, but there didn't seem to be any connection between him and Sara. Mr. Post has been writing letters like this for years. Why would he suddenly decide to kidnap and murder the senator's niece?"

"But you're still not ready to take him off the list as a possible suspect," Dana observed.

"Right. The letters from Mr. Post are in the file. You can see for yourself. They're mainly political rhetoric, like most of the casino-related letters; the Indians are spouting off about oppression and the loss of rights for the Confederated Tribes." Miller smirked. "Like they really need more money. The government is already doing more than they should."

Nate shifted in his chair, obviously having a differing opinion on the subject. He didn't seem too pleased with Agent Miller's comments. Even Agent Lauden looked a little uneasy.

"At any rate," Miller continued, "the letters are all postmarked at Warm Springs. You might want to take a look at them before we go on."

Mac, Dana, and Nate looked at each of the letters, skimming the contents for something of relevance.

"This is Therman's handwriting, all right," Nate said. "I've seen it before. He has an unusual way of signing his name." Nate pointed to the signature, which was a flourished TP with a stylistic Indian-style tent or tepee beside it.

"You said you had a second Native American suspect," Mac said.

"Person of interest," Agent Lauden corrected. "There was a second set of letters." He motioned to the file, flipping to another section.

"Another advocate for the casino?" Mac looked at Miller for an explanation.

"Maybe," Agent Miller admitted.

"What's the deal on these letters?" Dana asked, pulling another packet from the file.

"The letters from Therman Post stopped around the time Sara was reported missing. Then these started coming. They appear to be written by another person, but we're not entirely certain that's the case. They're computer generated, but they are also postmarked from the Warm Springs Reservation." Agent Miller nodded toward the case file. "These letters indicate that the author had kidnapped Sara and would harm her if the senator didn't allow the casino to be built in the gorge."

"How many letters like this did the senator receive?" Mac glanced over the letters in question.

"Three, total," Miller said. "The letters were all received within the first ten days of Sara's disappearance. Coincidentally, they stopped after we interviewed Mr. Post at his home in Warm Springs. He told us he didn't own a computer."

Nate nodded. "Therman speaks the truth. Which brings us to the second suspect, who is . . . ?"

"A guy named Milton Driver. He's a postal employee on the reservation. You know him?" Agent Lauden asked Nate.

"Yes, I do. How is he connected?"

"We lifted his print from one of the envelopes in the second series of letters that were postmarked at Warm Springs. Turns out Driver has an alibi, so he more than likely just handled the letters."

"How did the interview go with Therman Post?" Mac asked. "You said he wasn't very cooperative."

"Not very well. He wouldn't even let us in the door, and we ended up speaking to him through the screen door. He admitted to sending letters to the senator, but none after Sara disappeared. We asked if he would take a polygraph, but he refused and then slammed the door in our faces."

"Hmm." Nate rubbed his chin. "Like I said, Therman can be a little difficult. I don't see him driving to Portland and kidnapping a woman, though, let alone killing her for political gain. He values life too much for that."

"He may not be a kidnapper or a killer, and he may not have written the second set of letters, but we don't have a lot of leads on this case. And this is the closest thing we have to motive." Agent Miller frowned. "Sara's husband, her cousin, her co-workers, and even her neighbors have all taken the polygraph, and there's no indication any of them were involved. All we have is those letters—and you have to admit, there's a strong motive. A casino in the gorge stands to bring in a lot of money."

"Take a look at this." Dana pointed to the bottom of one of the letters that were mailed after Sara's disappearance. She held the letter so Mac and Nate could see.

"What am I looking at?" Mac peered at the paper.

"The pictograph on the bottom; look how it's signed."

"She Who Watches." Mac looked over at Nate. "I don't think that's a coincidence."

"Does this mean something to you guys?" Agent Miller asked.

"Not until now," Mac answered. "During the autopsy, we removed a leather pouch from Sara's mouth that had a stone with an odd carving on it. Nate identified the object as—what was the Native American name, Nate?"

"Tsagagalal," Nate pronounced the name with an ethnic dialect. He explained the reference, the legend, and the relationship to the English translation of She Who Watches.

"It looks like we definitely have a marriage between the letters and the evidence on the body." Miller leaned back in his chair. "If Sara's killer is a member of the Warm Springs Reservation, then we may have to retain control of the case." He pulled the file over to his side of the table.

"Only if we request your assistance in the investigation," Nate challenged. "We don't have any proof that the crime occurred on tribal grounds. Right now, I think we need a fresh set of eyes on the case. We'll be requesting that OSP continue to work the case with our cooperation."

Miller's features hardened. "But OSP has no jurisdiction on the reservation."

"That's where I come in," Nate said.

"That's right," Mac said, pulling the case file back to his side of the table. "We believe in the spirit of cooperation, as you know, so we can get the job done. We'll let you guys know if we need anything."

UPON LEAVING THE FEDERAL BUILDING an hour later, Mac, Dana, and Nate opted to eat lunch before heading back to the office. Downtown Portland offered a lot of great opportunities, Nordstrom's Café being one of them. Once they'd ordered and secured a table, Mac took out his notes. "Nate, do you think as a tribal member you'll be able to set up an interview with Therman Post?"

"There's a good possibility. Though I don't think he's your guy."

"Hopefully that's the case, but we still have to eliminate him as a suspect."

"It might be a good idea if I head back to Warm Springs after lunch," Nate said. "Do you suppose you could spare some photos of that beaded pouch and the stone we recovered from the body dump?"

"Absolutely. We have the digitals, so when we get back to the office I'll print them off for you."

Nate frowned. "Miller and Lauden seem pretty convinced that Sara's death is connected to the clash over the casino. I just hope they aren't right. As much as I hate to admit it, tempers have gotten hot and heavy over the issue."

"It's possible someone snatched Sara to make a statement, and the plan went south." Dana stirred her vegetable soup. "I'm just glad you'll be talking to the people who might be involved."

"I appreciate you giving me the opportunity."

Mac sipped his coffee. "While you're working the reservation, Dana and I will get going on the interviews here in Portland. If Post agrees to an interview, though, we'd like to be there. If he'll only talk to you, then go for it."

"I'll see what I can do."

"You want to start with Sara's husband?" Dana asked Mac.

"Yeah." Mac stabbed a fork into his blackened salmon salad. For once, he'd chosen healthy—Dana's influence. "I took a look at the notes Miller and Lauden had on him, and they were pretty sparse. I have a feeling they crossed him off the list too soon."

"Well, he apparently had an alibi."

"Right, but that doesn't mean much. He could have hired a hit. That seems to be the rage these days."

"I can't imagine him killing his little girl's mommy. Besides, he seems genuinely heartbroken." Dana sighed. "I know, I know. We can't rule out anyone."

"Darn right." Mac dug into his food. Talk dissipated as they ate in companionable silence.

AS PLANNED, Nate left for Warm Springs after lunch to look into the possible tribal connections to the case. He took with him digital photos of the stone and pouch that were recovered from Sara's mouth back with him, so he could show them to tribal members and local historians to confirm his interpretation of the image. He would also attempt to secure an interview with Therman Post; hopefully Post would grant a meeting with Nate based on his status as a tribal member.

After Nate left them at the OSP office, Dana phoned Scott Watson at his home. He picked up the phone after Dana started to leave a message.

"I'm sorry, Detective Bennett. I've had to screen my calls. The media won't leave us alone. They're camped out on my front lawn, if you can believe it."

"Oh, I believe it," Dana said. "Detective McAllister and I would like to come by for an interview. I can only imagine how difficult all of this is for you, but we are taking over the case from the FBI and really need to speak with you personally."

"Can't you just read the files? I told the FBI guys everything I know."

Dana apologized again. "Since this has become a murder investigation, we basically need to start over."

"OK. Um—why don't you come over now? Chloe's asleep and probably will be for the next two hours."

"Thanks, Scott. We'll be there in about thirty minutes."

"Do I need a lawyer present?"

"You're certainly welcome to one if you feel it's necessary." Dana glanced over at Mac.

"Am I a suspect?"

"No. However, we will need to rule you out as one."

"I understand."

"Good. We'll see you shortly." Dana pinched her lips together and ended the call.

"He didn't want to talk to us?" Mac straightened and moved away from the desk he'd been leaning against.

"No, and I don't blame him." Dana pulled on her suit jacket. "He's being hounded by the press."

"We will be too," Mac predicted. And they were. Reporters pressed in on them en mass as they maneuvered the car through them toward the Watsons' house.

As they pulled up into the circular drive, Mac noticed a woman holding a bag and ringing the doorbell. "Looks like he has company." Scott opened the door and took the proffered bag. He was thanking the woman as Mac turned off the motor. "What do you suppose that's all about?"

"Probably a casserole or something like it."

"Hmm. I wish somebody would bring me casseroles," Mac

mumbled as they exited the car. His fridge was empty again and would probably stay that way until they resolved Sara's death.

Scott Watson opened the door before they rang the bell. With a phone to his ear, he motioned them inside. "I'll be with you in a second; make yourself at home."

"You taking notes this time?" Mac asked Dana.

"Sure, I think I'm up." They both stood in the living room until Scott came in with some bottled waters and extended one to each of them.

"No thanks," they said in concert.

"We just ate," Dana explained. "Thank you, though."

"I've got a ton of food, getting more meals and drinks from friends and neighbors than we can eat. Guess I'll have to put some of the stuff in the freezer." Scott nodded toward the phone. "That was my secretary, Jackie. She's a lifesaver right now—been keeping my business afloat while I try to pick up the pieces. Everyone's been so helpful, from friends and family to complete strangers. Especially Claire. She and Allysa are still here, but I imagine they'll be going home after the funeral."

"She was here for a long time."

"She loved Sara. We both did." He frowned. "It's not what you think, Detective. There's nothing going on between Claire and me."

Having seen them together, Mac wasn't sure he believed him. He and Claire may have loved Sara, but what if they loved each other more?

EIGHTEEN

So what kind of work do you do?" Mac asked Scott, settling into the actual interview.

"I'm an engineering partner in a firm in old town—Watson, Simons, and Keller. Patrick Simons and Donovan Keller and I are good friends; we started the business from the ground up after college."

"That's right; I remember reading that somewhere," Mac said.

"So what can I help you guys with? I've given my statement, blood, and hair samples, and I've even taken a lie detector test. I didn't have anything to do with my wife's death." Scott's demeanor had changed since Saturday. He was back to looking like a professional.

"We've read through the interviews, but we'd like to have you go through the events that led up to Sara's disappearance and maybe ask a few questions that weren't asked before."

He bit into his lower lip and frowned. "Sure. I'm sorry; I know you're only doing your jobs. I feel like I'm outside looking in right now, you know? It has been so long since Sara disappeared, and I've gone through so many emotions—hope, anger, remorse. I'm glad it's over. Not the outcome I'd hoped for, but at least now I can get on with things. I just want her killer caught and locked up before he can do this to someone else. Where do you want me to start?"

"How would you describe your relationship?"

"Good. I mean, really good. I was crazy about Sara."

"Tell us about the day she disappeared," Mac said. "Did you notice anything out of the ordinary?"

"You probably already know this, but Sara got off work early because we had guests coming for the weekend. I got a message from my secretary that Sara had called while I was in a meeting to let me know her car had been broken into. I wish now my secretary would have let me know right away. Of course, she had no way of knowing what would happen. She feels terrible about it." Scott shook his head. "I'd have told Sara to call the police. I don't know why she didn't. Guess now I never will."

"You came home early that day?"

"Yes. About the same time I got the message about the car, our day-care provider called wanting to know when one of us would be by to pick up Chloe. That's when I started to get worried. According to the day-care worker, Sara was supposed to have picked her up around three. As soon as I got the message about the car, I tried Sara's cell phone. She didn't answer, so I went directly over to pick up our daughter and came home. Claire called while I was on my way. She got here around four and found the front door unlocked and Sara's car in the driveway with the window broken. Claire was pretty shaken up, and I called the police right away."

"So you knew that someone had broken into her car," Mac said. "Did you know the garage remote was missing too?"

"No, it wasn't missing," Scott clarified. "I told the FBI agents this, so it's probably in the notes, but Sara had given me her garage remote to replace the batteries about a week before she disappeared. She was using the keypad to get into the garage."

"OK." Mac made a mental note that the killer could have had the keypad combination to gain entrance to the Watsons' home.

"What kind of meeting were you in, and who was present?" Mac asked.

"Do you mean can someone substantiate my story? Yes. One of my partners, Patrick, was there, along with two of our attorneys and about a half-dozen clients on a major project we're working on. We're remodeling an old brewery into upscale condos and a shopping center. I supplied a list of the people at the meeting to the FBI."

Mac nodded. "Go ahead and continue with the events that day. What happened next?"

"After that, it was pretty much a blur. I called people Sara might have contacted, but no luck. The police came and the FBI. Dale got them involved right away. I couldn't believe she was gone. All those questions and. . . ." He paused and looked over at Mac. "I still can't believe it. Why would anyone want to kill Sara?"

"Has anyone attempted to contact you with regard to a ransom—anything like that?"

"No calls, just those threatening letters to Dale—her uncle, um, Senator Wilde."

Mac glanced at Dana, a little surprised that Scott knew about the letters when the feds hadn't even told the OSP detectives. But again, there had been mention of it by the press. "What letters are you referring to?" Mac asked, making sure he wasn't leading Scott in the interview.

"The letters from the Native Americans demanding that Dale change his position on the casino in the gorge. The FBI was looking into it. We didn't know if they were a hoax or the real thing. Dale thought whoever had written those letters might have been responsible for Sara's disappearance."

"Did you see the letters?"

"No, but he told me about them. The letters kept coming, even after Sara disappeared, only they got worse. The senator was told to back off and allow the casino to be built, or Sara would be killed. I thought the letter writer was the prime suspect."

"Where did you hear this?"

"From Sara's uncle. He had his staff turn the letters over to the FBI and told me to keep the information to myself so I wouldn't jeopardize the investigation."

"Do you have any idea how the media got hold of the story?"

"Not a clue. It wasn't from me, that's for sure. Dale and I were worried that those articles might have gotten Sara killed."

"How so?"

Scott shrugged. "Maybe they thought the senator was playing them, and they got mad. That's assuming the person who wrote the letters kidnapped her in the first place."

"What kind of relationship did Sara have with her uncle?"

"He was like a father to her. Her parents died when she was in grade school. Her uncle didn't come around much after we got married, but since she disappeared, he checks in with me and Chloe at least once a week, or he has Grant do it. His wife, Anne, comes over nearly every day. They've been supportive—they even hired a groundskeeper for us. Dale and Anne are devastated about the way things turned out. Dale blames himself."

"How so?" Mac reached for one of the water bottles and twisted the cap.

"He didn't change his stand on the casino situation. You can't succumb to demands like that. We both thought the FBI would be able to track down the person who wrote the notes. He'll feel even worse if it turns out to be true."

"If what turns out to be true?" Mac asked.

"If Sara's murder is related to his political position—you know, to opposing the casino."

"Tell me about this Grant person you mentioned."

"Grant Stokely. He's Dale's assistant; chief of staff, I think, is his official title. Grant is the one who usually calls to check on us and arranges times when the senator can visit. He'd be the one who told Dale about the letters."

Mac jotted the information on his pad. "Do you know if Senator Wilde took a polygraph? I see in the case file that he was interviewed."

"I wouldn't know. I assume so, since the rest of us were asked. I didn't really like the idea, but I didn't want to throw up any red flags or complicate things. You'd have to ask the FBI agents to be sure, but I'm sure Dale cooperated to the fullest."

"We'll look into it." Mac made a note to check the files. "Now, Mr. Watson, I have a few questions to ask that we could both do without. Let me apologize ahead of time as some will probably seem inappropriate, but we have to ask them."

"OK, you have my attention." Scott sat forward.

"Is there any indication Sara was having an extramarital affair or seeing anyone else?"

Scott sucked in his cheeks. "Boy, you really hit below the belt, don't you? I suppose anything is possible, but Sara and I were happy. If she was having an affair, she hid it very well."

"Do you suppose it's possible?"

"No. Are you thinking she was seeing someone and that I killed her?" He seemed defensive now and angry.

"I'm sorry to upset you, but like I said, we have to ask some very unpleasant questions if we are going to find out who's responsible for her death. We need to cover all the bases. Did you or Sara have any enemies, anyone who might want to hurt you or your wife?"

"No. Everything was aboveboard in my professional life. I mean, we bid jobs with other engineering firms, but I've never heard of professionals in my business holding grudges to this degree. Sara worked for an ad agency and got along with everybody."

"I've heard advertising is a cutthroat business."

"It can be, but Sara never seemed to have any problems."

"Do you owe any substantial debt to disreputable collectors?"

"We're financially sound. You can check my bank records if you want. We owe on our home, but that's about it. I only deal with banks, no loan sharks or anything, if that's what you're asking."

"What about you, Scott—any jealous girlfriends?"

Scott blew out a long breath. "Absolutely not. Sara and I were happy. We loved each other and Chloe."

"OK, that's all I have for now." Mac looked over at Dana. "Detective Bennett?"

"Yes. I have a couple of questions. Did your wife spend a lot of time on the Internet?"

"What, like she might have set up a meeting with some chat room predator?"

"It may sound far-fetched, but these days . . ."

"I see your point. I read about that attorney who set up a meeting with someone he met in a chat room, and they killed him. No, she didn't have time for stuff like that. Neither did I. She worked and came home and took care of Chloe. She has e-mail, but she even complained about that taking too much time."

"Did she have her own computer here?" Dana asked.

"We shared one in our office upstairs," Scott said.

"We may need to look at it."

"The FBI agents checked her files, but you're welcome to take another look." Scott leaned back against the cushions, avoiding eye contact.

"Thank you. If you don't mind, we'll take it with us."

"For how long?"

"Hopefully, just a few days."

"What if I refuse?"

"We'd get a warrant; but letting us take it will save us all a lot of grief."

He shrugged his shoulders. "Go ahead. I don't think you'll find anything on it anyway. Just try to get it back as soon as possible. I bring work home sometimes." Mac completed a search-by-consent form after Dana asked the question, handing the form to Dana for Scott to sign. Although Scott was cooperating now, the form would verify that he was consenting to the seizure of his computer and to have the hard drive analyzed by a forensic expert. The form might come in handy at trial if he was ever implicated. After explaining the form and the extent of the examination, Dana secured Scott's signature.

"We appreciate your cooperation, Scott." Dana slipped her notes into her briefcase. "Thank you for your time."

"Please contact us if you have any questions or need anything from us." Mac handed Scott a business card.

Scott's demeanor softened. "Thank you. I'm sorry if I seemed upset. If you need anything, call me. I assume you'll be in touch."

"Yes," Dana answered. "We'll update you as much as we can."

"What happens now?"

"We're working on the lead you mentioned earlier," Mac said, "regarding the letters to Senator Wilde. I can assure you we'll get to the bottom of that. We have an officer gathering background information as we speak. Even though the FBI interviewed scores of witnesses, we'll probably have to contact every one of them, and that could take a while."

Scott nodded. "Can you tell me anything else about Sara's death? I mean—do you know how she was killed?"

Mac hesitated, trying to be careful about the way he answered the question so as not to give out too much information. "The medical examiner found no obvious cause of death, I can tell you that much. We're still running tests and waiting for more forensic results."

"I'm glad you guys are on the case," Scott said. "Sounds like you're pretty thorough."

"We try to be." Mac glanced toward the stairs. "You said Claire was still staying here. Is she here now?"

"Yeah. Allysa's at school, so she's working in the guest room. Do you want me to get her for you?"

"That would be great." Turning to Dana, he said, "While we're waiting for her, why don't we take the computer to the car?"

When they came back inside, Claire was seated on the sofa, legs curled under her. Scott was sitting beside her, holding her hand. He let go when he realized they'd come in.

"Thanks for agreeing to meet with us, Claire," Dana said, taking over the role as interviewer.

Scott got up. "If you guys are done with me, I'll head over to the office. Jackie tells me I have some things that need my attention."

"That's fine."

The interview with Claire substantiated Scott's story about finding the house empty and Sara gone. When Dana asked about her living there, Claire insisted that she was there primarily to care for Chloe and be a support for Scott, who was taking Sara's disappearance and death very hard. "I can see where you might suspect the worst," she said, "but Allysa and I stay in the guest room, and I can assure you, Scott and I are not an item."

"Tell me about your relationship with Sara," Dana said.

Claire reiterated much of what they had already heard about Sara's becoming part of the family.

"How did you feel about that?"

"I loved it. Sara and I had always been close, but living together as sisters was an ideal situation." Claire's eyes misted over. "You're wondering if I had a motive to kill her. I did not. Neither did Scott."

"How did Sara get along with your parents?"

"Good, mostly. Sara went through some pretty tough times after her parents died, but she never acted out. I was a different story. I didn't like the political arena and left home after high school. Got married and pregnant and divorced. I had Allysa, settled down, and made peace with my parents. That's about as exciting as it gets."

"Are you seeing anyone now?"

"No." She sighed. "I got burned, and I'm not sure I want to get into a relationship again."

Dana licked her lips. "Claire, had Sara ever talked to you about Scott seeing other women?"

She shook her head. "There's no way."

"How can you be sure?"

"You're planning to pin Sara's murder on Scott, aren't you?"

"Not unless he's guilty."

She stared at her clasped hands. "He's not. I know Scott. We've been friends since before . . ." She paused, as if wishing she could take back what she said.

"Before?"

Claire bit into her lower lip. "OK, I wasn't going to say anything because it really isn't relevant. Scott and I dated briefly in high school. I introduced him to Sara, and it was love at first sight for them."

"And how did that make you feel?" Dana tipped her head to one side.

Mac was glad Dana was conducting the interview. She tended to have a lot more patience and sympathy than he did.

Claire smiled. "I admit I was a little jealous at first. But seeing them together made me realize they were right for each other. I moved on."

"Sounds like Sara has had a happier life, though. Does that bother you?"

"I made some bad choices. There are things I wish I'd done differently, but . . . ," Claire hesitated. "Look, you can dig around trying to find a motive for Scott and me, but you're wasting your time."

"Can you think of anyone who might want Sara dead?"

"Absolutely not. If I had to guess, I'd say it was a random act. Some pervert broke into her car and got the address, and somehow got into the house. Who knows what they were planning? I don't think it was ever a kidnapping."

"Do you know if anything was taken from the house?"

Mac wondered where Dana was going with her questions. They'd gotten the reports from the CSI team shortly after the kidnapping, and no one could determine that anything had been stolen.

Claire frowned. "It's hard to tell, you know. Scott said there wasn't anything of value."

"You seem unsure."

"Sara had a small collection of Native American art. No real artifacts that we know of, just items she'd gotten from her grandmother's estate."

"Her grandmother?"

"Her grandmother lived on the Warm Springs Reservation. I think she was from the Paiute tribe."

Mac sat up straighter. Coincidence? He didn't think so. They had another Native American connection.

Dana kept her gaze level on Claire. "What was her grandmother's name?"

"Margaret. Margaret Case."

Dana jotted down the information. "Go on."

"I could be wrong, but I think there might be a couple of pieces missing. Sara got the collection while she was still living with us. She kept it in her room, and then when she got married, she put the pieces in that curio cabinet over there." Claire pointed at the rounded-front, older style cabinet with glass doors. "I was dusting the other day and happened to look inside. There are two pieces missing—a carved stone and a small beaded bag."

Mac stopped breathing. Dana gave him a look that said, *Why don't you take it from here?*

"Are you sure?" Mac leaned forward.

"There's an empty space in the cabinet where she kept them. I suppose she could have given them away or sold them, but Sara loved that stuff."

"When did you discover that they were missing?" Mac asked.

She shrugged. "Saturday. I remember because I'd been putting off the dusting—just too many other things to do. Sara dusted every Saturday. I've been trying so hard to keep things up so the house would be perfect when she came home."

"Did you say anything to anyone?"

"I asked Scott, but he didn't know. We thought maybe she'd put them somewhere else." Her gaze flitted between Mac and Dana. "You're thinking I should have called the police?"

When neither of them answered, she added, "I didn't see where they could have been related to her disappearance."

"They may be."

"How? I don't understand." Claire ran a hand through her reddish blonde hair.

"It may not be relevant at all," Mac said. "Can we take a look at the other Native American items Sara had?"

"Sure." Claire padded over to the cabinet and, taking a skeleton key from the top, unlocked the door.

"She kept this locked?" Dana peered inside.

"All the time since Chloe's been old enough to crawl." She set the key back on top of the cabinet.

"How many people know about this collection?" Mac asked.

"I have no idea. It's no secret. Sara was proud of the collection and her heritage. I'm sure everyone who knew her knew about it."

That narrows down the field. "Did she have other family on her mother's side besides Margaret?"

"She may have. An aunt and some cousins, I think. I didn't know them very well."

A whimpering sound came from somewhere upstairs.

"That's Chloe. I'd better go get her. She's learned how to climb out of her crib. I'll be right back."

"Look at this stuff, Mac. There's a beaded handbag and some woven baskets. That pouch we found in Sara's mouth could easily have come from her own collection."

"I'd be surprised if it didn't." He looked at the contents of the cabinet. "The crime lab should have checked this for prints. The results should be in the file we got from the feds."

"I don't remember seeing anything. Maybe since it was locked, they missed the inside."

"We may have to call the lab to reprint. You have those photos of the stone and pouch, don't you?" Mac asked.

She nodded. "I gave Nate copies and kept a set for ourselves."

"Good. When she comes back, let's show them to Claire—see if she can identify them."

Claire came down, carrying the adorable, black-haired, round-faced little girl. Chloe hid her face in the curve of her aunt's neck and shoulder. "She's shy around strangers."

"That's a good thing." Dana grinned as she opened her briefcase and pulled out the envelope she'd tucked away earlier. "Claire, we'd like to show you some photos."

Dana laid several out on the coffee table.

Claire gasped. "Those are Sara's. At least I think they are. The stone looks like hers for sure, but the pouch looks like it's torn. Sara's had a flap on it. Hers was in perfect condition. Where did you get them?"

Chloe leaned forward, her tiny hand reaching for the pictures. "Mine!"

Dana gathered the photos and placed them back in the envelope.

"Why do you have those pictures? Did Sara have the pieces with her? What happened to them?"

"We can't share that information with you right now," Mac said. "What I can tell you is that by telling us about Sara's collection, you may have provided an important key to our investigation."

"I wish I'd noticed sooner."

"I'm just glad you noticed it." Dana took her digital camera from the briefcase. "I'd like to get some photos of Sara's collection."

Before leaving, Mac asked Claire to make a list of people who knew about the key, as well as a list of any enemies Sara might have had. He had more questions for her, but the toddler needed her attention more than he and Dana did at the moment. Mac could hardly wait to talk to Nate and hopefully learn more about Sara's family tree.

NINETEEN

Claire watched the detectives leave and then put Chloe in her high chair, absent-mindedly filling her cup with milk and setting it on the tray. Whoever had taken Sara had taken the beaded bag and the rock. Why? What significance did Sara's heritage play in her murder? The detectives had asked her who knew about the collection. Who knew about the key?

It wasn't a secret. She'd previously considered Sara's abduction a random act. Now she wasn't so sure. A burglar might have thought the pouch and stone were valuable, but wouldn't he have broken the glass? This person knew where the key was. But that didn't make sense. No one among their family or friends had reason to kill Sara. Did they? On the other hand, how well did she know the relatives on Sara's mother's side? They didn't seem that close to Sara, but she'd never heard about any problems.

Could Sara have been involved with someone? Or Scott? She moved her head from side to side. It wasn't possible. Claire forced herself to leave her suspicions behind and focus on Chloe.

The child's dark eyes followed her every movement. She still missed her mother and would often start crying for no apparent reason. What would happen now? Claire would have to leave soon, and Sara wasn't coming home. Chloe would lose her now too. Had coming here to stay been a mistake? At the time, she'd only thought about how Chloe and Scott needed someone to take care of them. She hadn't thought this far ahead.

A lump clogged her throat. "Oh, baby doll. What are we going to do?"

Detective Bennett didn't believe her when she told them she and Scott were not a couple. She'd been honest in saying they weren't sleeping together but not so honest about her feelings. The truth was that she was falling in love with Scott Watson.

She hadn't meant to, and he probably didn't feel the same way. But there it was. Claire set an animal cracker on the tray in front of Chloe. "Don't worry, sweetie. Auntie Claire isn't going anywhere— at least not yet. I can't leave until we find out what happened, can I?"

Chloe chewed on the cookie and then held it out for Claire to take a bite. She pretended to nibble on it, and Chloe giggled and pulled it back.

Allysa bounced in, her arms full of school things. Claire shoved aside her concerns and went back to being the mother both girls needed. She'd have to ask Scott about Sara's collection tonight. He'd know better than she did who had access to the key.

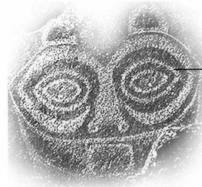

TWENTY

What do you think?" Mac asked, once they were buckled in. He didn't have an opinion as yet and was still trying to digest what they'd learned from Scott and Claire.

"I'm not sure. We can't really prove or disprove anything either of them said at this point."

"Gut feeling?"

"Scott loved Sara," Dana said. "I believed Scott and Claire when they said they weren't sleeping together."

"Why would you think that?"

She shrugged. "Just the look on his face when he talked about Sara. And Claire was being mostly honest."

"What do you mean?"

"They might not be sleeping together, but something is going on. I think she's in love with him."

"I'm more interested in how a bag and rock from Sara's collection ended up in her mouth. Suggests her killer knew her or at least knew about the collection."

"Maybe, but according to Claire, it could be anyone who's visited the house."

As they headed back to the office, Mac asked, "Are you up for another interview?"

"Sure."

"Good. I want to find out if Senator Wilde and Mr. Administrative Sidekick have been asked the tough questions."

"Before we get too far with our questioning," Dana said, "we'd better bone up on the reports we inherited. I want to check the lab results for prints on that cabinet."

"It'll take awhile to go through all those files, but you're right. We can contact Nate at the same time."

"I hope the senator can fit us into his busy schedule," Dana said.

Mac cast her a sideways look. "Oh, I think we can persuade him."

MAC AND DANA RETURNED to the Portland Patrol Office and talked to Kevin about their interview with Scott Watson and Claire Montgomery, as well as their plan to interview the senator.

"Lots of good information, kids. I'm especially interested in this Native American connection."

"So are we. We need to check the FBI files to see whose prints showed up on Sara's cabinet. Latents should be able to tell us who besides Sara was in there." Mac felt good about this one.

"I appreciate your wanting to interview Senator Wilde right away, but getting an appointment with the senator may take some doing. I'm sure he'll want to cooperate, but we have to go through the right channels." Kevin told them about the dignitary protection unit down in Salem. "We'll have to go through them to set up the interview."

"Humph," Mac grumbled. "Sounds like a lot of red tape to me."

"Unfortunately, yes, but we do what we have to do."

"I'd forgotten how much power these politicians have." Turning to Dana, Mac said, "How about we let the good sergeant work the political angle while we catch up on our reports?"

"Good idea," Kevin said. "I hope you're working the catch-'em-and-clean-'em method I taught you."

"Yes, sir," they said together. Kevin's method was simple: write up reports after the interviews so they don't back up on you. Detectives could easily interview dozens of potential witnesses in a day, turning into the hundreds during the course of an investigation. If they let the crime scene, autopsy, and interview observations grow stale, they might fail to document key elements or nuances in the reports. Mac tried to avoid more than a twenty-four-hour turnaround on the reports, but that wasn't always easy. Right now, he was more than two days behind.

"You want me to hang the paper on the interviews with Scott and Claire?" Dana asked as they exited the sergeant's office.

"If you don't mind." Mac stopped at his cubicle. "I'll do the crime scene and the post if you get the Watson interviews, FBI case review synopsis, and the evidence we took to the lab."

"Deal." Dana grinned. "I'm relieved that we're not interviewing the senator today. I'm not at my best this time of the afternoon."

"Yeah. I could go for some coffee."

"Me too. Want me to make a run to Starbucks?"

"No, I'll do it."

ONCE MAC RETURNED WITH THEIR COFFEES and they worked for a while, both dictated their reports into a tape recorder for their secretary.

"Any word from Nate?" Dana clicked off her tape recorder an hour later.

Mac tapped his recorder on his chin. "No, come to think of it. I haven't. I'll page him." He dialed in Nate's pager, pecking in his cell phone number in case Nate called him back after he left the office, then went back to dictating the report. Minutes later, his cell rang. "Hey, Nate, how goes it?"

"Not bad. I've talked to a number of folks, including Therman Post. Can you and Dana make it out to the reservation tomorrow? I have an interview set up with Therman."

"I think so. Hang on a sec." Mac hurried to Kevin's office. "Hey, Sarge, did you set up an interview with the senator yet?"

"No, I'm waiting to hear back from our guys in Salem. Why?"

"Good. Don't schedule anything for tomorrow. We're heading out to Warm Springs. Nate has an interview lined up."

"Good. I doubt we could have gotten in with the senator that quickly anyway."

Getting back to Nate, he said, "Tomorrow is fine. So Post agreed to talk with us?"

"Hopefully. Therman is skeptical, and I can't say that I blame him. He said we could come talk to him, but he needed to consult someone about it."

Mac felt the lead slipping away. "An attorney?"

"I don't think so. Though he might do that. I think he was talking in a more spiritual sense."

"So he's going to pray about it?"

"Yes, and probably talk to the tribal elders as well as our shaman."

"OK, well, let's hope he agrees. I don't want to drive all the way out there if he's going to change his mind."

Nate laughed. "I'll call you if anything changes. I think Therman will cooperate. He's just being cautious."

"OK. We'll plan on seeing you tomorrow, then. We should be able to get there by ten."

"Ask him about Margaret Case," Dana whispered.

"Oh, yeah. Nate, we might have something on the beaded bag and stone we found with Sara." Mac told Nate about the possible lead and connection to the Piaute Tribe.

"Interesting. The name has a familiar ring to it. I'll see if I can track it down."

"Well?" Dana asked when Mac hung up.

"Nate is one good guy. I wish he worked for our outfit. He has an interview set up for us with Therman."

"Cool." Dana sighed. "I'm almost done here. Can we talk details later?"

"Sure." Mac finished his own dictation and clicked off his tape recorder. He double-clicked on his e-mail icon, waiting a couple of seconds before the screen came up asking for his password. As he read through his e-mails, thoughts turned to his slain friend.

Mac scrolled through dozens of department messages, many from the agency head giving updates on the murdered trooper and the pending investigation. There was an e-mail listing a bank account that had been set up in the trooper's name to help the family with financial costs associated with their unborn child. Mac jotted down the participating bank's name so he could make an anonymous donation to the cause.

This donation would be in addition to the 1 percent of his monthly pay that all department members donated to the burial. It was tradition that all the OSP troopers donate 1 percent of their month's pay in the event a trooper was killed in the line of duty. The payment went to the surviving family to offset the burial costs. Unfortunately, this kind of thing happened often enough that the agency payroll system had an automatic deduction program to remove the money from the monthly checks. All they needed was an authorization notice to remove the money. There was always 100 percent compliance among the troopers.

Mac caught a glimpse of Philly carrying a stack of paperwork into Kevin's office. It was probably the search warrant return and the crime report from the biker clubhouse. Philly gave Mac a nod when he walked by, shoulders stooped, as though the burden of Daniel's death hung on them.

Mac felt he should say something, but he didn't trust himself to speak. All he could muster was a nod back to the big man. He peered into Philly's office when he spotted Detective Dustin Mitchell from the Salem office and a woman, probably his partner. They were seated at the small table next to Philly's desk. They had probably posted Trooper Revman today. Mac had never been to a fellow officer's autopsy and hoped he'd never have to. Urged on by curiosity and the desire to know more about Daniel's death, Mac pushed back his chair and walked into Philly's office.

"How's it going, Dustin?" Mac reached out to shake his hand.

"Mac. Good to see you." Mitchell's tired eyes turned to the woman. "Mac, this is my new partner, Jodi Creswisk. Jodi, this is Mac McAllister."

"Nice to meet you." Jodi and Dustin were both in their early forties. Jodi stood to shake his hand, and she must have been a good five-ten. She was an imposing, well-dressed brunette with a dark tan.

"You two up here for Officer Revman's investigation?" Mac asked.

"Yeah. We drew the short straw and had to attend the autopsy today." Jodi glanced down at the table. "Tough job."

"What was the cause and manner?" Mac asked. "Um—Daniel was a friend."

"Sorry." Dustin looked at Mac and then glanced away. "He had a torn carotid, frags in the head and chest, and probable shock from the massive blood loss. Take your pick, a grab bag of causes." Sarcasm, disgust, and grief layered his tone.

"The mechanism was grape shot and gasoline, fired up by that little makeshift cannon inside the light bulb." Dustin shook his head. "If I could get five minutes in a room with that filthy piece of . . ." He stopped midsentence. The autopsy had obviously taken an emotional toll on the detective. How could it not? It was bad enough watching the medical examiners cut into a total stranger, let alone someone you worked with. It made matters worse when the pictures in the papers and on TV had the victim wearing the same kind of uniform you had hanging in the closet.

"I don't envy you, and I really appreciate your seeing this through," Mac said.

Philly came back in and Mac left, but not before giving Philly an empathetic pat on the shoulder.

Mac returned to his cubicle and continued pecking away at the e-mail messages. Daniel's funeral was set for Wednesday. Mac would go unless the investigation was at a critical stage. It was the least he could do for an old friend.

Dana rounded the corner, sliding her arms into the sleeves of her suit jacket. "Are you finished?"

"Almost."

"I've dictated the rough draft to the reports and will proof them as soon as Cindy puts them on paper." She hesitated. "Did you see the e-mail on the funeral down in Central Point?"

Mac nodded. "Want to ride down with me?"

"Of course. You're my partner."

"I want to go in uniform. I'll pick you up at your place. I need help getting into my dress blues. I can never get that Sam Brown strap right." The Sam Brown was a traditional strap that went from the gunbelt over the shoulder and chest like the uniforms worn by police in a Norman Rockwell painting.

"Sounds like a plan," Dana said. "But the funeral isn't until Wednesday. What time do you want to meet in the morning?"

"How about seven? I told Nate we'd be there by ten."

"OK. Good night, Mac; get some rest." Dana slipped out of his cubicle, and Mac could hear her saying good-bye to Kevin and the rest of the detectives.

Mac finished up his e-mails and headed for Kevin's office, giving a rap on the door before pushing it open.

"Hey, Mac. C'mon in," Kevin looked up from the mountain of paperwork on his desk.

"Hey, Sarge, how are the new digs?" Mac looked around the office. The only thing that proved Kevin had changed offices was the picture of his wife on the desk. The heap of binders and reference manuals left behind by Frank Evans still occupied the two bookshelves in the cramped office.

"Still not used to it yet. I should have stayed across the hall in my old office."

"But this one's bigger, an office fitting a man of your importance," Mac grinned.

"Yeah, right." Kevin smiled back. He picked up a rubber band and shot it at Mac. Mac caught it midflight, then he slumped down in a chair.

"Are you doing OK?" Kevin asked, his face showing concern for his friend and former partner.

"Yeah, just bummed about Trooper Revman. Just like everyone else probably." Mac stretched the rubber band to occupy his hands.

"You know about the funeral on Wednesday?"

Mac nodded his head. "I'm going. At least I plan to."

"Are you interested in standing deathwatch? It begins tomorrow at midnight."

"I've never done that before. What does it entail?" Mac continued playing with the rubber band, stretching it around his fingers.

"For twenty-four hours, we'll post a ceremonial guard on Daniel's body. The post rotates every fifteen minutes. You'll have to stand at attention and rotate the post with a slow salute to your replacement. Since you and Daniel were pals, I think it would be a good idea if you were the representative from our detectives' office."

"Sure. What shift do I need to work?"

"I'll call the Honor Guard supervisor; see what openings he has with his team."

The OSP Honor Guard team was comprised of rank-and-file officers who were specially trained in drill and ceremony, much like the military burial teams. They wore the traditional dress uniform, complete with white gloves and leather polished to a high gloss.

The Honor Guard members were tasked with completing the burial rites for current and past members. Anyone who worked for the OSP was entitled to the use of the Honor Guard team at their funerals, regardless of the time they retired from active service. Most of the team's use was for memorial services, special ceremonies, and the funerals of retired members, although from time to time they had to participate in the grim task of burying an active member like Trooper Revman. Mac's presence on the deathwatch would be an honor and an obligation to his fallen friend.

Kevin searched through the paperwork on his desk. "I have a contact name and number for you on that interview with Senator Wilde. You and Dana can head down Thursday morning."

"Not until Thursday?"

"He's not available tomorrow, and with the funeral on Wednesday . . ."

"Right."

"Here's a contact number." Kevin handed Mac a slip of paper.

"Grant Stokely. He's Senator Wilde's aide."

"Chief of staff, actually." Kevin leaned back in his chair. "He was cooperative enough, although he gave pretty strict instructions that nobody was to talk to the senator without going through him. I found that a bit odd."

"Kind of territorial, isn't he?"

"Something else that was kind of odd." Kevin frowned.

"What?"

"He wanted to review any press releases on the case before they went out. He gave me the impression he was going to make sure he was present for any interviews with us."

"What do you make of that?" Mac asked.

"He's a politician, so who knows? He's either up to something, looking out for himself, or just plain weird. Maybe all three; you can never tell with these guys."

"I guess we'll find out Thursday morning. You want to come along?" Mac knew the answer.

"And leave all this?" Kevin spread his arms wide. "I'll let you and Dana sift through the answers and get to the truth."

"We'll see. I don't even know what the questions are yet."

"I have faith in you two. You'll come through."

Mac hoped that would be the case. He couldn't remember a time when he'd had so much trouble concentrating. The investigation didn't seem all that daunting, except for the fact that they were dealing with a five-week-old murder. But there was more to being a cop than solving crimes. Mac drove home, his mind in turmoil. He couldn't stop thinking about Daniel's swift and unexpected death and how it could just as easily have been him. Though he wasn't on the SWAT team, he was just as vulnerable. They all were. Even a minor traffic violation could turn into a gun battle. Mac shook the morbid thoughts from his head.

Once home, he took Lucy for a walk and spent some time in the park playing with her ratty old tennis ball, a favorite. By the time they got home, Mac felt better, more upbeat, his mind clearer. His focus right now was finding Watson's killer. Tomorrow they'd go to Warm Springs and see for themselves what this casino business was all about.

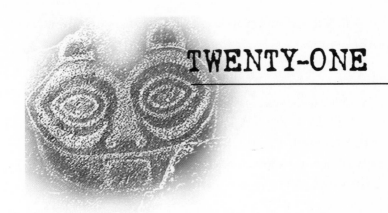

TWENTY-ONE

Mac groaned when the alarm clock went off at five thirty. He reached over and slapped the snooze button. After repeating the process three times, Mac finally dragged himself out of bed and took a long, hot shower.

He missed Lucy and then remembered he'd taken his dog over to Carl's the night before. He called Dana. "Hey, since we're both going to Warm Springs, want to bypass the office and just have me pick you up?"

"Sure. Sounds like a plan. We can at least skip some of the rush-hour traffic."

"My thoughts exactly." He finished getting ready and headed out to his car. Mac started the unmarked cruiser without getting in and reached over the steering column to hit the trunk-release button after turning the key. He had recently qualified with one of the department's new AR-15 rifles, the civilian model of the military's M-16. He kept the .223 caliber rifle in his trunk while off duty. Grabbing the weapon from the temporary storage and securing it in the roof-mounted rack of his cruiser, he tucked the shoulder strap around the rifle's forearm to keep it from hanging down in his rearview mirror.

Dana came out as soon as he pulled up to the curb. She looked nearly as tired as he felt, but that didn't detract from her appearance. Mac couldn't help admiring her khaki slacks and matching jacket with a lavender scoop-neck knit shirt. Not a lot of color, but on Dana, everything looked good.

She got into the car with a sigh. "Sleep well?"

"Not bad. Morning came too early, though."

"Tell me about it."

Mac drove to Brewed Awakenings to order coffee at the drive-through window.

"We're way too habitual, Mac." Dana's dimples creased when he ordered her usual.

He chuckled. "Keeps us from having to think too much until after we have coffee."

From the coffee shop, they headed south on 164th, then west on Highway 14 to the I-205 junction. It took them an hour to get to Highway 26 and another hour and a half to drive to Warm Springs. On the way, Mac called Nate to confirm their meeting while Dana began to pore over the case files they'd inherited from the feds.

"Any reports in there on Sara's cabinet?"

She shook her head. "Not that I could find."

"We'd better ask our CSI team for the results then. Hopefully they dusted it."

"It's possible they didn't. At the time of her kidnapping, we knew nothing about her Native American connection." She dialed the lab and asked that the reports in question be faxed to her at the OSP office.

Mac had reviewed Therman Post's infamous letters the night before while looking through his own copy of the file. In the first group of letters, Post alluded to but never actually made an overt threat. The second set of letters, however, had a cruel tone and a definite death threat: *Do as I say, or Sara dies.* "Did you read the letters?" he asked, wanting Dana's take.

"I did. Several times."

"And?"

"I don't think Therman Post wrote the second batch. They're too different. I really think we're looking for someone else."

"I tend to agree. The only corresponding evidence we have so far is the Warm Springs postmark on the envelopes. I'm sure Post isn't the only activist out there."

"Hopefully Mr. Post will be able to shed some light on things." Dana tucked the files back into her briefcase, set it on the floor behind her, and settled back against the seat.

"Tired?" Mac asked. She seemed more subdued than usual.

"Mmm. That guy called again last night, five times." She sighed. "I thought I'd catch up on my sleep on the way."

"Sure. Have you reported the calls?"

"Yes—to the Vancouver police. They suggested we get a trap trace on my phone."

"Sounds like a good plan."

"Maybe. He doesn't stay on the line long enough."

"Just phone calls?" Mac asked.

"I—I think so." Dana's hesitation spurred Mac on.

"He's following you?"

"I don't know. He may be parking outside my apartment complex at night. I've noticed this car, but it's always gone in the morning." She gave Mac a sidelong glance. "It's probably a new tenant or something."

"Just the same, next time you see it, jot down the license plate number. We can check it out."

"I already thought of that, but he's got no front plate and always backs into the stall. I haven't brought myself to walking out to look at it yet." She folded her arms and closed her eyes.

Concern for Dana etched its way into Mac's mind. Maybe he'd do a stakeout himself. He'd have to remember to mention it later.

The scorched earth gave evidence of the devastating forest fire as Mac entered Warm Springs around ten. He slowed to forty-five miles per hour when they entered town, heeding the reduced speed warning. Warm Springs was notorious about speed enforcement, with the proceeds of traffic citations going into their municipal budget.

Turning off the highway near the tribal interpretive center and museum, Mac made his way to the Warm Springs Police Department on the south side of town. The tidy brick building was one story, with two marked police cars and Nate's pickup parked by the front entrance.

"Hey, sleepyhead." Mac nudged his partner. "We're here."

She yawned. "You go ahead. I'll be there in a minute."

Mac stepped out of the car. Across the street in a school playground, at least a dozen school-age children played kickball, laughing and running in the sun. He smiled and waved at a young girl as she ran toward him to pick up an escaping red ball. She paused momentarily, but when an older woman called her name, she grabbed up the ball and hurried back to her friends.

Mac was taken aback by the woman's stern look, but he shouldn't have been surprised. He was a stranger here. He had no police authority and no professional contacts other than Officer Webb. The feeling left him a little unnerved. Being an ethnic minority was new to Mac, and it bothered him more than he thought it should. He'd never really thought about cultural divisions and felt a tug of guilt and embarrassment that he would be flustered by being the only white person other than Dana in the immediate area.

While waiting in the lobby for a receptionist to find Nate, he reflected on how he felt and vowed to make life easier on others when the roles were reversed.

The female receptionist returned a few moments later, tucking strands of long, black hair behind her ear as she slipped back into her chair. "Officer Webb will be with you in a minute." Her curious gaze lingered on him for several long moments before turning back to her work. Probably sizing him up.

While he waited, Mac admired the brilliant artwork displayed on the wall, most of which had a Native American theme. In the corner stood a beautiful bronze statue of an eagle, with the words *Brave at Heart* etched into the marble base. The small police department apparently had a great deal of pride in their community and heritage. Mac wished he had the same connection to his past. He'd never really felt as if he belonged anywhere except maybe to the OSP department and, of course, at home with his grandmother.

"You gonna stand there gawking all day?" Nate's familiar voice sounded behind him.

"Hey, Nate." Mac turned, catching a glimpse of Nate's broad smile. "I was beginning to wonder if you had gone without us."

"Wouldn't think of it." Nate shook Mac's extended hand. "Where's your partner?"

"In the car, waking up. She'll be in shortly."

"You want some coffee?"

"No, thanks," he chuckled. "I'd like to get rid of some, though."

"Right down the hall, past the drinking fountain. I'll meet you outside. I just got off the phone with Therman, and he's asked us to meet out at his place. We'll head over there first."

Mac walked out to the parking lot a few minutes later where Nate was sitting in his four-wheel-drive, crew-cab pickup. Dana, now looking revived and anxious to get started, sat in the backseat. "It's about time you got here," Dana teased. "We were about to leave without you."

"I'd be happy to drive," Mac offered.

Nate nodded toward Mac's Crown Vic. "Your rig wouldn't get us past Therman's cattle guards. You better leave that city-slicker car in the lot."

Mac chuckled at Nate's exaggeration. "Whatever you say." He popped the trunk on his cruiser and pulled out his large briefcase. It contained a portable camera and evidence collection kit, along with his interview gear, like notepads and a tape recorder. He adjusted his tie while peering into the case and looking over the contents of his trunk to make sure he wasn't leaving anything essential behind.

Satisfied that he had everything he'd need for the interview, he shut the trunk and set the alarm on the car with his keychain remote control.

"My rifle is in the car. Will it be OK here?" Mac asked as he climbed in on the passenger side.

"What, you think this is a bad neighborhood?" Nate asked, only half joking.

"No. I just don't want any of those kids getting curious."

"It'll be fine here at the P.D. We should only be gone about an hour. Therman just lives a few miles out of town."

Mac looked around the cab of Nate's pickup. A twelve-gauge shotgun was secured in a vertical mount on Mac's side of the cab, with a sidesaddle of spare ammo mounted to the stock. Although the outside of the truck was covered with dust and mud, the inside was clean and neat. Maps and resource books were crammed in every car door pocket and visor, just like any other cop car Mac had been in. A large brown feather with a white tip hung from the rearview mirror.

"What kind of feather is that? Eagle?" Mac flipped the feather with his left index finger.

"Close. It's from a red-tailed hawk. They're are all over the place in central Oregon."

"Does it mean anything—you know, carry any significance?"

"You mean like spiritually?"

"Or whatever, anything to your culture or to tribal members."

Nate looked up at the feather, then back to the highway. "To some, maybe. I just think it's cool. We can possess the feathers from birds of prey here on the reservation, whereas for you guys, it's a crime."

"Bit of a double standard, you think?" Mac softened his words with a smile. "I mean, it's not like you're using it for ceremonial reasons."

"I like your honesty, Mac, even if you are trying to put me on the spot. You're probably right. I shouldn't flaunt it. But it is one of the perks of being an Indian." Nate chuckled. "Just like you white guys get to wear all that gel and girlie stuff on your hair without anybody bothering you. We get to keep feathers." Mac ran his hand through his hair. "It's not gel; it's mousse. And they make it for men too. You could use some if you grew your hair longer than a quarter inch."

"Picked up the habit of short hair in the army; it makes haircuts a little cheaper when my wife cuts it at home."

"You guys are too much." Dana rolled her eyes. "If you can get serious for a minute, I have a question."

"What's that, Dana?" Nate eyed her in the rearview mirror.

"Should Mac and I be aware of any customs? The last thing we want to do is offend Mr. Post."

"Not really. Just show him the same respect you might show an elder in your own community. Therman is an old horse trader, a jack-of-all-trades kind of guy. I may not agree with some of his business dealings and the tactics he takes to get his message across, but I can't fault his dedication to the plight of some of our people on the reservation."

"Like the casino," Mac said.

"About that." Dana shifted positions. "How does another gambling casino in the state really help the tribe? Gambling is addictive. I wish the Native Americans had never gotten into that business."

Nate slowed the vehicle, turning off the pavement to a long gravel road. "Good question, Dana. The Confederated Tribes of Warm Springs holds a few records we're not particularly proud of, but we are trying to turn things around. Children on our reservation die at more than three times the statewide average and nearly twice that of other tribes in our nation. About sixty percent of those deaths are from accidents, alcohol and drug abuse, or domestic violence. Our unemployment rate is up around fifty percent."

"How many people live on the reservation who are actually members of the tribe?" Leaning closer, Dana rested her arms on the seat in front of her.

"We have nearly four thousand members on the rez, made up mostly of Warm Springs, Paiute, and Wasco tribes. Together, they comprise the Confederated Tribes, which are governed by an elected tribal council."

"So the casino they want to build in the gorge would help to combat some of the poverty and substance abuse?"

"Exactly. Our casino and resort here at Kah-Nee-Ta is a bit removed from the Portland market, but the placement of a facility in the gorge, with its proximity to the metro area, would attract many more customers. Our biggest competitors now are the larger casinos like Chinook Winds and Spirit Mountain, plus the video poker and lottery games in the local bars. If people can gamble right in their own neighborhoods, they are not as likely to travel two to three hours to central Oregon. We hope by opening the new market in the gorge, we can attract both Oregon and Washington customers to the casino. The extra revenue would go a long way for education and social treatment programs here at Warm Springs."

"I understand," Mac said. "But I'm not sure gambling is the right way to get the revenue you need."

"A lot of people would agree with you."

Mac looked out the window at the bleak landscape. The sagebrush and jack pines littered the landscape. A double-wide mobile home appeared on the horizon at the end of the washboard gravel road they were traveling on. "Say, did you get anything on Sara's grandmother?"

"I did, but we'll have to talk about that later."

Dana nodded at the buildings just ahead. "Is that Therman's place?"

"Yep," Nate affirmed. "He has about a hundred and sixty acres—not a bad spread. He has water rights to about two-thirds of the place. His wife, Emma, is a faith healer. She offers a voice for mother earth, guiding those who have strayed from the Creator."

"Come again?" Mac asked as they approached the front entrance of the residence. Not much of a yard, Mac noticed. There was, however, a rectangular plot that looked like a garden and shrubbery near the house with flowers coloring the otherwise bleak yard.

"We'd better save that conversation for when we have more time and less trouble." Nate gestured toward the house as he slipped out of his seat belt.

"Uh-oh." Dana drew in a sharp breath.

Therman Post stood on his porch, solemn faced and armed with a lever action rifle.

TWENTY-TWO

Mac eased open the door, slipping his .40 caliber out and holding the weapon at his right side. Dana pulled out her weapon as well, taking cover in the backseat.

Therman nodded toward them and then ducked around to the back of his house, his rifle at the ready. "What's he doing?" Dana asked.

"I have no idea," Nate said.

"Brandishing a rifle around the police isn't the smartest thing to do." Mac wasn't sure what to make of the older man's odd behavior.

"Hold on, Mac." Nate held up a hand. "Wait here while I see what's going on." Nate jogged to the corner of the house and then disappeared around the back. Less than a minute later, Mac heard a shot. "Please tell me this isn't happening."

"I wish I could," Dana said.

He crouched down behind the open door of the pickup, leaving room for Dana to squeeze out from behind the front seat. Mac leaned over, releasing the shotgun from the mount. He holstered his handgun and racked a round into the chamber of the twelve-gauge.

After waiting for what seemed an eternity, he yelled Nate's name. No response. Mac looked down at the open sights of the shotgun, running his thumb on the safety.

"Nate!" Mac yelled, then listened again. He heard nothing other than the wind rustling the nearby trees.

"He's not answering." Dana peered over the bed of Nate's truck.

"We have no authority here," Mac said, "but I have to do something."

"I agree. He could be bleeding to death out there. Or worse."

Mac looked over at the radio dial; the digital screen was blank. Even though the shotgun release was hard-wired, the radio was not and could not be turned on without the ignition key. He glanced over at the ignition. The keys were gone; Nate must have taken them with him. "We need to move in, Dana. You go to one side of the house, and I'll take the other." Mac thought about the last time he'd been in a situation like this. Dana had taken a bullet, and Mac ended up using deadly force. "On second thought, maybe you should stay here. We may be walking into an ambush."

"No way, Mac." The look in her eyes told him she was remembering the same incident.

"All right." He took a deep breath. "We move in. Go to the right, but be careful."

"You, too, partner." Dana headed toward the right side of the house, while Mac went left—in the direction Nate had taken. Since Therman hadn't come back, Mac figured the guy had either run or was waiting for them.

Please, God, not Nate. Mac whispered up a short prayer as he crept along the side of the house. He raised the shotgun barrel eye level and looked around the corner.

Therman Post was walking toward the house, rifle still in hand. He apparently hadn't seen Mac and was less than forty feet away—well in range of Mac's shotgun. Mac pressed the safety button again, assuring himself that it was ready to fire. "State Police," he yelled out. "I'm armed. Don't make me shoot you; drop the rifle!"

Therman stopped in his tracks and looked over to his right, showing no indication that he intended to drop the rifle. It looked like he was seeking an escape route. There was no route of escape that Mac didn't have covered with his buckshot, but Dana would be directly in the guy's sight. Mac held his breath. "Down on the ground. Drop the rifle."

Therman dropped to one knee. "D-don't shoot."

"Drop the gun!" Mac yelled one last time, closing one eye to secure his target and moving his index finger inside the trigger guard.

"Mac, no!" Nate rounded the corner on the other side with Dana close behind. "Don't shoot, Mac. Everything is OK." He was carrying what looked like a dead animal.

Mac slowly lowered the gun and put the weapon's safety on. "I heard a shot," Mac yelled to Nate.

"That was Therman. He was just shooting at a badger." Nate held up the animal with the dark fur and pointy nose. "They dig holes that'll break a horse's leg. Therman saw him just as we pulled up and, well, first things first."

"A badger." Mac blew out a long breath. "Man, I thought you were a goner."

"I'm sorry, Mac. It's just that when I saw what he was doing, I walked out with him to pick it up. It has a good hide, and I'm going to tan it for him. I'm so sorry."

Mac ran a hand through his hair and down the back of his neck. "I feel like an idiot." Mac pointed the shotgun barrel at the ground and glanced at Therman, who was struggling to get back up. "I thought you were in trouble. I bet the old guy's going to be ticked off, having a guy point a gun at him on his own place."

"You didn't know, Mac," Dana came alongside him.

"Give me a second with him. Here, hold this." Nate handed the badger to Mac, who reluctantly grabbed the tail. The badger looked bigger than it had at first. Mac held it away from himself as blood drained from its mouth and the open wound, spattering his shoes. He lowered the animal closer to the ground.

Dana grimaced. "That poor thing. It was only doing what badgers do. There should be some way to deal with them other than shooting them."

"The badger is the least of our worries." Mac eyed the two men. Nate was no doubt explaining what had transpired and why Mac had acted as he had. Therman threw back his head and laughed, and then the two of them headed back toward the house. He was probably in his late fifties, his face tanned and weathered. He had the build of a man who spent his days working the land. He held out a hand several strides before reaching Mac, holding the rifle with his left hand over his shoulder.

"That's the first time I've had a gun pointed at me since I was a young private in Vietnam," Therman said.

"I'm so sorry. I thought you'd shot Nate." Mac smiled as the two shook hands.

"No need to apologize; Nate already explained the matter. You had your partner's back, and I can appreciate that." He looked over to Dana. "And this must be Detective Bennett."

Dana nodded. "Pleased to meet you, sir."

"Come on inside and have a cup of coffee. Just brewed a fresh pot." Therman walked around toward the front of the house.

"You go on ahead, Therman. We'll be right with you." Turning to Mac, Nate said, "I'll take that critter from you. Unless you're growing attached to it."

Mac handed over the dead animal without hesitation. "I can't believe I'm standing in the middle of the desert, wearing a suit, and holding a shotgun and a dead badger. You never know where this job will take you."

"Pretty glamorous, huh? Welcome to my world." Nate strode to the truck and threw the carcass into the pickup bed. He set the shotgun back in the mount while Mac and Dana grabbed their briefcases and followed Nate inside.

Therman had four cups of hot coffee and a plate of cookies sitting on a rustic wooden table.

"I love Emma's oatmeal cookies." Nate made a beeline for the table. "You're in for a treat." He took one and passed the plate to Dana.

"Yum. They smell wonderful and they're still a little warm."

"Emma just baked them. She had to go into town." Therman chuckled. "Which is just as well. Glad she wasn't here for all the excitement."

Mac wondered if Nate wasn't being a little too friendly with one of their suspects, but he took a cookie anyway. The adrenaline rush had left him starving. "Wow, these are good."

Therman handed them each a napkin and sat down between Mac and Nate. Dana sat opposite him and took out a pad and paper, indicating that Mac should conduct the interview.

"So, what can I do for you?" the older man asked. "I assume you detectives didn't come up for the badger hunting."

"You know why we're here, Therman," Nate replied. "Detectives McAllister and Bennett are heading up Sara Watson's murder investigation in Portland. Your letters to the victim's uncle have caused a stir."

"Am I a suspect then?" Therman leveled his gaze on Mac as he took a drink of coffee.

"Yes, you are, Mr. Post." Mac met his dark gaze. The guy was a straight shooter. Good.

Therman's brown face lit in a wry smile, as if he enjoyed the attention. He helped himself to a cookie. "As long as we understand one another. Why don't you ask your questions?"

"I'm going to be direct with you," Mac said. "We understand you wrote several letters to Senator Wilde regarding your position on the casino placement."

"That I freely admit." Therman nodded. "I also admit that I dislike your senator more than that badger I shot this morning."

"Are you saying you want to harm Senator Wilde?" Mac set down his coffee.

"No." He chuckled and leaned back in the chair. "My days of harming men are over—they were a long time ago. I just don't like the man. Politicians like him traded lands, which is what your people like to call the treaties of old. Politicians like him want to bend the rules and restrict what we can do on our tribal lands. As you know, the Confederated Tribes is governed by our elected council and operates according to the will of our people. Our tribal business interests your elected officials only when it conflicts with their personal plans. Senator Wilde knows a casino so close to Portland would take money from your state coffers by competing with your lottery and video poker slots. If I'm not mistaken, a portion of your paycheck is probably paid out of gambling revenue, is it not?"

"You're correct, but I don't know how much," Mac said, deflecting the dig. "Now, tell me about the intent of your letters."

Therman leaned forward again, arms resting on the table. "My intent was to get the senator's attention. And I wrote those letters *before* the senator's niece disappeared—none after I read about his niece in the paper. I have a mission, based on my people's interest, but I'm no animal."

Mac glanced at Dana, remembering that the FBI agents had said Therman slammed the door in their faces when they asked him about the other letters. He didn't want to make Therman angry, but he did need some answers.

Turning to Therman, he said, "You say you didn't write any letters to the senator after you read about Sara Watson?"

"That's right."

"And you know that Sara is now dead and that we recovered her body just off the reservation by the White River?"

"Yes, Detective, I know about that also. Like I said, I read the papers. I'm sorry for the senator's loss, but with all due respect, what does her death have to do with me? Just because I wrote some political letters to an elected official, I'm now public enemy number one?"

"That's not the only reason." Mac hesitated.

"Because I'm an Indian, then?" Therman's dark eyes bore into Mac's.

"No. The letters sent to Senator Wilde after his niece was missing were postmarked from Warm Springs. The same as the letters you admitted to writing. There's also the matter of finding her body so close to tribal land."

"And that she was buried with what might be one of our artifacts," Therman added.

Artifacts? He raised an eyebrow and noted Dana's concern. Had Nate told him about those? Mac knew he was planning to talk to the elders, but Post was a potential suspect.

Nate cleared his throat. "I showed him the photos and asked if he recognized the rock and the beaded bag."

"And did you?" Mac directed his question to Therman.

He shrugged. "They look familiar. We have a number of pieces like them at the Warm Springs museum. Items like that are easy to duplicate, though. A number of women continue to do beadwork and weaving in the old ways." He gestured toward the bookshelves and cabinets. "My wife, for one." There were several baskets and beaded bags placed in prominent places throughout the room.

"So you would have had access to similar stones and beaded bags."

"I suppose that's true, but I assure you, I didn't have anything to do with writing that second set of letters. You may or may not choose to believe me, but I had nothing to do with that woman's death."

"Do you have any idea who might have sent the second set of letters?" Nate asked.

While Mac preferred to have only one investigator asking questions at a time, he deferred to Nate.

"I do not. You're well aware of my political involvement. I know the inner workings of the state legislature better than anyone in the tribe. I not only wrote to the senator, but I encouraged others to do so." He sighed. "I didn't know Senator Wilde was related to Sara Watson until the story connecting both of them came out in the news. If I didn't know about the connection, I doubt anyone around here did. Did you know, Nathan?"

"No. But obviously someone did," Nate replied.

"Mr. Post, can you think of anyone other than yourself who is as passionate about the casino issue as you are?" Mac asked.

Therman pursed his lips and after a moment said, "You know, my people are not the only ones who would profit from the placement of the casino in the gorge. We've been working with developers for the six-hundred-acre parcel that the gaming center, conference area, and hotel is proposed to sit on. We've also been in contact with gaming experts from St. Louis, Reno, and Las Vegas, recruiting some of the best talent to help run the gambling aspect of the venture. There are a lot of folks who stand to make some serious money if this project were to go through."

"He's right there, Mac." Nate seemed relieved. "The property owner alone stands to lose millions of dollars if the casino isn't built."

"I see your point," Mac said. "Could you supply us with a copy of those names?"

"I could, but it will take awhile to put it together. We're talking close to a hundred names of people who have been involved in the consulting alone. I'll have to make a few calls. When do you want it?"

"Yesterday." Nate finished off his coffee and grabbed another cookie. "I'll come back by this afternoon if you can put it together by then."

"I'll do my best. How about I bring it to you? I'll have to go into town anyway."

"We really appreciate this," Mac told him. The suggestion broadened their investigation, and Mac wondered if the feds had done any interviews along that line.

"Am I still a suspect?" Therman asked.

"You're more of a person of interest. Our job at the moment is to eliminate as many people as possible. If you don't mind, I'd like to get a taped statement of your whereabouts for the past few weeks and fully document your letters to Senator Wilde."

"I have no problem with that." Therman brought out a daily planner that accounted for nearly every hour of every day from before Sara went missing to the present. He apparently had an alibi for the time Sara disappeared, but the journal could have been doctored. It was almost too organized. Most people couldn't tell you what they did more than a day or two back. He had also kept copies of the letters he wrote to Senator Wilde, all handwritten and signed with his unique logo.

The second grouping of letters that had been sent to Senator Wilde had been computer generated. "Do you have a computer, Mr. Post?"

"No, but I have access to one. I use the one at the library to do my research."

Mac nodded. After taking Therman's detailed statement, he asked for a swab of Therman's gum line to secure a DNA sample, and Post readily agreed.

Mac secured the cotton swab inside a paper envelope, preparing the evidence for an eventual trip to the crime lab. Right now there was no evidence with which to compare the control samples.

"I think we're done here." Mac turned to Dana. "Unless you have something."

"No. I think you and Nate have covered everything."

"SO, WHAT'S YOUR READ?" Nate asked Mac on their way back to town.

"Too soon to tell. I try not to form an opinion this early in the game. He seems all right, but I've been fooled before."

"I'd be pretty disappointed if Therman was in on Sara's death. To be honest, I just don't see him pulling a stunt like this. Therman is proud and has definite opinions, but he's not desperate."

"How far out was the badger Therman shot this morning?"

"About a hundred yards, why?"

"Just curious. That's pretty good shooting, I'd say."

"Implying what?"

"Nothing." Mac tucked the information away. "Just an observation."

"I liked him." Dana leaned forward. "He's a no-nonsense guy who tells it like it is. Besides, Mr. Post wrote his letters by hand. Why would he change to the computer? I still think we're looking at two different people."

"Could be," Mac said, "but he might have decided to switch tactics to throw us off the track."

"Well, you're right about one thing, Mac," Dana said. "It's too early to make any kind of judgment call."

"I did come away with something, though," Mac said. "Therman might not be our killer, but I have a feeling he wasn't telling us all he knows."

"You think he's protecting someone?" Nate asked.

"Could be. All I know is that I'm not ready to let him off the hook."

Nate nodded. "You asked me earlier about Sara's ties to the tribe."

"Right. What did you find out?"

"Margaret Case grew up in these parts years ago," Nate said. "Her daughter, Denise Galbraith, lives in Portland. I have an address for you. No family left on the reservation. The daughter has a couple of grown kids. She was pretty upset about Sara and says she's willing to talk to you."

"That's great," Dana said. "It'll be interesting to see if she knows anything about the beaded bag and the carved rock."

"I'm sure she does. One of the things she asked me was if I thought Sara's family would be willing to give her the artifacts her grandmother had given to Sara. She didn't want to bother the family so soon, but since I'd called . . ."

"Artifacts? Does she think they're valuable?"

"Sentimental value, she said."

"Thanks, Nate," Mac said. "We'll contact her as soon as we get back to town."

TWENTY-THREE

Did you know Senator Wilde was going to the funeral tomorrow?" Dana asked on their drive home.

"I think Kevin said something about it. Dignitaries usually attend services like this. It's their way of showing support for the troops." Mac frowned. "By the way, I forgot to tell you—I'll be standing in on the deathwatch, which means I have to leave tonight."

"I talked to Kevin last night, and I'm standing in too."

"Good. So we can still ride down together. I'll pick you up at, say, seven. Maybe we can catch a bite on the way."

"Sounds like a plan," Dana sighed, "though I have to admit, I'm not too excited about driving five hours to Medford after this trip to Warm Springs. But at least we'll be able to take turns driving."

Before heading across the river to Vancouver, they looked up the name and address Nate had given them for Margaret Case's daughter, Denise Galbraith. The place was close to the freeway, so they decided to pay a visit.

The house, situated in Gresham, was older, small, but nicely landscaped. The woman who answered had mocha skin and wore glasses. She wore her long, salt-and-pepper hair pulled back in a braid that reached the middle of her back.

They introduced themselves and were immediately ushered in. "I've been expecting you. Can I offer you anything to drink?"

"Water would be great." They hadn't stopped since leaving Warm Springs, and Mac felt nearly as parched as the desert itself. He blamed it on the lingering smoke from the forest fire.

"That sounds good to me too," Dana said.

A corner of the living room had been converted to a craft area of sorts.

"I do beadwork," Denise told them when she caught them looking. "My mother taught me."

"On leather?" Dana asked.

"Sometimes. Mostly, though, I make and sell jewelry—necklaces, earrings. I do a lot with silver and turquoise. But I'm sure you're not interested in all of that. You wanted to talk to me about Sara?"

"Yes, we do. Margaret Case was her grandmother, so I'm assuming you were Sara's aunt."

"That's right."

"Were you close?" Mac asked.

"I'm not sure how to answer that, Detective. After my sister and her husband died and Sara went to live with the Wildes, she rarely visited. Not like before."

"Why would that be?"

"Perhaps we reminded her too much of her mother. The Wildes are very rich, and we . . ." She smiled. "We are not. I don't think Sara ever really thought about it. She lost herself in the white world with too many things to do and too little time. The last time I saw her, outside of her wedding, was at my mother's funeral."

"Her cousin, Claire, said that she received an inheritance."

"Yes. My mother listed a number of things that she wanted left to

Sara. Some are very old and have been in the family for generations."

"So they really are artifacts?" Mac asked.

"A few are. My mother was an artist much as I am. We've tried to preserve the old ways when we can."

Mac signaled Dana to bring out the photos. "I'd like you to take a look at these pictures—see if you recognize the items."

She looked over the photos and nodded. "I believe these were in the collection Sara received. I would have to see them up close to be sure. And the bag is torn—it wasn't when we gave it to her. It's one of the oldest pieces and can't be replaced. How did this happen? And how did you come to have them?"

"I'm not at liberty to say." Mac handed the photos back to Dana. "Officer Webb told us that you'd asked about Sara's collection."

"Yes. I don't mean to sound callous, but they probably wouldn't mean a lot to Scott or the Wildes. They were my mother's and my sister's. I realize they now belong to Scott, but I am hoping he'll be willing to give them to me."

"I'm afraid we don't have any say in that."

"I understand." Her warm gaze swept over him and went to her hands.

"Do you have family, Mrs. Galbraith?" Mac felt uncomfortable with the woman's request and wanted to move on.

"Yes. A grown son, Aaron. And a daughter who lives in Port Orchard. My husband died last year. Heart attack."

"I'm sorry. Does your son live here with you?"

"He did this past winter. Aaron moved out a few months ago when he was laid off."

"Where does he live now?"

"On the reservation. He's staying with a friend. Got a temporary job at the casino at Warm Springs. He has a teaching certificate, so he's hoping to get on at one of the schools this fall."

"How does he feel about the casino being built in the gorge?"

She hesitated. "He believes it will help the schools and would like to see it pass. We both would. Why do you ask?"

"Just curious. My partner and I would like to talk with him, if he wouldn't mind."

"I'm sure he'd be happy to. Though he saw Sara less than I did, so I don't know what he could tell you."

"We need to talk to everyone who might have had a connection to Sara."

Denise pushed herself out of the chair and went to the kitchen. From a basket near the phone, she took out a pen and pad, on which she wrote her son's name and phone number. "I can tell him you will call."

"That would be fine." Mac gave her a card. "We appreciate your being willing to talk with us. You've been a big help."

AFTER DROPPING DANA OFF at her apartment, Mac went straight home to check on Lucy and talk to Carl. He then showered and packed before changing into his uniform. He'd have preferred driving in more comfortable clothes and changing once they reached Medford, but they were going straight to the deathwatch, and there might not be a place to change. Besides, he wanted to make sure he had everything he'd need.

The OSP dress uniform had remained the same since the 1930s, even though they had gone to a more functional uniform for day-to-day use. For occasions like the funeral, the members of the department would wear the uniform that the early troopers wore on duty every day. The current day ankle-length slacks and functional lace-up boots had taken the place of slacks that came just below the knee to meet the leather knee-high boots that were polished to a high gloss.

The uniform fit Mac a little more tightly than he remembered, giving evidence to the ten pounds that had slipped up on him over the past year or so. Their traditional dress uniform was built more for looks than comfort. Once he put on the heavy wool coat, the gun belt would be supported by the leather Sam Brown, which was clipped to the heavy-duty belt in the front and worn over the shoulder to be connected to the back of the belt.

He thought briefly about what it must have been like to work an entire career wearing this stiff uniform and to be in foot chases wearing these boots. Back in the old days, all three divisions of their department wore the uniform, even the investigators. That was back in the day when the only undercover work or covert operations being conducted were by the military or the federal government. Local and state cops were content to be a visible presence in their community, the uniform a symbol of their pride in their respective community.

So many things had changed, but the common elements had remained. The troopers in their department still took pride in their uniforms and in the role they played in their communities.

After checking a few e-mails, Mac headed over to pick up Dana.

As Mac walked up to her apartment, his stiff leather boots creaked. "Hey, partner," he said when she opened the door. "How does it feel to be back in uniform?"

"Don't ask." Dana also had on her dress uniform, the same style Mac wore. On her, the dress blues looked professional and attractive.

"Ready to go?"

"Almost. I can't get this stupid strap on."

He took the Sam Brown strap from her. "It's almost impossible to do this without help. I decided not to wear my jacket and gun belt until we got down there."

"I wasn't going to, either, but I didn't want to take a half hour to dress in front of everyone when we got there. I can hook up the front if you can get the one in the back."

Mac stood behind Dana, breathing in the subtle scent of her

perfume and waiting for her to pass the strap over her left shoulder. He liked the scent and thought about telling her so, but didn't. She might not take it the right way, and he definitely didn't want her to get the wrong idea.

Mac lifted up on her gun belt slightly to secure the strap to her belt keeper, then let go and stepped back. "How's that feel? Too heavy on your shoulder?"

Dana flexed her arm and then lifted it up to her shoulders. "It's definitely not comfortable, but it will do. Thanks."

As planned, after grabbing a light supper, they took turns driving and resting for the long trip. Around 1:00 a.m., they reached Central Point just outside of Medford, where they stopped at the OSP office to get directions to the high school where Trooper Revman's body was being held. The two of them were scheduled to stand watch between two and two-thirty Wednesday morning. After getting instructions from the Honor Guard supervisor, they joined the other participants in the hallway just outside the gymnasium.

Shortly after two o'clock, the lieutenant supervising the event signaled for Mac. He slipped on his white cotton gloves and stood in the doorway to the auditorium. Then, after getting the nudge from the lieutenant, he began to march toward the stage area, where Trooper Revman's flag-draped coffin sat in the center, flanked by two uniformed troopers that he didn't know. He walked down the left side of the aisle, while a second trooper from another field office walked down the right side. It was their job to relieve the two troopers by the coffin and then stand their fifteen-minute watch. This had gone on for the past twelve hours and would continue throughout the ceremony the next day. Troopers from all over the state were participating in the traditional deathwatch.

Once he reached Daniel's coffin, he came to attention in front of the trooper he was replacing, their felt campaign hats nearly touching. Mac slowly raised his right hand to his hat and lowered it in the traditional salute. The second trooper was dismissed to leave the room, then Mac performed an about-face and stood at attention.

Initially, Mac had thought that fifteen minutes was a relatively short time and had hoped for a longer watch. But by the time five minutes had passed, he was more than satisfied with the briefer time. Standing at attention next to Daniel's coffin felt like an eternity. He went through a lifetime of memories and was glad to see Dana enter the room to relieve his post.

Fifteen minutes later, Dana met him in the waiting area, and they drove to their hotel and checked in.

"This is me." Mac pointed toward his room.

"I'm a couple of doors down." Dana motioned with her bag. "You want to grab breakfast or sleep in?"

"I think I'll sleep in, if I can," Mac slid the key card inside the door. "Just give me a call when you wake up."

"Mac." Dana lowered her bag to the floor, holding out her arms for a hug. "I know you would never initiate this, which I appreciate, but I think we could both use a hug right now." As usual, she was right on. They hugged, like two old friends should at a time like this. Dana rubbed Mac's arms as she stepped away. "Get some rest." She turned and picked up her bag.

"You too." Mac smiled and watched her enter her room. Then he went into his own.

The day had been long and tedious. It seemed days ago that they had talked with Therman Post, but it had only been about sixteen hours. Mac was glad he'd made the trip south for the watch and for the funeral tomorrow and even more pleased that Dana had come down with him. She didn't have the same connection with Daniel and had come primarily to support him, and he appreciated that. The department didn't pay overtime for these types of events, and the hotel costs would be coming out of their own pockets. So Mac didn't take the gesture lightly. Dana was a good friend.

TWENTY-FOUR

Mac awoke to the phone ringing and rolled over to grab the phone from the nightstand. He groped around and eventually realized that he wasn't at home, and the ringing was coming from the desk on the other side of the room. He yawned and glanced over at the clock. It was after nine.

Mac picked up the receiver and peered out the curtains at the bright sunlight. The thick drapery had kept the room dark as a crypt. "Hi."

"You hungry?" Dana asked.

"Yeah, I could eat. Are you already dressed?"

"Yeah. I've been up for an hour. I woke you up, right?"

"Not exactly. I had to get up to answer the phone." Mac let go of the drapes, noticing he was holding them a little too far apart for his current attire.

"I'm sorry, Mac. You can go back to bed if you want."

"No, that's OK. Give me a few minutes, and I'll get dressed. There's a restaurant here in the hotel. We can grab something there."

"That's what I was thinking."

Mac patted his stomach, making a mental note not to eat too big a breakfast. The uniform was a little too tight already. He remembered that when he'd first worn the dress uniform, he actually had to wear his bulletproof vest under his jacket to make it fit better. He really needed to lose some serious weight. He got dressed and met Dana down in the lobby. She was wearing sweats and wore her hair up in a ponytail.

After ordering, Dana picked up her coffee and sipped it. "We may have a discrepancy in Scott Watson's timelines between the two interviews."

"What?" Mac had been staring out the window. "You brought the files with you?"

She shrugged. "I thought I might have some time to go through them. I couldn't get to sleep right away last night, so . . ."

Mac felt a little guilty. He hadn't brought anything and hadn't even thought about the case. "What inconsistencies?"

"Nothing major, but something we need to address. Scott told the FBI investigators he was interrupted from his meeting by his secretary. You know, when she gave him the message that Sara had called about her car. But he told us that he didn't get the message until he was out of the meeting after the day-care provider called him. It could be something or nothing at all."

"You're right. We need to check it out."

"I'm anxious to get that list of possible suspects from Nate. That's an angle we need to pursue. There's a lot of money at stake, and that equals motive."

"Hmm." Mac sipped on his coffee. Strong, hot, and black. He needed the caffeine this morning, for sure.

"I think we should make another run out to Warm Springs." She leaned back as the waitress brought their meals. "I'd like to find out more about Margaret's grandson. There might be some jealousy on his part. Sara's rich, and he's without a job. Maybe he went to her house to confront her about the artifacts their grandmother gave her. Or maybe she caught him stealing them."

"Possible, but he wouldn't need to break into her car to get the address."

"Maybe he wanted it to look like a random act. Shoving that beaded bag into her mouth seems like an act of revenge."

Mac spread some salsa on his omelet. "Maybe, but if it was an artifact and worth a lot of money, why do that? I'd like Nate to handle the interview with Aaron and some of the others. Remember, we have no police authority there."

She didn't seem happy about the idea. "I suppose you're right. He can tell us if the guy needs to be investigated more thoroughly."

"We can trust Nate, Dana. I'm sure of that. He's in a better position. The FBI couldn't even secure an interview with Therman Post, and Nate was able to get an interview in less than a day." Mac thought about the little girl in the park and the chilly reception he'd gotten from the older woman. They might get the same reception from others. "I think we can trust Nate to do right by us."

"You have a point. It's just that I—I mean, I know we need to be here for the funeral, but the case is already cold, and Sara's killer is still out there. We were fortunate to find these leads. I wonder if the feds even realized Sara had a history with the Warm Springs tribe."

"I know what you mean, but we need to get through this funeral today, and tomorrow we'll be in Salem all day. Nate can save us some time by covering for us on Aaron Galbraith and any of the others on Therman's list." He tackled his ham-and-cheese omelet.

AFTER BREAKFAST, they returned to their rooms and prepared for the actual funeral. They met in the lobby and then drove over to the high school, where troopers were still participating in the deathwatch. As the time for the ceremony approached, Mac and Dana stood in formation with several hundred members of their department. They made an impressive sight. Officers from all over the country, and even some Royal Canadian Mounted Police in their brilliant red uniforms, stood in formation in another part of the parking lot. Members of the Central Point office stood alone in front. This was the office where Daniel had worked, and by tradition they would be the first seated in the auditorium.

By the time Mac and Dana entered to be seated, there were more than two thousand officers in the room. While watching the officers funnel through the door, Mac spotted Nathan Webb. Seeing all of the officers gave Mac a sense of pride. He'd done well in choosing law enforcement as a career. No matter what part of the country you came from, you were a member of a unique brotherhood.

"That's Senator Wilde down there." Dana pointed down into the crowd.

"Where?" Mac squinted at the line of dignitaries toward the front.

"Down there, three seats to the left of the governor."

"I see him." He wore a gray suit and was seated in the front row in an area reserved for family members and VIPs.

The funeral service began as the department chaplain offered an opening prayer while everyone stood at their seats. After the prayer, Daniel's wife was led into the service by their department head. Tears smeared Mac's vision. This was the hardest part.

When Jennifer had been seated, the chaplain offered one more prayer. The bagpipers played "Amazing Grace" as they entered the auditorium, followed by the Honor Guard, who would be carrying the coffin to the awaiting motorcade after the service. The flag-draped coffin was still in the front of the room, where it would remain throughout the rest of the ceremony. Flag bearers entered the room, and behind them came the professional drill team, the finest in the state. Many of them were prior military. The troopers on the drill team practiced regularly for these events, which, thankfully, were infrequent.

At the end of the service, the Honor Guard carried the coffin from the room and placed it in the back of a hearse for the motorcade trip to the gravesite. Following tradition, before anyone left the service, Trooper Revman's radio number was broadcast over a loudspeaker.

A dispatcher called out his number. "Thirty-one thirty-four." Except for an occasional sob, everyone maintained silence.

"Thirty-one thirty-four," the dispatcher called out again.

"Thirty-one thirty-four." The final call was given. "Gone but not forgotten."

Most attendees in the room, who had been to a police funeral, knew this statement marked the end of the service. Mac and Dana stood and began the slow trip to the car, wading through the crowd of mourners.

Hundreds of police cars, fire trucks, and ambulances led the solemn motorcade to the gravesite. The local streets were closed to allow the vehicles to travel in procession, each with a wailing siren and emergency lights activated. Once the motorcade arrived at the gravesite, the mourners gathered on the grass to pay their last respects. A lone bugler played taps in the distance, followed by a volley of shots from the Honor Guard.

When Daniel's body was lowered into the ground, most of the troopers, even those who rarely cried, fought tears. Mac pulled out a handkerchief and blew his nose.

Then it was over. Mac tipped his head back, relieved to have some closure.

On the way to his car, Mac spotted Senator Wilde and pointed him out to Dana.

"Want to say hello?" Dana asked.

"Sure, why not? But I don't want to get into an interview with him. Let's just say hi and firm up our plans for tomorrow. I'm not in the investigative mood right now."

"You and me both."

"Senator Wilde?" Mac said as they approached the man.

"Yes." His questioning gaze darted from Mac to Dana.

"Senator Wilde, I'm Detective Mac McAllister and this is Detective Dana Bennett. We are the investigators on Sara's case."

"Yes, I recognize you. You were at Sara's house the day she disappeared." He shook hands with each of them.

"Excuse me," a smaller man interrupted. "I believe you have an appointment *tomorrow* at nine, yes?"

"And you are?" Mac asked, irritated by the man's brusqueness.

"Grant Stokely. The senator doesn't have time to talk with you now, so if you'll excuse us . . ."

"We saw the senator and thought we would introduce ourselves." Mac held his ground.

"As I told your sergeant, no one speaks to the senator without going through me first. The senator is a busy man. We'll see you tomorrow at nine." Stokely lead the senator toward the line of sleek black limousines.

The senator looked as though he wanted to say something, but a reporter chose that moment to shove a microphone in his face, so he complied. He shook hands with a number of people and told the reporter how sorry he was to have lost Trooper Revman and how the Oregon State Police were doing a great job and how he wanted to alter the budget so they could hire new troopers.

"That Stokely's a piece of work." Dana set her hands on her hips.

"Yeah." Mac watched in disbelief as Stokely arranged for the photographer to take pictures of the senator and Daniel's widow. She was still holding the burial flag in her arms, folded in a neat triangle by the Honor Guard.

He hadn't been in the mood to investigate the murder moments ago, but he was now. He couldn't wait for their interview with the famous senator. Mac put a hand to Dana's back. "Come on, let's get home."

TWENTY-FIVE

Mac slept much better Wednesday night in his own bed and awoke by six Thursday morning, eager to get back into the investigation. Daniel's death and the funeral had been a huge distraction. That was over now, and though his grieving would go on for some time, he needed to get back in the game and back to normal.

Stokely's unprofessional rebuke yesterday still irked him, but it only served to sharpen his resolve. He was committed to finding Sara's killer, now more than ever. Unfortunately, their primary leads involved the letters mailed to Senator Wilde. The letters indicated that they were from the kidnapper, who had supposedly taken Sara and threatened to harm her if Wilde didn't swing the decision for the placement of a tribal casino in the Columbia River gorge. Even the beaded bag and rock from Sara's collection pointed to a revenge killing.

He was beginning to wonder about the authenticity of the second set of letters, though. They'd been written after Sara's death. Why would the killer write those letters when he'd already killed her? Maybe the killer hadn't written them at all. Suppose someone like Therman or another tribal member had used Sara's disappearance to pressure the senator as a kick-'em-while-they're-down tactic?

He and Dana might be getting into the investigation late, but it was far too early to be discouraged. The investigation could still take any number of turns. Maybe the murder had been meant as a message from one of the Native American proponents of the casino, or, as Therman Post had suggested, they could be looking at someone with a great deal of money to lose if the deal fell through.

They would also be looking at family and friends. So far the husband's story checked out, but that didn't mean he wasn't dirty. Mac frowned, remembering the discrepancy in the story he'd told the FBI and the one he'd told him and Dana. Then there was the cousin, who'd actually moved in with Sara's husband. Jealousy? Wouldn't be the first time. This Native American cousin they just discovered looked pretty interesting too.

One thing was for certain: they were not without possible suspects. These thoughts and more accompanied Mac while he showered, shaved, and got dressed for work.

While Mac and Dana had been in Medford, Sergeant Bledsoe had scheduled a polygraph appointment with one of their own detectives to review the FBI polygraph reports so they could either eliminate people as suspects or take a closer look.

Scott Watson was still cooperating for the time being, so they were taking full advantage. Hopefully, they would find Senator Wilde just as cooperative. Mac was less than impressed with yesterday's encounter and concerned the senator and his aide might prove difficult. He intended to give Stokely a close look as well.

MAC PICKED DANA UP at her apartment at seven thirty. They stopped for coffee, and Dana got on the phone to let their sergeant know they were on the way to Salem. She switched to speakerphone so Mac could hear the conversation.

"Listen, kids," Kevin said, "as you know, this is a high-profile case, and like it or not, with the senator involved, everything we do is going to be scrutinized to death. The brass is monitoring our investigation all the way."

Dana sighed. "Which means what exactly?"

"Solving the murder is high priority, but the agency budget is important as well, so no big surprises. Wilde not only has a say in the casino, but he also has a lot to do with our funding. Like it or not, that's the nature of the beast."

Dana rolled her eyes at Mac. "So what else is new?"

"Be diplomatic, Mac," Kevin warned. "I know that's not always easy, but don't be ruffling any feathers with the state's political powerhouse."

"Me? What about Dana?" Mac grinned. He doubted Dana had an undiplomatic bone in her body.

Kevin chuckled. "I think you know the answer to that one."

"Oh, I don't know, Boss. I came pretty close to losing it yesterday." Dana told him about the encounter they'd had with Stokely and Senator Wilde after the funeral.

"That doesn't surprise me. I guess that's why I felt like I had to stress the point with you. I don't care what kind of guff they give you, keep your cool. You have a big audience."

"We'll be on our best behavior, Sarge," Dana said.

On the way, Mac filled Dana in on his theory about the second set of letters not being from the killer.

"I think you may be right, Mac. Why kill her and then write threatening letters?"

"Unless . . ." Mac hesitated. "Unless the killer was trying to get us off track."

Dana shrugged. "That too."

They talked more about Mac's concerns as they traveled down to the Capitol Mall complex in Salem, where their own general head-quarters was located, along with other agency heads. The Capitol Mall was also the location of the state capitol building, where state legislators and senators worked.

They parked in the official lot and made their way to the entrance. Mac and Dana walked along the marble entryway to Senator Wilde's private chambers where they announced them-selves to the receptionist. A good ten minutes later, Grant Stokely came out to greet them.

"Good morning." Mac offered his hand, determined to start off on the right foot. "We're here to meet with Senator Wilde."

Stokely ignored Mac's proffered hand and nodded toward a couch near the door. "Have a seat."

Keep your cool, Dana's warning glance told him.

He would, but the guy certainly wasn't scoring any points. Once they were seated, Stokely, with his air of self-importance, remained standing.

"Before we begin," he said, "I have some instructions for you. First, I want to review all the questions you have for the senator. Second, if I determine they are acceptable, I will forward a written copy of the questions to the senator, and you will await his responses. If we decide it's necessary, he may respond in person. Finally, there are to be no press releases from your agency. Any press releases will come from my office." With a smug and condescending smile, he added, "Are we clear on the conditions?"

Mac glanced over at Dana and cleared his throat. He wished Kevin were here to respond and tried to think of what Kevin might say. Mac knew what he wanted to say, but his superiors might not appreciate his tact. He got to his feet, his own arms folded and his legs slightly separated. He had a height advantage and could intim-idate with the best of them. "Condition number one, not a chance.

Condition number two, no way. We will, however, agree not to talk with the press—for now."

Dana bit her lip, trying not to smile. This was too good.

"I don't think you understand who you're dealing with, Detective. Let me remind you of your authority here." Stokely's jaw twitched, his hands balled into fists.

"No, Mr. Stokely." Mac settled his hands on his hips. "Allow me to do that for you. I'm a sworn peace officer in the state of Oregon, which means I can write search warrants and compel testimony through a subpoena to a grand jury if the prosecutor deems it appropriate. I'm here to investigate Sara Watson's death. At the moment, this interview is purely voluntary on Senator Wilde's part. If he doesn't want to talk to us, that's his call; but I'm putting his refusal to cooperate in my report, which, as you know, is a public record. That means the public and the press can get a copy of it."

Stokely sputtered about having them removed from the premises.

"I understand your desire to protect the senator," Mac went on, "but you are obstructing a felony investigation by insisting on these conditions. I'm sure with your knowledge of the lawmaking process, you are fully aware of that. Perhaps you've forgotten. You see, Mr. Stokely, obstructing our investigation could land you in jail and have *you* barred from the building."

By now the man had turned an unflattering shade of red. "Wait here." He spun around on his heels and went back into the senator's office.

Mac blew out a long breath. "That went well."

Dana smiled. "Good job."

"Hope I didn't mess things up too badly."

"You were terrific. I don't think Stokely appreciates your talents, though. If looks could kill, we'd both be lying on a slab in the morgue."

"Yeah." Mac relaxed his pose and rubbed the back of his neck.

"You are in the right, Mac." Dana stood and touched his arm. "That guy is a pompous—"

The door to the senator's chambers opened, and Stokely, looking slightly more composed, gestured for them to enter. The aide led them through the reception area and into a double set of doors. Senator Wilde himself must have granted them an audience. He sat in a leather chair in front of a large oak desk, a phone pressed against his ear. Mac hoped he wasn't talking to the brass. Tangling with Stokely like he had could get him a reprimand—even if he was right.

Senator Wilde nodded toward two chairs, a sofa, and a coffee table in the corner while he continued his phone conversation. "Yes, I understand. I'll see you at the budget meeting tomorrow." He smiled. "You too."

Hanging up the phone, he turned to Mac and Dana. "I hope you haven't been waiting long. I didn't know you were here until Grant announced you. Please, may I offer you something to drink?" Senator Wilde came over to the small furniture grouping and shook their hands. "Detectives McAllister and Bennett, right?"

"Right. Nothing for me, thanks." Mac answered.

"I'm fine." Dana told him.

"All right, then." The senator lowered himself onto the sofa. "That will be all, Grant." He nodded toward the aide. "I'll let you know when we're through here."

Stokely glared at Mac and hesitated at the door, looking as though he wanted to say something. Then he stepped out and closed the door behind him.

"Thanks for meeting with us, Senator Wilde," Mac said.

"Quite all right." Wilde looked at the burgundy and beige oriental carpet. "I'm afraid I owe you an apology for Grant's behavior this morning and after the funeral yesterday. He was out of line in treating you the way he did, and I've talked to him. I have the utmost respect for our law enforcement officers and expect my staff to show the same respect. Grant is a good man and a great chief of staff, but he tends to be a bit overprotective where I'm concerned. He thinks he has to protect me from everything and everyone, which is not the case. I assure you I want to cooperate fully with the investigation and will do anything to assist you in catching Sara's killer." He pressed his lips together and blinked back tears. "I'm sorry. It's hard to think about what happened to her."

Mac was a little taken aback by the senator's show of cooperation and his overt grief. "I understand, Senator. We're sorry for your loss." Apparently Stokely had acted on his own regarding the interview conditions. He made a mental note to look into Stokely's relationship with Sara later on. "We'll start whenever you're ready." Right now, he needed to give this rare interview with the senator his full attention.

Wilde nodded. "Thanks, but I'm fine. Go ahead."

Mac began the interview by asking about some background information. "Could you tell us about your relationship with Sara?"

"That girl was like my own daughter. I still can't believe she's really gone. In these past few years, I haven't spent as much time with her as I would have liked. This job of mine has taken time away from my entire family." Wilde got up, walked to the window, and stared outside. "Since her marriage, I was lucky to see her at weddings and family get-togethers. People get too busy these days."

"How did you learn she was missing?"

"From my daughter. Claire called our home, and I happened to be there." Wilde turned back toward them. "As soon as I heard, I had Grant cancel my meetings and drove to Portland to offer any assistance I could. I was the one who requested the FBI and insisted they utilize the Oregon State Police to assist in the investigation."

"I thought that directive came from the governor's office."

Wilde offered a wan smile. "It did, but I instigated it."

"Detective Bennett and I have been involved from day one, but didn't assume the lead in the investigation until her body was discovered. We were disappointed to learn that the FBI had withheld some valuable information from us."

He sighed. "You're talking about the letters regarding the casino."

"Yes." Mac leaned back in the chair.

"I'm afraid that wasn't entirely the FBI's fault. I recently learned that there was substantial pressure from my office to keep the letters confidential so we wouldn't receive any negative press."

"Let me guess," Mac said. "Stokely?"

The senator nodded.

"Could you tell us about the letters and how they were received?" Mac asked.

"Of course. I assume you know about Mr. Post?"

Mac nodded. "We've been in contact with Therman. With the help of the Warm Springs P.D., we interviewed him on Tuesday. I can't go into too many details, but he was cooperative."

"Did he admit to writing the letters we received after Sara disappeared?"

"Like I said, I can't go into too many details, but I will tell you this much." Mac chose his next words with care. "Mr. Post admits to writing the letters prior to Sara's disappearance to convince you of his position on the casino placement, but he denies writing the letters indicating that Sara would be harmed if you didn't change your allegiance."

The senator frowned and sat back down. "I'm glad to hear that, actually. Therman is a political activist and a good one. I'd hate to think he'd resort to murder or even kidnapping. Do you have any idea who might have written those letters?"

"No, but we're looking into the matter." Mac glanced at Dana, who was taking notes. "Senator, you said earlier that Grant didn't want information about the letters leaked to the press, yet as I recall there were several articles in the *Oregonian* talking about the letters and speculating on tribal members kidnapping Sara in an effort to get you to change your mind. Do you have any idea how the press might have gotten that information?"

"None whatsoever, unless the person who wrote them contacted a reporter."

Mac made a mental note to find the articles and talk to the person who'd first written them. "Did you talk about the letters to anyone?" Mac knew he had, but wanted to hear it from the senator himself.

"Yes. Scott and I discussed them. I thought he should know."

"Could he have told anyone else?"

"I doubt it. I asked him not to." He cast a long look at Mac and paced back to the window. "I hope you two don't consider Scott a suspect."

"We're casting a pretty wide net right now," Mac replied.

"And the husband is always suspect?"

"We really haven't focused on any single individual yet. Do you have any thoughts on the matter, any suspicions you'd like to tell us about?"

"I have my theories, but nothing concrete." Wilde went back to the chair behind his desk this time. "I sincerely hope the tribal members were not involved. If they were, then I misjudged them. I didn't take any of those threats seriously." With an elbow on the desk, he rubbed his forehead. "Maybe I should have, but that wouldn't have changed my mind. I refuse to be swayed by terrorist actions."

"Sounds like you're feeling guilty."

"I've had my moments. I suppose one of the tribal members could have killed Sara, but I prefer to think that Sara's death was a result of a robbery gone bad. You know that her car was broken into the day she disappeared?"

"Yes, we're aware of that," Mac said. "We always consider the possibility of a random act—that Sara may have been killed by a stranger." Mac didn't mention the beaded pouch and stone found in her mouth. That and the fact that her body had been buried near the reservation made the crime seem like more of a personal vendetta.

"Good. I'm glad you aren't being too quick to narrow your investigation."

Mac realized he still hadn't gotten an answer to his question about the letters. "How did you actually receive the letters, Senator? Were they delivered to your office directly from the post office, routed from the mailroom . . . ?"

"I don't get the mail directly. My staff always goes through the mail first. Then they pass pertinent letters on to me."

"So you have people who open all your mail."

"Right. My administrative assistants work under Grant. I receive a lot of mail, and the staffers read and respond to the bulk of it. They bring some of the letters to my attention, but to be honest, I see maybe one out of a hundred. The staff either sends a form letter in response, or they write a letter and provide my stamped signature to the document. Because of their somewhat threatening nature, I did read the letters from Therman Post and the letters that came after Sara disappeared, but they were among hundreds of others that were either in support of or opposition to the casino placement."

"What was your understanding of these initial letters from Mr. Post?"

"I took them at face value. Mr. Post represents a group of people who stand to gain financially if the casino is placed in the gorge. For every letter I received in favor, I received ten that are opposed to the placement. It's evident that the majority of the population is opposed, but it's also evident that the matter will be decided in a legal battle and not a popularity vote."

"Would you elaborate?" Mac asked.

"Sure, glad to." Wilde sat forward in his chair and put his hands together. "You see, the battle is over treaties and legal rights afforded to the tribes. It was never a popularity issue. I don't plan to cast a vote in the senate. All I can do is offer my opinion and hope for the best. Though I'm against the casino going in, the Oregon Supreme Court will make the ruling, which will eventually go to the Ninth Circuit Federal Court of Appeals. The courts will make the final decision."

"So there's no vote on the issue, and you really don't have the power to change the outcome."

"That's what we explained to all the letter writers, but they continue to write. That's OK; it is their right, and I'm here to represent them. It goes with the office, and I can appreciate that."

"The FBI made it sound like Therman Post was public enemy number one, although I get the impression from you that he was more of an inconvenience than anything else. He was just another letter writer your staff had to respond to."

"That's essentially correct, but please note that 'inconvenience' is your word, not mine." He smiled. "I'd rather not go on record saying a concerned citizen of our state was an inconvenience."

"Noted and understood." Although Mac had been looking forward to the interview, the senator didn't have much information relevant to their case. His pager vibrated, and Mac glanced over at Dana. "Do you have any questions, Detective Bennett?" He pulled his pager from his belt after passing off the interview, looking to see who was calling.

"Just a couple," Dana replied. "Tell us how you learned about the second set of letters, the ones indicating that Sara was kidnapped and would be harmed if the casino plans didn't go through."

"From Grant. With the first one, a staffer opened the mail and brought it to him, and he immediately turned it over to the FBI. I never actually read the letter until later. Apparently they wanted as few prints as possible. I read it after the FBI provided a copy. They were hoping I'd be able to provide some clue as to who had sent it. I mentioned Therman, and they collected all the letters he'd sent. I'm afraid I wasn't much help. I had never seen any other letters with that kind of signature, and neither had my staff. We turned over all the letters from Warm Springs, many of which were legitimate letters of correspondence. All of those were returned to us for a proper response."

"You saw the first letter in the second group. What about the others?"

"After that first letter, all letters from Warm Springs were confiscated before anyone could open them, but Agents Miller and Lauden filled me in on the contents. They did a good job of keeping us informed when they could."

"Agents Miller and Lauden are still involved in the case, and they are both very concerned about finding the killer," Dana assured the senator.

The senator glanced at his watch. "I don't mean to rush you, but I have an appointment in about ten minutes."

Dana gave a slight nod. "Just one more thing. How well do you know Sara's family on her mother's side?"

"I know them, but not socially. That is, we don't spend time together. You don't think there's any connection . . . ?" Senator Wilde's gaze darted between Mac and Dana. "They cared about Sara as much as we did."

"I'm sure that's true." Dana pulled the photos of the beaded bag and rock from her briefcase and showed them to the senator.

"Do you recognize these items?"

"Yes—at least I think so. They look like the same ones in Sara's collection." His Adam's apple bobbed up and down as he spoke. "She was so proud of those."

"Do you have any idea what will happen to them now that Sara is dead?"

He shook his head and looked out the window. "That would be up to Scott, I suppose, unless Sara stipulated something in her will."

"That's all I have for now." Dana turned toward Mac. "Do you have any more questions?"

"We're set for now, but we'll be in touch." Mac took out a business card and handed it to Wilde. The senator glanced at it and thanked both of them for their service. Wilde also passed along his condolences to Mac and Dana over Trooper Revman's death.

Grant Stokely was standing a few steps outside the door. Mac said good-bye to him but received a mumbled response. The aide gave Mac a wide berth as he entered Wilde's office. Mac would have liked to take a few minutes to interview Stokely, but that would have to wait.

"What now?" Dana asked.

"To the crime lab. They paged me during the interview. Angela has some breaking news for us."

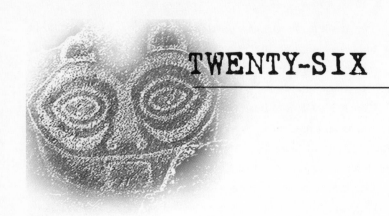

TWENTY-SIX

Mac and Dana made their way back up I-5, but true to form, a jackknifed semi and trailer near Tualatin brought them to a dead stop just north of Woodburn. Half an hour later and tired of sitting in gridlock, Mac initiated the emergency lights and drove on the shoulder. "I'll just head up to the wreck and see if the trooper needs a hand with traffic."

"Yeah, right," Dana mused. "You're abusing your authority, partner. Don't lie to me. I heard the trooper say he was just waiting for the wrecker."

Mac did feel guilty, but he was trying to solve a murder, after all, not make it home to catch a movie. Dana was right, but he wasn't about to admit it. One way or another he'd prove her wrong, even if it meant delaying them longer. He pulled his cruiser up behind the wreck, parking behind one of the two OSP motorcycles on the shoulder. Mac exited the car and approached the helmeted trooper, who was talking to the truck driver. "I didn't do anything wrong, Officer. This stupid guy driving a sports car was weaving in and out of traffic—cut right in front of me, then he brakes, you know. I had no place to go except the shoulder. You ought to be thanking me for avoiding a pileup, not questioning me like I'm some sort of criminal."

Although the trucker seemed to be providing a good argument, his actions and the slur of his words told Mac another story.

"Hey, Mac." The trooper gave Mac a nod, still keeping his attention focused on the truck driver.

"Hi, Roger. Do you need any assistance on the crash?"

"I could use some help with traffic control." The trooper then faced away from Mac, holding two fingers down at his pant leg to indicate he was considering a custody arrest and wanted Mac to stick around. "Sir, would you wait right here by your rig for a second? I want to speak with Detective McAllister."

"Detective? What for? I didn't do nothing wrong. Sheesh." The heavyset truck driver begrudgingly turned and walked a few yards away, lighting a small cigar butt that he had in his pocket.

"What's up?" Mac asked.

"I think our trucker friend here is under the influence of some type of stimulant. I'm going to run him through some field sobriety tests. I have a female witness who tells me that he'd been driving next to her since Aurora. Guess he was trying to flirt with her. She was pretty scared and tried speeding away from him, but he kept up. It sounds like this business of being cut off by another driver is bogus, but I can't say for sure until I test him. His mannerisms and pupils are giving me some pretty strong suspicions he has something in his system besides coffee."

"I'll stand by while you run him through the tests. I can call for a transport if you need one."

"Thanks. Let's see what we have." The trooper ambled toward the suspect.

Feeling a little smug, Mac stood back to observe the field sobriety tests. After all, the trooper did in fact need a cover officer. Dana joined him, and he filled her in.

She shook her head. "I arrested my share of users."

"Me too." Drug use was a common problem in the trucking industry—commercial drivers using illegal stimulants so they could stay awake and drive longer. The methamphetamine monster that was sweeping the country provided a cheap and easily accessible drug for the drivers. Although trucking companies publicly discouraged drug use among drivers, the unreasonable expectations placed on the drivers to deliver goods created an undue hardship on commercial drivers. One or two experiences with the highly addictive drug were enough to hook them. Intoxicated drivers in any sort of vehicle posed a potential danger on the highway, but the drivers operating forty thousand pounds or more of truck and trailer were lethal.

The trooper ran the trucker through a regimen of tests designed to gauge how the driver could perform under circumstances of divided attention, just as a driver must perform while operating a motor vehicle.

Dana leaned toward Mac. "The guy's obviously a user."

"I almost feel sorry for the guy," Mac said.

"Not me," Dana said. "He made the choice; he pays the price. His drug abuse could have easily led to a fatal car crash. It happens much too often."

With the driver arrested and awaiting transport, Mac and Dana merged onto the freeway and resumed their trek to the crime lab. He checked his cell phone and saw that he'd missed a call. Noting the eastern Oregon area code, he hit the redial button. Nate answered.

"Hey, Nate. What's up?"

"Just wanted to let you know that I interviewed everyone at the Warm Springs post office to cover our bases on that print we recovered on one of the second set of letters to Senator Wilde. No red flags. The background on the postal employee is squeaky clean, and he has no connections to Sara or her family. He isn't into politics and wasn't even sure who Senator Wilde was—says he doesn't care one way or the other about the casino. He's agreed to a polygraph. Thought I'd have him come in since we have the polygraph examiner coming to do Therman. Thought we might do Therman's wife while we're at it."

"So Therman agreed to the polygraph?"

"Yeah. You didn't know? I talked to Sergeant Bledsoe earlier today, and he set it up."

"He'll probably give us the news when we get back. Dana and I have been in Salem interviewing Senator Wilde."

"How'd that go?"

Mac gave him a brief overview and asked him to look up Margaret Case's grandson, Aaron Galbraith, and hopefully get a set of prints to match with any that might have come up on Sara's cabinet. "Try to get him to agree to a poly too." After making plans to connect the next day, he ended the call.

"Nate's been busy." Mac stuffed his phone in his jacket pocket and repeated the message.

"So the polygrapher is giving how many exams on the reservation?"

"Three, maybe four: the postal employee whose latents were on the letter, Therman, and Therman's wife. Maybe Aaron Galbraith, too." Mac adjusted his rearview mirror. "With all this cooperation, I'm beginning to wonder if there's a connection at the reservation at all."

"Have you had a chance to read through the results of the polygraphs the feds did?"

Mac shook his head. "Did you?"

Dana reached into the backseat and brought up her briefcase. "I started to, but my eyes were getting blurry."

"Do we have the actual test results from the polygraphs—the narrative from the polygrapher?"

Dana took out the files and thumbed through them. Pulling one out, she said, "Here's Scott's. According to the FBI examiner, there were some hitches, but the inconclusiveness comes from medications Scott was taking."

"What kind of meds?" Mac asked.

"He was taking antidepressants at the time."

"Great. Those things can interfere with the testing." He'd learned that much on his first homicide.

"The report says he started taking the prescription drugs after Sara went missing. Some of those medications can be pretty addictive. Sure hope he doesn't end up using them as a crutch forever."

"Why the concern?" Mac glanced over at her.

She tossed him a wry smile. "I want him drug free so we can run another polygraph on him."

"Good thinking. We'll have a look at the results again after one of our OSP polygraphers reviews the charts. I want someone we know to give the FBI polygraph charts a glance. Not all of the polygraphers are as good as our OSP guys. Anyway, the polygraphs aren't all that valuable unless you can score a confession out of a suspect who thinks the machine actually works. We've had plenty of innocent people get 'deceptive' results."

"I still haven't seen anything about the prints captured at the scene."

"Hopefully the lab will have faxed them over." Mac pulled into a parking slot marked Police Only in front of the Justice Center in downtown Portland. It was two o'clock when they made their way up to the crime lab on the twelfth floor. Dana had tried calling while they'd been stuck in traffic to see what Angela had for them, but she was in a clean room and couldn't accept the call. The contaminant-free room was where the scientist performed her DNA work.

The receptionist asked them to wait in the reception area for Angela. While they were waiting, Kevin came in. "Glad to see you made it. I heard about the accident."

"What's up, Sarge?" Mac asked.

"I'm assuming you got my page. Did Angela tell you what she had?"

"No, but I figure it's something good if she wanted us down here." Mac looked at his watch. They had a lot to do, and a phone call would have been nice. But Angela liked handing off important finds in person.

"She probably has a suspect for you. I'm guessing she's recovered some DNA from the post or some of the other trace evidence you two submitted." Kevin sounded excited, and Mac couldn't help but absorb some of it.

"Did she tell you that?" Dana asked. "Who is it?"

"I have no idea. Her message was on my voice mail. She wanted someone connected to the Watson case down here right away. I sent you the page but couldn't respond myself. I had to be present on an arraignment for Trooper Revman's killer. I knew you were either in Salem or on the road, so I got here as soon as I could." He sat down and rubbed his hands together. "I know you two can handle this just fine, but since I'm here . . ."

"Might as well stay," Mac finished for him. While they waited, Mac and Dana filled him in on their visit with the senator. "The senator was great, but for a while there, I was afraid we weren't going to get to see him at all."

"Why's that?" Kevin asked.

"His aide, Grant Stokely, came out to greet us with a long list of restrictions."

Dana smiled. "And Mac told him exactly what he could do with them."

"Oh, yeah? Even after my lecture on diplomacy."

"You would have done the same thing, boss," Mac said. "I told him very politely that if he planned to obstruct justice I'd have to arrest him, or at least make him think I would."

"Stokely was furious," Dana said, "but a few minutes later he came out to get us and looked like a puppy with his tail tucked between his legs."

Kevin chuckled. "I'd like to have been there."

Mac leaned forward, pressing his elbows into his knees. "Like I was saying, the senator couldn't have been nicer. That assistant of his is something else. He may just be a royal pain, but I'm planning to take a long, hard look at the guy. I wouldn't be surprised if he tries to get us fired. Me, anyway. I don't see why the senator keeps him around."

"Don't worry, Mac." Kevin slapped the back of Mac's shoulder. "Sounds like you did fine."

Angela came out to greet them wearing a white lab coat, her hair still neatly tucked under a white cap. "Sorry for the delay. Come on back to the conference room."

Angela had her business face on, and Mac knew she had something good for them. Even though Angela was a scientist, she was still a State Police employee and had the same love for catching the bad guys as the detectives and the troopers working the road. Mac had a hunch that this passion kept highly skilled scientists like Angela from seeking higher-paying jobs in the private sector. She led the investigators to the conference room and then excused herself for a moment to remove her lab attire.

She returned in a few minutes dressed in a suit and slapped a file folder on the table. "Thanks for coming down. I have a strong suspect for you in the Sara Watson murder." She pushed the folder over toward Mac.

"Really?" He opened the folder, pulling out a digital photograph and other documents. "Who is this guy?"

"Owen Sinnott." Angela took a seat next to Dana.

Dana leaned closer for a look, and Mac moved the folder over for her. "How'd you hook him?"

"You know that fingernail you found in the dirt?" Angela asked.

Dana beamed. "It *was* a fingernail. I knew it."

"That's the one. Did you get DNA from the nail?"

"I sure did. I couldn't extract DNA from the fingernail itself, though I think we can make a circumstantial case that the clipping is from our victim. What is truly amazing is that I found a skin sample on the bottom half of the nail clipping. DNA linked to Mr. Owen Sinnott."

"How do we know it was him?" Mac asked. "I mean, where'd you get the control sample to compare it to?"

"I didn't. You guys did," Angela reached for the file folder, pulling a criminal history sheet from the stack. "At least law enforcement did, not you guys personally." She pointed at a line on his record.

"He was arrested for Rape First Degree back in 1999." Mac's gaze slid from Dana to Kevin. "He's a registered sex offender."

Angela grinned. "This means we had his court-required DNA sample in our database. Once I recovered the DNA standard from the nail, it took me a day to type the standard. After that, I began comparing to the standards you brought in for comparison but struck out. This morning, I ran it through our statewide database computer for a standard check, and bingo! Owen Sinnott popped up."

"This guy's a pretty bad dude, Sarge." Mac continued to read the criminal history sheet. "Assault, sex offenses, dope charges—he's a real career criminal."

"Is this conclusive, Angela, or just an RFLP test?" Kevin began looking over the file Mac handed him.

"A what?" Dana asked.

Angela smiled. "The RFLP is a DNA test for Restriction Fragment Length Polymorphism."

Dana grinned. "Whatever you say."

"That's what I was working on after I called you. We are good to go; the test is conclusive now. One in twelve billion odds, he's our guy. Since he doesn't appear to be the kind of person she'd be giving a back scratch to, one can assume she retained the sample under her nail during a defensive act. Of course, that's an educated guess. It's up to you guys to find out what the link is. All I can tell you is that his DNA is under our victim's fingernail."

"If it really is our victim's nail." Dana frowned. "I don't like the circumstantial part of this. Why can't you do a DNA on the nail itself?"

"The fingernail is like hair, bone, and teeth—I can't extract DNA from them unless I have the component that contains the sample. In hair, it's the follicle; the bone is the marrow; and in teeth, it's the root. If you had found the end of the nail that was connected to tissue, that would be a winner; but I'm afraid the end of the fingernail is a dry well for me. Sorry."

"He lives in Gresham." Kevin handed the sex offender registration readout back to Dana. "At least that's the address listed here."

In Oregon, convicted sex offenders must register with the State Police. In addition to providing a DNA sample for future comparisons, they had to notify the OSP whenever they changed addresses, jobs, or automobiles. Their addresses, registered vehicles, and work locations were all kept in a statewide database. The program had been invaluable for detectives working cold cases or stranger-to-stranger cases. And it looked like that's what Sara's case was after all.

"Either of you recognize his name?"

Neither had. Mac and Dana had recently worked on the list, but Sinnott's name never came up. His listed address was nowhere near the victim's residence, so he was outside their range of interest.

Angela continued, "Was there anything else to link him to Sara's murder? Fingerprints at the scene, maybe?"

"Sorry. That's it. We lifted a lot of prints during the initial visit to the house. All of them are accounted for with family and friends.

By the way, Dana, I did get your message and faxed the reports back. They should be waiting for you at the office."

"Thanks. Did the feds have a copy? I couldn't find anything in the files they gave us."

"As far as I know." Angela pursed her lips. "Like I said, there were no prints other than family and friends, so they may not have felt the need to include it."

"Says here he's a general laborer," Mac said. "There's no actual address for employment, so that's another reason we wouldn't have hit on his work location for our sex offender roundup." Dana read from the form. "He has a 1979 Buick LeSabre as his listed vehicle; not much more information here."

"Enough to get started," Kevin said. "You two get on the residence, and I'll get SWAT tuned up for a callout. You better use the undercover van at the office; the keys are on my desk. I'll get Philly and Russ on the horn after they're done with court. They can help out on the warrant for the house if you can get me a description when you get out there. Don't try any heroics, kids. If the house can be watched, then fine. If not, c'mon back, and we'll try it when we have everything in order."

"Got it." Mac sighed. Adrenaline pumping, he nearly tripped on the leg of the chair as he stood up and started to leave.

"Why the SWAT team?" Dana asked. "Can't Mac and I just go arrest him?"

"Too dangerous with a predator like Sinnott," Kevin said. "We'll be following our risk protocol to the letter on this one, Dana. I know we've gone in like cowboys in the past, but I like to play by the book. With this guy's criminal history and his recent conduct, I want the SWAT team in my hip pocket. I'd rather send them home than wait three hours for guys to arrive from all over the state if we need them in a pinch."

"What if he's not there? Isn't that a wasted effort?"

"It's not uncommon for us to kick the door on an empty house. The warrant allows us to do that and to search the place. If he's not home, we go find him."

"You ready, Dana?" Mac asked.

"Let's go."

TWENTY-SEVEN

Mac parked his car and jogged into the OSP office with Dana to grab any gear they would need to work surveillance. He found the keys to the undercover van—a newer tan Dodge, complete with a fixed camera and video system. More importantly for long surveillances, it had a bathroom, a feature that really came in handy when you were sitting in a vehicle for hours on end.

They both changed into a set of street clothes, jeans and T-shirts, which they routinely kept in their lockers for circumstances such as this. They didn't want to look like cops, just a couple hanging out on a sunny afternoon.

After donning his jeans, an Oregon Ducks T-shirt, and running shoes, Mac went out to start up the van. Dana joined him a while later, wearing a loose purple T-shirt and jeans.

Before pulling out of the parking lot, Mac grabbed his ballistic vest, raid jacket, and AR-15 rifle from his trunk. He was going to suggest that Dana do the same, but she already had her trunk open.

Before driving to Gresham, Mac had one more stop to make.

"Where are you going?" Dana asked when he headed north off I-205.

"Home." He tossed her a sly grin. "We're picking up Lucy."

"Really? May I ask why?"

"She's a great prop, and since dogs love to stop and sniff things, her dallying will give us time to look around. Besides, nobody would expect a dog as sweet as Lucy to be anything but a pet."

"Good thinking, Mac. I take it she's been on surveillance with you before?"

"A few times. Once, I even had a suspect pet Lucy before going into his house." Mac chuckled. "You should have seen the guy's face when I handcuffed him an hour later."

Lucy could hardly wait to get inside the van. Mac tossed her leash and food and water dish into the back and returned to his apartment for a cooler and some sodas.

On the way out, they stopped at Brewed Awakenings for twenty-ounce iced lattes and returned back to the Oregon side, taking the I-84 exit toward the gorge. They pulled off at the 181st Avenue exit, eventually taking a winding road that followed Johnson Creek on Gresham's east side. Dana navigated for Mac as they worked their way into the residential area where their suspect supposedly lived.

"There it is, Mac. Nice home for such a sleazy guy."

"Yeah, but it probably isn't his." It was an older two story on some acreage with a small barn and a shed of some sort. They were in a rural area, where most of the homes had an acre or two of land, which meant they probably wouldn't have neighbors to worry about in case things went south.

Mac drove past the house without slowing, to avoid drawing attention to themselves.

"I don't see anything." Dana examined the house and yard as

they passed. "I couldn't tell if there were any cars in back; nothing out front, though."

Mac drove a half mile down the road and turned around, then he backed the van into a driveway of a fenced utility area. The driveway allowed them to watch the house in an unobtrusive manner. "Shall we take a walk?"

Lucy's tail thumped on the side of the van, recognizing the key word in Mac's question. She loved going for walks and runs, and one in the middle of the day was a special treat for her. Mac removed his pistol from the holster and slipped it into the small of his back, pulling his shirt over the weapon for concealment. Dana put on a lightweight vest to cover hers.

"Ready?" Mac asked.

"Yeah. Does she have a leash?" Dana motioned to Lucy.

"I put it in next to her water dish, but we don't really need it out here. Besides, you don't have to worry about Lucy. She does really well off leash, especially if I have my ultimate control tool with me." He reached into the back of the van and pulled out a ragged tennis ball. "She won't get two feet from me when I have this thing. I think she likes this ball more than me!" Mac slapped his leg, and Lucy jumped out of the van, excited when she saw the tennis ball. "Let's go, girl," Mac began the short walk toward Sinnott's house, bouncing Lucy's ball on the road.

Dana activated a tape recorder she'd hidden in her vest pocket. "Testing 1-2-3," she said in a normal speaking voice. She then rewound the tape to make sure the sensitive recorder had picked up her voice. She would record her observations while walking along with Mac and Lucy.

Mac tossed the tennis ball for Lucy a few times on the way to the house. Each time, the dog caught the ball in her mouth after it bounced twice on the ground and brought it back to her master.

They rounded a deep five-foot hedge on the south end of the property, and Dana started talking into the recorder as they came closer to the house. "Two-story, wood-framed residential dwelling." She looked at Mac as she spoke to give the appearance of having a conversation. Her observations would be used in the search warrant affidavit.

"Primary color is taupe with dark maroon trim, wood shake roof, the numbers 3161 prominently displayed on the east entrance, next to an apparently wooden door. The numbers are painted black and appear to be metal. There is a paved circular drive, with two large outbuildings in the back of the residence. One appears to be a metal pole building, cream in color, and the other a wood construction that is similar in paint and material as the primary structure." Dana pushed the pause button and looked around to see if there was any more relevant information she needed for her warrant.

"I don't see any cars in the back, do you?" Mac hunkered down and ruffled Lucy's ears.

"I can't tell," Dana craned her neck as they walked in front of Sinnott's house. "We need to go down the driveway a bit to see."

"I have an idea." Mac threw the ball, putting a curve on it so it would land in the side yard. As the ball bounced toward the back of the house, he whispered, "Fetch it up, girl."

The dog tore off after the ball, and Mac jogged after her, playing the part of dog owner who was concerned that his pet might be trespassing. "Hurry up and get the ball, Lucy. Come on." Mac jogged to the end of the house where he could see around the back. There were no vehicles in the back of the house that he could see. The doors were closed on both of the outbuildings. The smaller building was large enough to hold a car, but not much else, so it was probably more of a storage building. The second building, however, was big enough to hold several cars.

Mac wanted to have a look inside the buildings, but that would be an illegal search and his observations would be tossed out in court. He had known officers who would fudge on fine lines such as these, but Mac wasn't one of them. No case was worth losing his integrity, not even a murder case.

Lucy grabbed the ball and ran back to Mac, who immediately took it from her mouth and tossed it back toward the main road. He hurried after his dog, not looking back at the house. Dana caught up and jogged alongside him. "See anything?"

"Nothing, but his car could be stored in the larger of the two buildings. Let's get back to the van and call our description in to Kevin so he can get the paper started on the warrant."

Once they reached the van, Mac called in, stating their vehicle's location while Dana relayed the description of the house.

"I ran a power and utility search on the residence," Kevin told them. "The owner of the home is an elderly woman named Alma Sinnott. Probably the suspect's grandmother or another relative."

"I'm not surprised," Mac said. "There's nothing going on here— at least not that I can see."

"Keep a watch on the house while we make an application for a search warrant based on the DNA evidence and the fact that Sinnott listed this address as his home." The warrant affidavit would seek permission from a circuit court judge for both the search of Sinnott's person and the home for evidence of the murder. "We're also asking permission to search his vehicle when we find it."

"Did you get anything on the car?"

"It's registered to Alma Sinnott as well. I suspect Owen is using it, though, as she no longer has a valid driver's license. We'll get there as soon as we can," Kevin assured him, then hung up.

Mac told Dana about the older woman. "I suspect Alma Sinnott is only guilty by association in this case. No doubt Sinnott appealed to her sympathies with a promise to walk the straight and narrow."

"That's so sad. She's about to have her whole life turned upside down just because she took pity on her grandson or nephew or whatever."

"I wonder if he's there," Mac said. "Too bad I couldn't get a look inside the barn."

"We'll find out soon enough."

The tinted windows in the van concealed their identity, but they had to be careful to avoid any movement that might indicate that they were inside. Lucy snuggled down in the back of the van, content with the amount of exercise she'd had.

Mac and Dana slipped into their ballistic vests and raid jackets, preparing for the eventual SWAT team assault on the house. Mac thought how tough it would be on the tactical team members, this being their first call out since Trooper Revman had been killed less than a week ago. Emotions would be running high, but these guys were pros and would be able to check their feelings at the door. They were trained to react appropriately during high-stress situations.

Mac pulled his AR-15 rifle from the black carrying case, seating the thirty-round magazine in the weapon. He propped up the gun on the side slider door of the van so he'd be ready in a moment's notice to charge the weapon and exit the van. He and Dana then settled in for the duration. A nice breeze came through the open window on Mac's side, keeping the van at a comfortable seventy or so degrees.

"Did Kevin say how long we'd have to wait?" Dana asked.

"Nope. We're probably looking at a couple of hours at least."

Dana sighed. "No offense, partner, but I hate waiting around."

"Me too, but orders are orders."

They watched the house without speaking for a time. Dana finally broke the unnatural silence. "You talked to Kristen lately?"

"No. I think she went back to Florida. I haven't heard from her, and I've been too busy to call."

"That doesn't sound good." Dana tipped her head to the side. "Are you losing interest?"

Mac shrugged. "I have no idea." He didn't especially want to talk about Kristen. The whole deal with her rushing back to Florida to see her ex frustrated and confused him. Dana confused him, too, so what else was new?

"I hope things work out for you and Kristen. She's perfect for you."

"Why would you say that?"

"Think about it, Mac. She knows what you do and is OK with it. She understands your hours, and from what you've told me, she's pretty flexible. And she's nice. And if you and Kristen were together, I could worry less about you."

Mac pulled his gaze from the house. "Where did that come from? Since when do you worry about me?"

"Um . . . that sort of slipped out." She chewed on her lower lip. "I know splitting up with Linda was really tough on you, and when you started dating Kristen, you seemed happy. Now . . . I don't know, Mac. You seem lost."

He shook his head. "I'm not lost. I had a friend die, remember?"

"I know, but . . . I'm sorry. I have no business butting into your personal life."

"Yeah, actually, you do." Mac felt the heat creep up into his neck. Maybe this would be a good time to pull out the stops. "You're one of my best friends, and that's reason enough. Anyway, I don't think you really want me dating Kristen. I think you want me for yourself. I could be totally wrong, but I'm thinking all this garbage about not dating a cop is bogus. Why don't you just admit it?"

Dana stared straight ahead for several long moments. "Mac, I love you, but I don't *love* you. If I've given you that idea, then . . . It was letting you stay at my place the other night, right? And driving with you to work? I know a while back I said that I liked you, but . . . The hotel, when I hugged you?"

"No." It was Mac's turn to stare out the window. Had he really misread her intentions? Dana was just being Dana. His cell rang, and he managed to answer.

"Hey, boss."

"How's it going over there? Are you and Dana having a heart-to-heart?"

"How'd you guess?" Mac tried to make light of the question.

"Because I've been sitting on houses since you two were in diapers. You always get down to the nitty-gritty with your partners on a surveillance. I just wanted to read what I have on the affidavit. See if there are any changes." He read through it.

"Sounds fine to me." Mac said.

"The SWAT team is standing by at the Portland OSP office, awaiting the word to get started."

Much to Mac's disappointment, Kevin hung up, bringing back the tension between him and Dana.

"Are you getting hungry?" Mac asked, hoping to draw her attention away from their discussion. It was after seven.

"Not getting, I'm there." Dana rubbed her stomach. "I should have thought to grab something. Do you have anything to eat?"

"Just Lucy's dog treats." The dog's ears perked up, but the conversation apparently wasn't worth her full attention, so she went back to sleep after a couple halfhearted tail wags.

"In the rush I didn't think to bring food. I hope this isn't an all-nighter."

"Me too." Mac blew out a long breath. "Dana?"

"Mac?" They both spoke at once.

"You go first," Mac said.

"No, you go."

He thrummed his fingers on the wheel. "OK. I'm sorry if I read you wrong. It was probably the funeral. I really appreciated you coming with me, and maybe I did misread your intentions."

She nodded. "It's hard, Mac. If we weren't both cops, maybe . . . But we are cops and we are partners, so we can't go there, not even in our dreams. Besides, I've met someone."

"Yeah? Who?"

"Remember the attorney I said I was dating?"

Mac nodded. "You haven't mentioned him for a while."

"Well, we've seen each other a few times. He came over last night and . . . I really like him."

"I'm happy for you, Dana." In a way he was.

"By the way, I got another call last night, but not until after Jonathan left."

"Same guy?

"'Fraid so."

"Is he watching the place?"

"Probably. I never seem to get calls when someone's there."

"Maybe we should bring the van over to your place and set up surveillance. I'll bet the guys would volunteer to help me around the clock for a few days."

"Maybe."

Mac thought it best to end the conversation before he got into more trouble. He didn't want to overstep his boundaries with Dana. He scrutinized the house. The sun would be setting soon, and the lights would come on. They'd soon find out if anyone was home. "What's the description on this Sinnott guy again—height, weight, that sort of thing?"

"The report said five-eight—190 pounds. He'd be stocky." She reached for her case and took out a file. "Here's his picture. He's wearing a tank top that shows off his tattoos." Dana handed Mac the photo from Sinnott's last registration visit. "He's muscular, probably worked out in prison."

"Looks tough." He had dark hair and was clean shaven. Several tattoos accentuated his shoulder muscles. Mac made a mental note to ask him about the tats. They might be a good interview lead to soften him up for a confession. Most people with tattoos were fairly open about discussing them—at least, that had been his experience. Mac brought out the sodas and they chatted for a while, then lapsed into silence.

"Bingo." Dana hit his arm to get his attention.

Mac looked up, expecting to see a car or Sinnott walking down the street. "What is it?"

"The house. A light just came on in an upstairs window."

Mac trained his binoculars at the open window. "Looks like a bedroom. Can you see anything?"

Dana used her binoculars as well. "Nothing—not even a shadow."

The light went off after a few minutes. Mac looked at his watch. It was after eight. He reached for the phone to call Sergeant Bledsoe, but it rang before he could hit the talk button.

"McAllister," he answered.

"I'm going over to Judge Morgan's house right now to get the warrant signed," Kevin said. "The SWAT team is heading your way. They're driving the V-150, so it'll be slow going."

"Someone is home. We noticed a light go on and off. Hopefully, whoever is inside won't leave before you guys get here. And hopefully it's Sinnott and not Alma."

Mac hung up and filled Dana in. "Won't be long now. The ninja boys will be here to do the dirty work in a few minutes. Once they make the arrest, we'll have our turn with Sinnott."

Dana nodded. "I know he's our guy, Mac. DNA doesn't lie. But something doesn't feel right."

"I know what you mean. Seems like all our work so far has been for nothing. Sara's death still feels like a revenge killing to me, not a random act. Be interesting to see if Sinnott has ties with Sara or someone who knew her."

"Like her cousin Aaron?"

"Or her husband."

TWENTY-EIGHT

Mac and Dana waited in the van for another hour before receiving a call from their sergeant saying he had just turned off the freeway with the SWAT team and a signed warrant to search Sinnott's house and outbuildings. The first order of business would be to secure the residence, interview Sinnott, and finally search for evidence of the crime.

Several lights came on in the house, but they still couldn't see the occupant. They finally heard 12-33 over the police radio, the code indicating the SWAT commander was calling for radio silence so his commands could not be talked over by an unsuspecting trooper who was not familiar with the operation. The members on the tactical team had a scrambled radio channel of their own, but they wouldn't go to this encrypted frequency until they had exited their vehicles. The encrypted channels scrambled the officers' conversations so someone with a police scanner couldn't monitor them.

Big Johnson, a large black armored command vehicle with the lights blacked out, pulled past the target house. The van was equipped with light armor and looked like a UPS delivery truck on steroids. It had been designed for the military but was very popular among police agencies for its ability to safely carry twelve officers into dangerous perimeters like this one might prove to be. Twelve perimeter officers jumped from the back of the van, taking positions outside the house and around the foliage. With scoped rifles and high-power binoculars, their job would be to monitor the outside of the target location for escaping subjects. The officers, dressed in black, disappeared into the night as quickly as they had arrived.

Mac's heart pumped hard and heavy with anticipation. He opened the door to the van slowly, making sure Lucy didn't escape when he and Dana stepped out. After grabbing his rifle, he closed the van door and stepped to the back of the vehicle.

He could hear the distant rumble of the heavy armored assault vehicle, the department V-150, coming up the road. It, too, had been designed by the military. The fifty-caliber machine-gun turret had been deleted on a civilian order and replaced with a heavy bulldozer blade and long metal ramming bar. The V-150, with its oversize tires and thick armor, was virtually impenetrable to light arms fire.

Many who weren't familiar with the law-enforcement version thought the ramming bar, a thick hollow metal tube, was a cannon protruding from the front of the menacing-looking vehicle. The look of the vehicle alone had convinced many suspects to give up their barricaded strongholds and surrender.

The V-150 carried a hostage negotiator, who served as the driver, along with the SWAT entry team. If the negotiator could not convince the suspect to give up, the entry team would enter the residence and locate their bad guy. The team would try peaceful negotiations before sending in the big guns. In every case, however, they were prepared for the worst-case scenario. The SWAT commander in the first armored vehicle directed the driver of the V-150 to

motor up to the front of the residence and begin so-called negotiations, which were essentially, "Give up, or we will destroy your house
and hurt you in the process."

The diesel engine revved as the heavy vehicle lumbered down
the driveway. Diesel exhaust clouded the air.

The lights went out in the house as the V-150 approached, but
the floodlights from the SWAT vehicle went on, illuminating the
entry and the area around it.

Mac charged his AR-15, slamming a .223 round into the
chamber with a thud of the rifle's bolt. He wrapped the sling around
his left arm and took aim from behind the van. Dana did the same
with her handgun, though it wouldn't be much use from this
distance.

"Flight or fight time," Mac said in a hushed voice.

"This guy's going to fight," Dana said. "You can just tell."

"He looks tough, but I'll bet he's a wimp. Either that, or he'll
explode out of there with guns blazing."

"Suicide by cop?" Dana shrugged.

"I wouldn't put it past him." Desperate suspects sometimes
convinced themselves that suicide was the only answer, so they tried
to take as many cops as possible with them before they were gunned
down.

"He'll fight." Dana seemed too sure of herself.

Mac knew better than to make a wager with his partner. She
read people far better than he did. Still, he couldn't pass up the
opportunity. "Coffee for a month?"

"You're on." Dana's lips curled in a know-it-all smile.

Mac leveled his front sight on the entrance, alternating between
the door and the window where he and Dana initially saw the light go
on. He hoped Alma Sinnott wasn't around for this. Nobody decent
should have to live through a SWAT team assault on their home.

"I just hope he doesn't use Alma for a hostage," Dana whispered, echoing his thoughts.

The loudspeaker from the SWAT negotiator would serve to get the innocent parties out. If no one came out, officers would assume it was the bad guy, an empty house, or a hostage situation. Of course, the woman could be physically unable to get out. Mac hoped that wasn't the case.

The negotiator in the V-150 began his verbal assault on the house over the vehicle's loudspeaker, reading from a prepared card that was intended to protect the department from civil liability as much as it was intended to get the suspect to come out. The general rule of thinking for the police was to warn the suspects that they may be shot, so there was no surprise if they actually had to do it. It seemed inane, but in the day of civil lawsuits, officers were trained to protect their financial interests as well as their physical well-being.

"Occupants of the house, this is the Oregon State Police. We have your home surrounded and are in possession of a valid search warrant. Occupants, you are ordered to come out the front door with your hands over your head. Failure to obey this demand may result in serious physical injury or death. Occupants, come out of the house now." The negotiator paused for a moment, all eyes on the front door.

Mac clicked the safety off his rifle and released a long, steady breath. There was no movement in the house, no sound.

The negotiator repeated the commands three more times. When attempts for a peaceful resolution failed, the SWAT team leader gave the green light for a tactical assault on the house.

The V-150 roared to life, lowering the bulldozer blade with the long rammer bar to a height of four feet and then surged forward. The ram bar met the front door seconds later, splintering the wood and surrounding frame into a thousand pieces. The operator of the SWAT vehicle then raised the blade and backed away from the house, the rammer bar taking a huge chunk out of the front of the house twice the size of the original doorframe. The gaping hole would allow the team a point of entry wide enough for multiple officers to raid the house.

As the V-150 backed away, ten SWAT officers rolled out both sides of the armored vehicle in two single-file lines. Bright light reflected off the goggles as they charged the building. The first officer pulled a metal canister from his vest, which Mac immediately recognized as a flash-bang grenade. The diversionary device would explode with a large boom of sound and light, designed to distract and disorient a suspect. The officer pulled the pin on the flash-bang and threw the device in the front door.

The SWAT officers stepped back and ducked, plugging their ears as best they could. Since they had to have all their senses when they entered a house, they didn't wear ear protection.

After the loud explosion and flash of light, the entry team charged into the house, barking orders and yelling. The yelling continued for several minutes before he noted a shift in dialogue. Mac couldn't tell what they were saying, but he gathered they had located Sinnott, and there was some type of standoff. The SWAT members shifted over to their encrypted radio frequency, and Mac and Dana were unable to monitor the situation on Mac's radio.

Mac groaned. "He's not giving up."

"I just hope they don't kill him."

"You and me both." Although they felt certain they had Sara's killer, Mac really wanted a crack at Sinnott to put closure on the case.

The yelling subsided after the negotiator exited the V-150 and entered the house. It was his job now to try to establish a rapport with whomever they had in the house and hopefully get the suspect to give up. If not, the team's last option would be to gas the house. Not only did tear gas ruin the dwellings where it was deployed, it sometimes forced confrontations and was used as a last resort. Mac shuddered to think about what it would do to the elderly woman.

"Stay here." He motioned to Dana. "I'm going to get closer—try to get a better idea of what's going on."

"Sure."

Mac made his way over to one of the perimeter members, who stood near a lilac bush. He made sure the SWAT member recognized him as one of the good guys before he approached. The officer pulled down his black mask to reveal his entire face. It was a trooper from the Portland office, a guy Mac knew.

"What's the deal?" Mac asked.

"Those of us on the perimeter can stand down for the time being; the suspect is holed up in an attic and threatening to shoot anyone who goes up the ladder. The negotiator was able to get a cell phone up to him so they can talk without yelling. Looks like they are making progress. I think if he wanted a shootout, he would have done it by now. He's got no bargaining chips and no hostage—at least that we know of. Doesn't appear to be anyone else in the house."

"Thanks for the heads-up." Mac returned to the van to use the facilities and found Lucy cowering and whining in the back—probably from the flash-bang. "What's the matter, girl? Those noises scare you?" Mac wished now that he hadn't brought her. His past covert operations with Lucy had gone more smoothly than this one. He used the bathroom, then leashed her and took her outside and behind the van where she relieved herself. He'd just put her back inside when Kevin made his way toward them.

"I wondered what had happened to you," Mac said.

"I've been standing on the other side, trying to figure out what's going down. You heard anything?"

"They have someone holed up in the attic."

"Right." Kevin nodded. "Owen Sinnott. Now if they can only get him to give up without a fight."

"Doesn't look good so far," Mac said.

Kevin sighed. "You two can go on in and monitor the negotiations. Bring a tape recorder and take notes."

"You want us to go in there?" Dana asked.

"You'll be safe enough."

"It isn't that, exactly. I didn't think the SWAT team wanted us."

"Our SWAT members are very good at what they do, but they try to avoid taking part in actions or conversations that will tie them up in court. They want us in there monitoring the conversation in case Sinnott mentions anything about the case."

"Why didn't you say so?" Dana climbed into the van to retrieve her tape recorder and grabbed an extra tape and writing pad.

Mac took the pad and pen and shoved them into his jacket pocket, glad to be doing something other than sitting around waiting. He soon wished he were back out by the van. The bathroom was cramped and uncomfortable, and they weren't learning anything about their case. Sinnott and the negotiator talked on forever, the topics general and neutral. Their negotiator was among the best; but at this point, he wasn't looking for a confession—nothing adversarial or confrontational, just conversation that might encourage Sinnott to give himself up.

At about two in the morning, Sinnott finally agreed to come down.

"I don't have a gun," he admitted. "The only reason I'm coming down is 'cause I have to go to the bathroom and I need a cigarette. Just don't cuff me 'til I'm done using the john."

The negotiator reluctantly agreed. "Don't try anything. I have five officers pointing their guns at you."

"I hope for his sake he doesn't have a shy bladder," Dana whispered to Mac.

Mac swallowed back a chuckle. "We'd better get out of here."

They watched from one of the bedrooms while the SWAT officers took positions of cover in the hall and Sinnott backed down the steep ladder.

"I don't have a gun," he said again. He reached the bottom and shoved his hands into the air, then turned to face the officers, as instructed. He was wearing a pair of faded jeans with holes in the knees. His body was heavily tattooed, both ears and nipples pierced.

"On your knees." The negotiator then had him lie prone so he could be thoroughly searched. A second officer searched the bathroom, even inside the toilet tank, for potential weapons. Satisfied there were none, they allowed Sinnott to use the restroom at gunpoint.

He was then handcuffed in flex cuffs by one of the SWAT officers and led down the stairs to the dining room. Mac and Dana followed.

"He's all yours, Detectives." The SWAT supervisor slapped Mac on the back. "I'm going home." The bleary-eyed officer greeted Kevin before rounding up his team.

The detectives soon heard the V-150 rumble to life again.

The conversation Mac and Dana had overheard between Sinnott and the SWAT negotiator almost gave them the impression that Sinnott could be pleasant. Unfortunately, that wasn't the case.

"Mr. Sinnott, I'm Detective McAllister, and this is my partner, Detective Bennett. We're with . . ."

"Save your breath, pig." Sinnott spat on Dana's running shoes. "I got nothing to say to you."

Dana looked down at her foot, folded her arms, and with more composure than Mac could have mustered, said, "Wouldn't you like to know why we're here?"

"I know why you're here," he growled, "and I've got nothing to say to you. This isn't my first rodeo, so read me my rights and put in your little notebook that I think you're a piece of crap. Now shut up and take me to jail. I'm getting cold." Sinnott glared at Mac and spat in his direction. The spit landed on the carpet, which was probably a good thing.

"Fine. Have it your way." Scum that he was, he'd make the police prove their case without a statement from him. Mac was radioing for a uniformed trooper to take their suspect to jail when Philly and Russ strode in.

"Hey, guys. You missed all the fun." Mac hoped Philly wouldn't try anything with their suspect. Philly loved a good confrontation with a con and was often successful at getting them to talk. But having just come off a bust gone bad, Mac feared Philly might go too far.

"Watch out, Philly," Mac warned. "He's a spitter."

"Yeah?" Philly glowered at Sinnott and received a savage look in return. "What's the deal?"

"He's invoked his rights, and we have a transport coming in for him."

Sinnott swore and sent another mouthful of spit in Philly's direction.

Without a word, Philly walked past the chair where Owen Sinnott was seated and set his briefcase on the kitchen table.

"What's he doing?" Dana tipped her head toward Mac.

Mac shrugged.

Philly opened the case and removed a donut-shaped object. He shook it out, and Mac realized it was a woman's nylon stocking. While Sinnott was going into another threatening litany of curses, Philly approached him from behind and stretched the hosiery over his head, pulling it over Sinnott's head and tightening it around his throat.

Sinnott twisted in rage, but Philly put him in a chokehold and pulled him down to the floor. "You like spitting, boy? Well go ahead and spit. You can disrespect me all you want, you pervert."

Sinnott's face turned from red to blue as he gasped for air.

"You're choking him!" Mac grabbed the big man's arm, attempting to pull him away.

"That's enough, Philly!" Sergeant Bledsoe yelled.

Philly immediately let go but didn't remove the nylon stocking. The stocking was actually an acceptable tool to combat spitters. The guy could breathe, but the spit would just roll down his face.

"He was a spitter, Sarge," Philly responded in defense. "He got a little froggy when I put the nylon over his head."

"Well, he's not spitting now. Read the warrant, Mac, and get on with the search."

Mac read the warrant aloud, which was required by Oregon's search-and-seizure laws prior to the search of a home for evidence. After reading the warrant, Mac supplied Sinnott with a copy by folding up the document and stuffing it in his back pocket.

Though the crime lab wouldn't come to the house until detectives requested them, Mac and Dana and the rest of the crew were going to have to pull an all-nighter.

The first order of business was to bribe the graveyard-shift trooper who was transporting Sinnott to the county lockup. The bribe involved the trooper's promising to bring back coffee and snack food if Mac sent along the money when he returned to assist with the search. The second order of business was to let Lucy out of the van again before she had an accident and he had to pay for a carpet cleaning.

Mac met the uniformed trooper, Sean Dewitt, at the door of Sinnott's house. Either Mac was getting old, or they were recruiting teenagers these days. The boyish face and the fact that he'd pulled the graveyard shift, told Mac that Dewitt was probably a trooper in training who had just been released on his own for solo patrol, which meant he was about three months out of the academy. The trooper looked sharp and fit in his campaign hat and pressed uniform, reminding Mac he needed to hit the gym a little more often. He was that trooper not all that long ago.

Mac introduced himself to Dewitt and escorted Sinnott to the patrol car, explaining the charges as they walked. He turned to go back to the house for the probable cause affidavit that the jail would require before lodging. "Get him into the car. I'll be right back."

Trooper Dewitt patted down Sinnott for weapons, as he'd been trained to do before accepting the custody. Sinnott made a comment Mac couldn't quite hear.

"Detective!" Dewitt yelled.

"What the . . ." Mac whipped around, his heart dropping to his knees. Sinnott had somehow gotten free from the soft restraints that SWAT members had placed on his wrists and was struggling with the trooper.

Mac raced toward the two men. He was only a few feet away when Sinnott pushed Dewitt to the ground.

"Look out! He's got my gun!"

The warning came too late. Sinnott had the trooper's weapon leveled on Mac.

TWENTY-NINE

$\mathbf{M}$ac stopped dead in his tracks. Instinct kicked in, and he dove to the ground at the front of the patrol car. As he went down, he grabbed for his sidearm, cursing the jacket that got in his way.

Sinnott pulled off a shot, puncturing the front tire and hitting metal.

Mac made it to the opposite side of the car and, using it as a shield, took aim at Sinnott.

Sinnott fired again, the bullet deflecting off the patrol car's hood.

Two shots came from the porch. Mac heard the *thunk, thunk* as they hit their target. Sinnott fired off one more shot into the grass before slumping to the ground.

Dewitt scrambled to his feet. "He said the cuffs were too tight; I was only trying to swap out the flex cuffs for my metal ones." He ran both hands through his hair. "I'm sorry."

Kevin checked Sinnott. "He's dead."

Mac managed to get up but leaned against the front of the car for support. The rookie mistake had cost them their prime murder suspect, but at least the kid was alive. Mac took a moment to thank

God for that. The entire scene had gone down in less than ten seconds, but to Mac it had seemed a lifetime.

"You OK, Mac?" Dana hurried toward him.

"Yeah. Who got him?"

"Philly."

Mac made his way back to the porch. Philly was handing his service weapon to Kevin.

"Thanks, buddy," Mac said. "I owe you one."

Philly patted him on the back. "You'd have done the same for me."

Mac struggled to maintain his composure. "I should have seen that one coming. I shouldn't have left the kid alone with a seasoned criminal."

"It's not your fault, Mac." Dana gripped his shoulder. "Come on. Let these guys handle the details of the shooting. We've got a scene to process."

Mac would find time to deal with what he had just witnessed later on, but Dana was right. They still had a job to do, and they had limited time to do it. They had both just witnessed a justifiable homicide and would be subject to lengthy interviews by detectives from out of the area. Mac wanted to get a look at Sinnott and gather as much evidence as possible before the captain yanked them all from the scene. Now they had the original murder investigation that was complicated by the officer-involved shooting. The only good thing that came from Philly killing Sinnott was the fact they didn't have to do the reports.

Before Sinnott was taken to the morgue, Mac retrieved his digital camera from the van and snapped dozens of pictures of his hands, face, and torso. Mac hunkered down beside their suspect. "Take a look at this, Dana. On his face. Look like old scratch marks to you?"

"I'd say so. They're healed now, but it looks like they were fairly deep."

"I got some good photos. This will be excellent circumstantial evidence to go alongside the DNA recovery."

"Sara Watson fought back, and the killer clipped her nails to remove evidence," Dana said. The irony was not lost on the officers that a moment of bravery on Sara's part may not have saved her life, but it provided crucial evidence to link Sinnott to the crime.

Mac mentioned the scratches to Kevin when he came over to them.

Kevin nodded. "I noticed that too. We got a lucky break this time, depending on how you want to look at it. I know you two are up to it, but I'm having Multnomah County Sheriff's Office investigate Sinnott's death to keep things clean. The medical examiner gave us permission to remove the body, but that's as far as we're taking it. I want outside investigators with a clean plate to document his death."

"Good call, Sarge," Mac said, knowing his time at the crime scene was limited. Kevin was going through the paces, but he was cutting Mac and Dana a little slack to complete their parallel investigation. It was amazing how times like these could be considered normal, but everyone went about their business like this type of thing happened every day. "What about Dewitt?"

"I sent him home. He'll go in for counseling, maybe take some time off. I think he'll be OK."

"I hope so."

"In the meantime, we'll count ourselves extremely fortunate to have found Sara Watson's killer."

"You're right about that," Mac said. The investigative process was exceptionally fragile on these crimes. If the body had not been discovered when it was, the fire would have charred the remains and destroyed the evidence. Sara could well have been labeled a missing person, her name forgotten by all except her family and friends. Such was the case with thousands of missing people. Law enforcement officers either didn't get their lucky break or didn't have the technology or the right detective to put the pieces together.

But, like Kevin had said, they had gotten lucky, and now it would be up to Mac and Dana to put together the pieces of Sara's murder. Since a confession was not in the cards, they had to figure everything out on their own. There were still a lot of unanswered questions, and they needed to prove Sinnott's guilt before they could put the case to rest.

They started the search in the home in what appeared to be Sinnott's bedroom. Inside the room, detectives located the typical items they would expect from a registered sex offender. Stacks of pornography littered the floor, along with user amounts of marijuana and what appeared to be crystal meth. Besides heaps of dirty laundry and fast-food bags, they didn't find much more of evidentiary value. A lengthy search of the rest of the house yielded few additional results, taking them up to daybreak, when the search was complete.

Mornings on these all-nighters were the hardest time for Mac. Sunlight burned his eyes as he made his way from the house to the larger outbuilding. They had learned that the Buick was in the shop at the rear of the property and, although they planned to wait for the crime lab to process the vehicle for trace evidence, he wanted to have a look and take some photos.

A dayshift trooper arrived at sunup, offering to get some more coffee for everyone, but Mac declined. Sergeant Bledsoe, Philly, and Russ had all gone home to get some shuteye. They had all pulled their share of overtime, and it wouldn't do the department any good if all the investigators were exhausted at the same time. This way, the other half of the unit would get some rest and be ready to return to work when Mac and Dana called it quits.

Mac wondered how Philly was handling the shooting. He'd have to go on administrative leave, and that would be tough for him. Even temporarily losing another detective, especially one as seasoned as Philly, would be hard for the entire department.

He and Dana needed to stay on duty until the crime lab responded to recover the car and the house was secured. Once they were done, they could have Sergeant Bledsoe return the warrant to the judge, which was required after the warrant had been served, with a complete list of evidence that had been seized.

"The lab will be here by eight," Mac told Dana.

She was photographing the outside of the Buick with her digital camera. "Good, I'm dead on my feet. How long do you think it'll take them to process?"

"Couple of hours, I suppose, unless they find an area they really want to dig into. I can hang out if you want to go back home and grab some sleep. We'll need to let Sara's family know about Sinnott and look for any connections there."

Dana arched her back, placing her hands on her hips to stretch. The digital camera hung from her neck by a narrow strap. "Actually, that sounds pretty good. The only problem is I'm not leaving my partner behind while I go home to sleep." She brought the camera to her face and continued with the photos. "Besides. We came together in the van, remember?"

Mac appreciated her dedication. He walked back to the van to let Lucy out, taking a few tosses with the tennis ball so she could stretch her legs. Then after putting her back into the vehicle, drove it up to the house and into the driveway. The blue crime lab pickup pulled up behind him. Mac got out and waved. Angela was sitting in the passenger seat, and the driver was a male lab technician who would act as her assistant while she processed the vehicle and whatever else Mac and Dana requested at the scene.

"Morning, Mac. Heard you got our guy." Angela exited the truck with a cup of coffee in her hand. "Sorry it turned ugly in the end, but Sinnott probably saved us taxpayers hundreds of thousands of dollars by getting himself killed. I feel bad for the trooper; he must be kicking himself. At least Sinnott didn't take one of you with him."

"For sure." He shook hands with her and then greeted the driver. "Thanks for coming out. I'm Mac."

"Morning. I'm Richard Anderson." The man shook Mac's hand. "What happened to the house?"

"We had a minor standoff with Mr. Sinnott, which took us into the wee morning hours. You can see the patch job we had to do on the front door after the V-150 came knocking." Mac pointed to the front door. Uniformed troopers had covered the gaping hole left by the rammer bar with two plywood sheets and some two-by-fours to protect the integrity of the house.

"SWAT does tend to make a mess at a crime scene." Angela took a sip of coffee from her lidded cup. "Almost as bad as firemen with their water hoses and axes."

Mac laughed at the observation. "Sinnott kept us busy for a while, but we were able to perform a thorough search of the house."

"Yield anything?" Angela asked.

"We didn't find much in there, just some porn and a little dope in his bedroom. No smoking guns. Oh, before I forget," Mac said. "Sinnott had what looks like three scratches on his face, consistent with our theory about Sara fighting with him when she received the DNA transfer under the fingernail."

"I knew it." Angela slapped the hood of the truck. "Good for you, Sara. At least you hurt him."

Mac nodded toward the back yard. "We found the Buick he'd listed on his registration form in a pole barn at the back of the property. We haven't gone through it yet, just photographed the outside. I have a key, and we'd like you two to give it the once-over if you don't mind."

"Sure, glad to. Anything concrete that tells us Sara was transported in the car?"

"If Sinnott worked alone, this was probably his only means of transportation. As you know, Kristen is thinking the cause of death is asphyxiation. There were ligature marks on her neck and some bruising. Also, there's an indication he used duct tape to restrain her. I'm not expecting a big pool of blood or anything, but we are still looking for any connection between Sinnott and Sara. And the Indian reservation. I'd like to know why he stuffed that bag and stone into her mouth." It still bothered Mac that there had been no prints at the crime scene, but a seasoned criminal like Owen Sinnott had probably used gloves.

"Right. That is bizarre. Wonder what the connection is."

"The jury's still out. We were thinking a connection to the Indian casino or the Warm Springs Reservation because of some other evidence, but this really throws me for a loop. There's no obvious connection with Owen Sinnott and the tribe or with Senator Wilde. On the other hand, Sinnott claims to be of Native American descent. Every indication is that this guy is a predatory sex offender who raped and killed Sara and then got rid of the evidence. It may be as simple and horrible as that. But why bury her that far east? And why stuff a carved stone and beaded leather pouch in her mouth as if he were making a statement? I don't see a guy like Sinnott taking up the plight of the tribe or being politically motivated. He strikes me more as the type who's only in it for himself. You should have seen him last night—pure arrogance."

She glanced at the house. "All right, what say we get started, Richard?"

Richard and Angela pulled their truck around and then opened the canopy to access their tools. Both applied latex gloves and grabbed separate tool kits from the back of the car and followed Mac to the barn.

While Angela dusted for prints on the exterior, Richard took a second set of photographs, far more detailed than the set Dana had taken. He would photograph every inch of the car, giving special detail to the tire tread and the areas where Angela was able to lift prints. Once the car was released and the warrant returned, their authority to search the vehicle would end, so they took meticulous care to capture all the evidence they might need.

They started by processing the driver compartment of the vehicle. The interior of the car was a mess, fast-food wrappers and want ads tossed in the backseat. There was so much filth in the car that fruit-fly-type bugs were swarming all over the vehicle. Apparently, Sinnott had created his own ecosystem in his grand-mother's car by failing to throw out his refuse. Richard and Angela donned masks in an attempt to cover the sickening smell of the garbage.

While Angela was printing the front passenger area of the car, Richard began examining each item of garbage in the backseat. "This is why we get the big bucks," he muttered under his respira-tory mask as he searched through the trash.

Angela printed the front driver and passenger portion of the car, then began vacuuming the area with a special tool that gathered the collected items in a receptacle for future examination. Angela main-tained DNA and hair samples from Sara Watson back at the lab, so finding evidence in Sinnott's car that matched Sara's would put the nail in the coffin and they could officially close the case.

When Angela turned off the vacuum, Richard emerged from the backseat. "I think I've found something." He pulled the mask down and lifted up a torn paper bag with a half-eaten corn dog inside, garnished with hardened mustard.

"A corn dog?" Dana asked.

"Not the corn dog, the receipt that was inside the bag. Look at the date on the receipt. He got ten bucks in gas, a forty-ounce Coors, a lotto ticket, and two corn dogs," Richard read from the receipt before handing it to Dana.

"It's dated the day after Sara was reported missing," Dana said. "At eight in the evening from the Summit Chevron."

"Isn't that the gas station between Government Camp and the reservation?" Angela asked. "The stop-and-rob place that looks like it's in the middle of nowhere along Highway 26?"

"That's the one," Richard said. "I always stop there for a Big Gulp when I'm heading to Bend."

"Right, and it's only about twenty miles from where Sara's body was dumped. Good job, Richard." Mac slapped the young tech on the back. "This will be one more piece of circumstantial evidence to close out this case. We'd better take a trip up to the Summit Chevron tomorrow, Dana. In fact, we should get a trooper up there in case there are some surveillance tapes we want to check out."

"Good idea. I'll get on it right now." Dana pulled her cell phone from her vest to call dispatch and make the request for a Government Camp trooper to contact the store manager. They would still have to make a personal visit to the location, but they didn't want to find out the owner had recycled the videotape. Five weeks—almost six weeks now—was a long time. They would also have to make sure the receipts the cash register was issuing had the correct time and date.

After Richard and Angela completed their search of the back-seat garbage, Angela vacuumed the floor like she had done with the front seat area to collect trace materials like crumbs and hairs. There was so much debris, she filled up three of the hockey-puck-sized canisters before completing the task. Most of it would be plain old filth, but there may be a hair or two belonging to Sara. For this hope, Angela would assign a scientist the painstaking task of searching through all three canisters for trace evidence. Once the vacuuming was complete, they photographed the vehicle in a cleaner state before returning all the non-evidence items to the backseat.

All that remained now was the trunk of the car, which Mac thought bore the greatest potential of holding evidence. He popped the trunk after ensuring that Angela had completed her search for latent prints. After turning the key and lifting the trunk lid, Mac peered inside. "The trunk looks pretty clean." A spare tire sat in the back, along with a set of jumper cables and some motor oil. Off to one side, Mac spotted a roll of duct tape and pointed it out to Angela, who took photographs and bagged it. They also found some dirt. Mac stepped back to let Angela complete her forensic examination.

She pushed the trunk lid all the way up, lifting her camera to photograph the top. "Whoa. What do we have here?"

Mac and Richard leaned forward. "What is it, where?" Richard asked.

"On the trunk lid." Angela bit into her bottom lip.

Richard shined his flashlight to highlight several scratch marks. The scratch marks had gone through the paint, in parallel patterns of three or four scratches.

Angela grimaced. "These were made by human fingernails, guys."

Mac whistled. "If these were made by Sara Watson, she was still alive when he transported her."

He looked around for Dana and found her just outside, taking pictures of a flower garden.

"What are you doing?" Mac asked. "Find something?"

"I don't know." Dana pointed to the flowers. "I was admiring Alma's flowers and noticed that all the beds were overgrown except for this one. Look how the soil has been disturbed."

"Maybe Sinnott was getting the yard in shape so he could sell the place." Mac doubted that was the case.

Dana shook her head. "Beautification would start in front of the house. Sinnott doesn't strike me as the type to care about the flowerbeds in front or back for any reason."

"You're right about that. Do you suppose he's buried something there?"

"Like bloody clothes?" Dana looked hopeful.

"We'd better have a look. I'll go back to the van and get a shovel. Say, Angela," he stepped back into the barn. "Dana might have something. Someone's been digging in the flowerbed. Disturbed soil in this guy's yard is mighty suspicious." He glanced at the smaller shed. "Maybe we'd better take a look at the shed. Confiscate any shovels we might find. We should do a soil analysis of those as well as the dirt we found in the trunk. We might be able to put one of his shovels at the body dump."

"Good thinking, Mac." Dana took several more photos of the flowerbed. "There's a good shoe print here. Let's capture that too."

"Will do," Angela said. "We'll finish up the car first. You guys can do the print if you want."

Dana photographed the print, exchanging her digital camera for a 35 mm in their crime-scene kit so she could photograph in black and white. The black-and-white film was always the best for tire tracks and footprints, almost bringing a 3D appearance to the image. Mac mixed up some plaster from a box of the powder in his kit, applying the sticky solution to the ground on and around the print. After it dried, they would be able to lift a plaster cast of the print for future analysis.

"You ready for Big Foot now?" Dana joked as Mac stood up to admire his handiwork.

"I've wanted to try this out for some time; it looks easier in training class. I've never done it at a real scene, because the prints have never been in good soil like this. They're always in sawdust or mud or something."

Mac got a shovel from the van, while Dana grabbed the supplies needed to secure the shoe print cast after the plaster dried. Once they'd salvaged the print and gotten a soil sample, Mac started moving the soil. In less than five minutes, he had unearthed a human hand.

THIRTY

Mac made a call to their sergeant, who promptly turned this new crime over to the East County Major Crime Team, an investigative group comprised of city and county investigators within Multnomah County. Mac was a member of the team, representing OSP, but their resources were maxed with the investigation involving so many victims. They were also down one homicide team with Philly out of the game and Russ placed in a support role for him. The jury was still out on whether the captain would place Mac and Dana on administrative leave, complete with a mandatory psych exam, just because they had witnessed Sinnott's shooting.

With a new crime scene, Dana and Mac would need to go back and write an addendum to their warrant. While Angela and Richard completed the forensic examination of the Buick, Mac and Dana made one more cursory search of the house and then released their scene to the local police, who would deal with the new crime and the body they had found. They did, however, stick around to assist the OSP lab, a deputy medical examiner, and the local authorities in exhuming the body.

Silver hair attached to part of the skull suggested the body might be that of Alma Sinnott. That and the fact that throughout the search there'd been no sign of anyone other than Owen Sinnott living in the house. They had, however, found a recent Social Security check among some papers in the kitchen. This grave, like Sara's, contained lime, which in this case had helped to decompose the body. Time of death would be hard to pinpoint, although the CSI techs would narrow it down to a best guess depending on the level of decomposition. Mac hated to give up the subsequent death investigation, but there'd be no argument from him. He and Dana already had a full plate and more.

It was after two in the afternoon when Mac and Dana finally got back to the office and dropped off the van. They went inside to meet with Sergeant Bledsoe, handing over an itemized list of the evidence seized for the search warrant and briefing him on their findings in the car's trunk.

Sinnott's move to cut off Sara's fingernails made sense, especially after she'd scratched his face. He probably wanted to make sure they didn't discover any trace evidence under her nails. Sinnott had been smart to cut nails but stupid and careless not to account for all of the trimmings, and beyond stupid to have left damning evidence in the back of his car.

Mac had to spend another half hour typing a witness statement for county investigators who were documenting Philly's shooting. He would submit to a formal interview later, in addition to an eventual grand jury review to see if the shooting was justified. Mac wasn't worried about that; the shooting was clean, and the review was nothing more than a formality at this point. This wasn't Philly's first officer-involved shooting. He'd bounced back OK from the others—that is, if you consider alcoholism and ruined marriages bouncing back.

Mac and Dana would close out the Sinnott case with reports, as it related to Sara Watson. Now that Sinnott was in the morgue, they had time on their side and could tie up loose ends later. His death would be documented by outside investigators, who would also look into the second grave unearthed in the back of the house. Hopefully that would be the last corpse they had to deal with that was associated with Sinnott or his grandmother's home.

Mac thought about taking a nap and coming back to work later, but he decided instead to call it a day and hit it hard again tomorrow. Maybe even take the weekend off. They had their bad guy, and everything now would be a matter of making sure all the paperwork was in order.

With Lucy in tow, Mac dropped off Dana and started for home. He drove on autopilot, parked in his driveway, and went straight to bed.

Unfortunately, Mac couldn't sleep. They had their guy, and Mac should have been happy with that—but something just wasn't adding up. Sinnott was a rapist and a killer with no apparent motive. The place where Sara had been found and the talisman shoved into her mouth just didn't jive with Sinnott's MO. That part of the crime didn't make sense. Add that to the fact that the beaded bag had likely been taken from Sara's collection, and he had a giant puzzle with some of the key pieces missing. He still thought the murder had a revenge feel to it.

Mac punched his pillow. "Unless Sinnott was hired to do the job." He made a mental note to go over Owen Sinnott's phone records and bank statements when he got to the office—see if there had been a substantial deposit made around five weeks ago. There had to be a direct connection between their killer and Sara, and he intended to find it. On the other hand, would Sinnott even have a bank account? A guy like him would probably deal on a cash-only basis.

MAC AWOKE AROUND SEVEN in the evening to the phone ringing. He decided to let it ring; if it was important, they had his pager number. He didn't want to disturb a trancelike sleep for a sales call. Hearing his recorder pick up, Mac rolled over and closed his eyes. 7:00 p.m. Did he want to get up now and try to get to bed at a normal time, or stay in bed for fourteen hours? While trying to make up his mind, he fell back to sleep.

He woke up at five and was back in the office by six thirty, dictating reports and tying up loose ends. Dana had told him the night before that she'd meet him at the office around seven.

"Morning," Kevin greeted when he came in.

"Morning, Sarge." Mac clicked off his recorder to greet his old partner. He'd been dictating for half an hour.

"You get any sleep last night?"

"Too much." Mac yawned as if to punctuate the statement. "Slept right through the night without getting up. I was beat, still feel beat."

"Understandably. You and Dana did a great job yesterday, Mac. I wanted to let you know that before the crew gets in. I know the crime lab gave us a big boost, but we wouldn't have a case without the hard work you and Dana put in."

"Thanks."

Kevin folded his arms and leaned his hip against the desk. "Changing the subject, what's on the agenda for today?"

"First thing is to pay a courtesy call to Scott Watson, the victim's husband. We need to tell him about Sinnott. Then we're going to head back up toward Warm Springs and meet Officer Webb at that Chevron Station near the reservation. I have a few questions on the receipt and want to double check to make sure there are no surveillance tapes."

"Nothing panned out when the trooper went by?"

"Nope. I just want to make double sure before we close out the lead."

"It looks as though we have a clean case." Kevin seemed pleased, and Mac hated to disillusion him.

"I'm not so sure. Even with Sinnott's record, his DNA found on the fingernail, and the scratches in the trunk of his car, this is by no means a slam dunk." The doubts from the night before crept into Mac's mind. "I still have some concerns, motivation being one. Sinnott's attack on Sara may have been random, but some things aren't adding up."

"I've been thinking the same thing, Mac." Dana came around the corner of the cubicle. "I've been trying to come up with an explanation for the beaded bag and stone. It doesn't fit into the equation. Neither does the burial place. Sinnott buried his grandmother in the back yard, and there may be others. So why bury Sara out by the reservation?"

"We don't know for sure that the body is his grandmother," Mac said.

"No, but the point is, he didn't travel three hours to dump her body."

"You make a good point, Dana." Kevin narrowed his eyes. "You're thinking someone hired him?"

"The thought crossed my mind." Mac glanced at Dana.

Kevin nodded. "Then we'll want to do some more detailed investigating into who among Sara's friends and family might want to see her dead—maybe we can find someone with a connection to Sinnott. I don't want you to put too much time and resources into it, though." Kevin turned to Dana. "I was just telling Mac what a great job you two did. Finding that key piece of evidence was a real feather in your cap, Dana. I'm very proud of you both."

"Thanks, Sarge. We have great mentors."

Kevin didn't refute the comment. He glanced at his watch. "Philly and I have a nine o'clock, so I'd better go."

"Say no more; we're just leaving." Mac stood and pulled on his suit jacket.

Mac had no doubt the meeting was to discuss Philly's behavior on Thursday night. He was glad he hadn't been the one to kill the guy, but he felt bad for his co-worker. Unfortunately, Philly had some other things to answer for as well. Mac hated to think what might have happened if they'd had to go to court. A good lawyer could have hit on the police brutality and gotten Sinnott some sympathy from the jury or even a few bucks on a lawsuit.

Kevin sighed, no doubt reluctant to have to confront his long-time friend and former partner. "Hey, Mac, Dana. I'll get Sinnott's phone records while you're gone. We'll want to go through them—see who he's calling and who is calling him. Bank records as well."

"Appreciate that, boss." Mac gave a wave as he walked out.

On the way to the car, Mac called Nate to see if he wanted to meet them for lunch at Government Camp, and they agreed to hook up around eleven.

Dana made a second call to Scott Watson to let him know they were coming. She let it ring several times. "Hmm. He's either not answering, or he's out. His machine isn't picking up."

"Maybe he's gone into hiding. I'm sure the press went into a feeding frenzy when they heard about Sinnott." Thankfully, the OSP public information officer was fielding all the calls so Mac and Dana could remain free to work the case.

"Think we should leave him alone?"

"No. If I were Scott, I'd want details." Mac kept driving and they arrived at the house ten minutes later.

"Are you planning to go see the senator? I'm sure he'll want the details too."

"We don't need to. Superintendent Clark is contacting him personally this morning." Although Mac usually liked to contact the relatives himself, he didn't miss making that particular house call. "To be honest, I don't care if I ever meet up with Grant Stokely again. The senator, too, for that matter."

Dana smiled. "I know what you mean. But what if one of them hired Sinnott?"

"That's doubtful. What would the motive be?" Both men made him uncomfortable for different reasons. Stokely was just plain condescending, but Senator Wilde's disposition was a little tougher to put a finger on. Mac decided it was because he was a politician.

She shrugged. "Maybe Sara knew some secrets about the senator or Grant. It wouldn't be the first time."

"True. Essentially, we're back to square one. We can't rule out anyone at this point. And her being buried with her own Indian artifacts may mean we're still looking at Therman Post or someone else on the reservation. As far as that goes, the cousin could have hired a hit, or the aunt."

Mac pulled his car into the driveway and waited while Dana rang the doorbell. Maybe they'd get lucky and Scott would be home. After a couple of minutes, she opened the storm door and left her business card wedged between the door and frame.

"Let's hit the road, Mac." Dana climbed back into the car. "He's either not home or doesn't want to talk to us. Either way, I vote we head to Government Camp and check in with Scott later. I really doubt he hired Sinnott, but you're right. We need to look at everyone connected with Sara very carefully."

After a quick stop at the coffee drive-through, they drove east again. They arrived at the Summit Chevron, on the east side of Mount Hood, in about an hour and fifteen minutes. It was ten thirty, which gave them just enough time to interview the store manager.

Within minutes, they made contact with the store manager and showed him a copy of the receipt they had recovered in the back of Sinnott's car. He confirmed that the receipt was from his store and that he had been working when Sinnott bought the stuff. Mac showed him a photo. He glanced at it and handed it back. "Sorry, I couldn't say whether he was here or not. We get hundreds of people coming through here every day. Heck, I can't even remember what I had for breakfast this morning, let alone who bought a corn dog five weeks ago."

"'I can appreciate that. Do you mind if we check the time on your register? We need to make sure we have the right time on the receipt.'"

"No problem."

Mac bought a pack of gum so he could get a receipt from the store's single register. "Right on the money." Mac compared the time on the receipt to his own watch.

"One more thing, and we'll let you get back to work," Dana said. "We asked one of our troopers to pick up a surveillance tape if there was one available."

The manager shook his head. "We've got two of them, but neither one of them is working. Sorry. They stopped working over a year ago, and I haven't replaced them."

They thanked the manager and started back toward Government Camp.

Nate's police truck was parked outside the Huckleberry Inn restaurant, and Nate was seated in a corner booth.

"Good morning, Mac, Dana." Nate stood and reached out to shake hands with them.

"Morning, Nate. Have a good drive?" Mac waited for Dana to scoot in and then sat down beside her.

"I was a little early, so I stopped in at your ODOT shops and chatted for a while with the road crews. Several tribal members work up here, so we knew some of the same people."

"Have you ordered yet?" Mac grabbed a menu.

"Just coffee." Nate handed them each a menu and then opened his.

"Thanks." Dana took the menu. "What's good here? I'm starving."

"Me too." Mac perused the featured items. "I haven't eaten an actual meal for about twenty-four hours." He slapped the menu shut. When the waitress came, he ordered biscuits and gravy with eggs, hash browns, and ham.

After ordering their meals, Mac and Dana brought Nate up to speed on the case's latest events. Nate wanted all the details about the forensics process and Sinnott's eventual arrest and death. They talked all through their meal, eventually coming to the end of the tale.

"Now that you have your guy, I don't suppose you want me to follow up with Aaron, right?"

"Who?"

"Denise Galbraith's son. Sara's cousin."

"Yeah, what did you find out?" Mac drained his coffee cup.

"Not much. Aaron seems like a nice guy. Says he couldn't care less about the beadwork and the stone. That's his mother's thing. He liked Sara, had no problems with her. She had money, but that never got in the way of their friendship."

"You believe him?" Dana asked.

Nate shrugged. "No reason not to. Besides he has an alibi for the time Sara was killed. He was working at the casino, and his friend, the guy he's staying with, says he's been on the rez for the last three months."

"Alibis aren't worth much at this point," Mac said. "Find out if he knows Sinnott or if there's any connection."

"Sure. I'll run the name past Therman too."

"Did you get that list from Therman?" Mac asked.

"I did, but no red flags there. I'll check again, though, to see if anyone knows Sinnott."

At twelve thirty, Mac announced that they needed to get back to work.

"Anything else I can do to help?" Nate asked.

"Yeah. Find out who might have hired Sinnott." Mac grinned.

"The more I think about it, the more convinced I am that Sinnott didn't act alone."

"I have to agree." Nate reached over and grabbed the check when the server approached.

"Oh, no you don't." Mac tried to grab the check out of Nate's hand.

"Don't worry, I'll get my money's worth out of you when you come out to the farm." Nate went to the counter to pay the tab.

Mac and Dana walked out into the sunshine, and Nate followed them out a few moments later. "Hey guys. I got something for you. Hang on a sec."

Leaning into the cab of his truck, he pulled a brown grocery sack from the passenger seat and handed it to Mac. "I wrapped it myself." He grinned.

Mac reached in and pulled out a thick animal fur hat. "Let me guess; it's the badger hide." Mac slipped the hat over his head. "How do I look?"

"Like a nut." Dana laughed.

"Oh, I think he could pass for Daniel Boone. Besides, it'll keep your head warm. You're right, though. It is a badger, but not *the* badger. I haven't finished tanning that hide yet. This one is from my place."

"Thank you, Nate." Mac admired the sturdy stitching.

"This is for you, Dana. My wife made it." Nate handed her a beautiful blue and white beaded necklace.

"Oh, my goodness, she made this for me?"

"Yes, wear it in good health. I told my wife you had blond hair and blue eyes. She thought you would enjoy these colors."

"It's gorgeous, thank you." Dana gave him a hug and slipped the beaded necklace into the pocket of her jacket.

He laughed. "You're welcome. Shelly said you should come out to the farm with Mac. She'll show you how to bead."

"I just might do that."

Nate took a step back. "I guess I better get back to my side of the mountain and get to work. Good to see you both again."

"I sure like that guy," Mac said as he folded himself into the Crown Vic.

"Me too. Wish he worked for our department. Are you really going to go to his place and drive a tractor?"

"You bet I am. I may just quit this job and become a farmer. You never know."

"Yeah, Antonio McAllister, the farmer. That'll be the day."

Mac laughed right along with her. The job could be exhausting and maddening, but he loved it. And right now, he wanted nothing more than to figure out who had hired Sinnott to kill Sara.

MAC AND DANA WERE DISAPPOINTED and relieved when their call to Kevin resulted in both of them taking the rest of Saturday and Sunday off to rest and regroup. They'd been working nonstop and Kevin insisted they take a much-needed break.

Mac had mixed feelings, but he didn't argue the point. He took Lucy out and did some walking down in Vancouver's riverfront park. On Sunday, he went to church with Nana and took her and Dana to lunch. Once home, he caught a Mariners game, played catch with Lucy, and napped. By Monday, he felt refreshed and ready to tackle the case again.

The first item on their agenda was to talk to Scott Watson to let him know about Owen Sinnot. They called early to catch him before he left for the office. He seemed reluctant, but finally agreed to wait for them.

"Come in." Scott opened the door for them and stepped back to let them in. "I thought you'd be by yesterday. Saw on the news that you caught the guy who killed Sara."

"We tried to call," Dana said, "but you didn't answer."

He nodded. "I had to run to the office. I was there most of the afternoon trying to get caught up." He closed the door behind them. "Have a seat. Um—I can't tell you how much I appreciate all you've done. You guys are good, I'll give you that."

"Thank you, but it's not over yet."

He frowned. "Why's that?"

"We still have to make sure everything checks out," Mac said. "But, yes, it looks like we have the man who killed Sara."

Scott sank onto the sofa. "I can't begin to tell you how relieved I am to have this case closed."

Mac kept his gaze on Scott. "It may not be as simple as that."

"What do you mean?" Scott's eyes widened.

"We're not sure Own Sinnott was acting on his own. We think Owen may have been working for or with someone."

Scott frowned. "You're saying someone hired him to kill Sara?"

"Possibly. We have a photo of Mr. Sinnott." He nodded toward Dana, who was already taking it out of her briefcase. Mac handed the mug shot to Scott. "Do you recognize him?"

After studying it for a moment, he said, "I can't say for sure, but he may have done some work for our firm. I don't see how that's possible. I make it a point not to hire felons—especially guys like him."

"But you've seen him before?"

"I think so."

Mac took the picture back. "Could you check your personnel files?"

Scott shook his head. "He wouldn't have worked for us directly, but he might have been hired by one of our contractors."

"We'll want to talk to whoever hired him."

"I'll look into it and try to get you a name."

"Thanks." Mac would do some checking on his own.

"I can't believe this." Scott stared down at his hands. "You try to protect your family from scum like this and . . ." He brought both hands up to cover his face and then drove them through his hair.

Genuine shock or overacting? Mac couldn't be sure. "We're having to work the investigation from scratch, and I wonder if you'd be willing to take another polygraph for us."

He jerked to his feet. "Another one? No. I already went through that. They told me it wasn't accurate because of the antidepressant I'm on. Nothing has changed." He paced to the kitchen and back. "I didn't kill Sara, and I didn't have her killed. I loved her."

"No one is saying you didn't." Mac stood.

"You guys have been on my case since day one." He turned to face them. "Well, no more. If you want to talk to me, you do it through my attorney. I've had it. You catch the guy who killed her, and even that isn't good enough for you." He strode to the door and opened it. "Now get out."

"We'll be in touch," Mac said as he and Dana stepped outside. The door slammed shut behind them.

"Whew." Mac glanced back at the house. "We hit a sore spot."

They got into the car and Mac started down the driveway before Dana responded. "I could be wrong, Mac, but I don't think his anger was a sign of guilt."

"Why?" Mac didn't blame the guy for being upset. Truth be told, he might have reacted in a similar way.

"He was fine with us until you mentioned the polygraph. He even told us he thought he'd seen Sinnott before. If he was the one who hired the hit, I doubt he'd have given us that information."

"Maybe."

"At least we have a possible connection between Sinnott and Sara."

"Let's get back to the office and have a closer look at Sinnott's records. Kevin should have them by now."

THIRTY-ONE

On the way back to the office, Dana's cell rang. "Detective Bennett."

"Dana, this is Claire Montgomery, Sara's cousin."

"Yes, Claire." She glanced over at Mac. "How can I help you?"

"I just spoke to Scott, and he's terribly upset. He didn't have anything to do with Sara's death. You have to believe him."

"I'm sorry, but we really can't rule anyone out at this point."

"I understand. It's just that . . . if you want someone with motive, you should look at Grant Stokely. Sara hated him, and he felt the same way about her."

Dana fumbled around for a pen, and Mac handed over his along with a pad from his jacket pocket. "I'm interested. Tell me what you know."

"Maybe he didn't exactly hate her, but he didn't like the idea of her appearing in public with my father."

"Why not?"

"B-because of her other family and her political views."

"Her political views?" Dana asked for clarification. "I'm not seeing a motive for murder."

"Grant has great aspirations. He'd like to run for office. Sara didn't like him, and she knew something about him that could have ruined any chance he had of running for office."

Dana questioned that but prodded Claire for more.

"It goes deeper than that, though," Claire went on. "Grant wanted to date her, and I think she went out with him once before she married Scott, but . . . I'm not sure—she never would say, but I think he may have used that date-rape drug on her."

"If that's true, why wouldn't she go to the police?" Dana was reeling with all this late information that Claire had mysteriously withheld earlier. "And why didn't you say something to us sooner?"

"It's complicated. Grant's father is very wealthy. He and my father are good friends. Grant's dad got him the job. She couldn't very well say anything, or Stokely would have cut his financial support. And she didn't really have any proof. I told her to at least tell Dad, but she wouldn't and told me not to tell either."

"Why didn't you tell us this sooner?" Dana repeated.

"You told me to think about any enemies she might have. I didn't remember about Grant until the other day. Grant was in Salem when Sara disappeared, but if he hired that Sinnott guy . . . Anyway, he's the one you should be looking at, not Scott."

"All right." Dana jotted down the rest of the information. "Thanks for the call. We'll follow up on it."

"Thank you."

"What was that all about?" Mac asked when she closed her phone.

"Claire thinks we should look more closely at Grant Stokely." She relayed the rest of the conversation.

"Interesting."

Dana smiled. "I thought you might say that. Let's set up an appointment with Grant for tomorrow. We need to check this out."

"I have a better idea. Why don't we take a run to Salem right now? The phone records can wait." Mac grinned. "Or better yet, let's call Kevin and see if he can assign someone else to that detail."

"Now you're thinking." Dana called and placed the speaker on so they could both talk to their sergeant. Dana related her conversation with Claire.

"We thought we should follow up on Stokely right away and maybe tackle the phone records and bank statement when we get back. Unless someone there can do it."

"I'm for you going to Salem," Kevin said. "I'll get Russ on Sinnott's phone and bank records. I'll run Stokely's name through our Law Enforcement Data System and Equifax records and see if I can come up with anything on criminal associates or credit history problems."

"The FBI didn't find anything," Mac said. "I read through all their profiles. Except for a few traffic violations, the family and friends are all clean. But it's been five weeks, so it wouldn't hurt to check again." Fortunately, the feds had gotten baseline prints and DNA samples from most of the players as well, so a lot of the groundwork was done.

"I doubt we'll find anything, but you never know. I don't think the senator would keep him around if he weren't clean."

"Anything else?" Kevin asked.

"We asked Nate to follow through on the people connected with the casino and with Aaron Galbraith—he's Sara's cousin—who lives on the reservation. We're focusing mostly on finding any kind of connection any of them had with Sinnott. I hope that was OK. I probably should have asked you first."

"That's fine, Mac. In fact, it's more than OK. Philly will be out for a few weeks, so we can use all the help we can get."

"Good. My thinking is that he'll get farther and faster than us." Mac maneuvered them onto the I-5 freeway and pointed the Crown Vic toward Salem. Traffic was heavy and Mac moved into the left lane.

"Sarge, one more thing." Dana thumbed through an open file she'd pulled from her briefcase. "I didn't see any mention in the FBI files about Aaron Galbraith. I can't believe they missed that part of the family. We should run his name through LEDS and the Portland Police Data System too."

"I'll do that. Want me to give the agents a call? Maybe they inadvertently left out some stuff."

"Yeah. Thanks, Sarge." Dana raised an eyebrow at Mac. "Heck of a thing to leave out."

"I agree," Kevin said. "You two be careful out there."

He hung up, and Mac initiated the siren and lights. They reached the outskirts of Salem in forty minutes. Kevin called just as they exited on Hawthorne. "I talked to Lauden. He says you should have the report on the Galbraiths. He and Miller talked to Denise and her son. They had alibis for the time Sara disappeared, so they didn't follow up—no reason to."

"That's it?"

"You have to remember that at the time, they didn't have a body or that Indian beadwork."

"True. So why don't we have the paperwork?" Dana asked.

"Lauden said he'd check into it. It's probably a clerical error. Not that it will be much help, but he's faxing over the information."

"Did you find anything on Stokely?" Mac asked.

"Just what you might suspect. He was a straight-A student, class president in his senior year, and he has a father with money and pull. His father and Senator Wilde are friends. Just one thing you need to know, though. He has a permit to carry a concealed weapon."

Mac promised to call Kevin as soon as they finished their interview with Grant Stokely.

They parked in an official space near the senator's office and started in. "You want to take the lead on this guy, Dana?"

"You bet."

Stokely smiled when he greeted them, but his eyes clearly indicated that he was not happy to see them. "Detective Bennett, McAllister. This is a surprise. You should have called. I'm afraid the senator is in meetings all day." He looked smaller and thinner than Mac remembered.

"Actually, Grant," Dana said, "we're here to see you."

"Me? I'm afraid I don't understand." His gaze darted from one to the other. "I thought you'd already caught the man who killed Sara."

"The investigation is far from finished." Dana moved forward, forcing him to take a step back. "Do you have a more private place where we can chat? Mac and I have a few questions for you."

"S-sure." He turned slightly and gestured toward the hallway. "My office is back here."

He led them in the same direction as before, going just past the senator's office and into the room with the open door. Unlike the senator's overly tidy office, this one looked lived in. Stacks of paper covered the desk and tabletops as well as the one extra chair. "Um—sorry about the mess." He grabbed a stack of papers off the chair. "You can sit in my chair, Detective McAllister. I'll get another chair from the office next door."

"That's OK, Grant," Mac said, taking notice of his uncharacteristic politeness. "I can stand."

"All right." Grant didn't like the idea, but he rolled his chair back slightly and sat down. "What can I do for you?"

Dana had pulled a pad and pen out of her briefcase. "You can start by telling us about your relationship with Sara Watson."

"S-Sara . . ." A flush started at the base of his neck and worked its way up into his cheeks. "I didn't have a relationship with her. She was the senator's niece. I knew her. That's all."

"I heard that you and Sara had a history—that she didn't like you, and you didn't like her."

"Then you heard wrong. I knew Sara in high school. Claire, too, for that matter, but we ran in different circles."

"You wanted to date her, and she rejected you."

"Wait a minute." He eyed them warily. "You think I had something to do with Sara's death?"

"Did you?" Dana kept her gaze steady on him. Mac crossed his arms and leaned against the wall.

"No! Of course not."

"But you do admit that you didn't like her, that she was a threat to your political career. What did she have on you, Grant?"

"She had nothing, because there was nothing." He shook his head. "I don't know where you got this information, but it's a lie."

"You're saying that there was not a problem between you?"

He sighed and licked his lips. "It's true that Sara and I didn't like each other, but I tolerated her and she tolerated me."

"Why?"

"Why what? Why didn't she like me? I have no idea. I was beneath her, I guess."

"Now see, Grant, that doesn't make much sense." Dana inched closer. "You were class president and on the dean's list. Your parents have money—in fact, isn't it true that your father and the senator are friends? Your father helped you get this job, right?"

"So what? I do a good job."

"A girl doesn't agree to date a guy and then turn around and hate that guy for no reason. What did you do, Grant? Did you do something to her that could land you in prison, maybe involving a date-rape drug?"

His flush turned scarlet. "This conversation is over."

"I'LL HAVE TO START CALLING YOU BARRY," Mac said to Dana as he pushed the elevator button to the first floor.

Dana looked at him as though he'd just sprouted horns. "Why?"

"Short for barracuda." Mac chuckled. "Wow, you were smokin' in there."

She sighed. "You think I was too hard on him?"

"Not at all. I'd say you gave him a lot to think about."

"Mmm. Maybe, but we don't have anything on him other than Claire's suspicions."

"Yeah. It would have given me great pleasure to have read him his rights."

"So what do we do now?" Dana looked worried. "Think we should take our information to the senator?"

"Not yet. I'm for letting Grant sweat for a while."

Minutes later, back in the car, the detectives called Kevin to tell them about their interview with Stokely. "We don't have anything concrete," Mac told him. "Just the cousin saying she thinks he might have raped her. He denies there was a problem but agrees they weren't crazy about each other. It may indicate motive, especially if Sara confronted him. But why would she wait so long?"

"Let's leave him dangling for the moment," Kevin said. "Sinnott's phone records don't show any calls to Stokely or the senator's office, but I have another possible lead. Sinnott made two calls to Scott Watson's business. There's no way to figure out who he talked to there, but the receptionist might remember."

"Great. We'll head over there right away." They were finally getting somewhere, and Mac had the feeling they might be closing in.

It was almost 4:00 p.m. when they pulled into the parking lot of the remodeled building near Montgomery Park where Watson, Simons, and Keller had their offices.

"How do you want to handle this?" Dana asked. "Unless I miss my guess, his secretary is going to be defensive if she thinks we suspect Scott."

Mac pursed his lips. "You're right about that. Claire, his mother, his mother-in-law, his secretary. They're like mother hens where Scott is concerned. Makes you wonder. We want to be careful not to implicate Scott. You want to handle this one?"

"I think you should. She might respond better to a guy."

Jackie's eyes widened when Mac and Dana walked into the suite. "You're the detectives who've been working on Sara's murder investigation."

"Hi, Jackie." Mac came forward, offering a smile that he hoped was friendly and nonthreatening.

She got to her feet. "Did you want to talk to Scott? He just got back in the office, but . . ."

"Actually, I was hoping to ask you a couple of questions."

"Me?" She tilted her head to the side. "OK. I'm not sure I can help. Anyway, I thought you caught the guy who killed her."

"We did." Mac glanced around the reception area and nodded toward some chairs. "Jackie, do you mind if we talk over here?"

"Not at all." She moved to the grouping he indicated, her features tense. The three of them sat down.

Mac opened his briefcase and brought out Sinnott's mug shots. "Do you recognize this man? Ever seen him before?"

Her chest rose and fell as she focused on the pictures. "I don't think so."

"Take your time, Jackie."

She swallowed hard, on the verge of tears. "Is this the man who killed Sara?"

"We believe so, yes. We're trying to find a connection between him and Sara."

She looked at the mug shots again and shuddered. "He was never here. I would have remembered. He's creepy looking, and all those tattoos. . . . You don't forget someone like that."

Mac nodded and took the photos from her. "Does the name Owen Sinnott mean anything to you?"

"Sinnott." Jackie moved her head from side to side, but she seemed unsure.

"We know he made at least two phone calls to this office. We were hoping you might remember who he talked to."

"I don't. I'm sorry."

"Scott told us the guy may have done some work for one of their contractors."

She shrugged. "I wouldn't know about that. I don't usually have anything to do with them unless it's to deliver plans or messages or something."

"Do you have a list of the contractors Scott and his partners may have used over the last couple of years?"

"I could get them for you, but I'd have to ask Scott if it's OK." She glanced at her watch. "I can let him know you're here, and you can wait for him if you want. I'm leaving early today for a doctor's appointment."

Mac nodded. "Sure. Go ahead."

Jackie hurried over to her desk and picked up the phone, letting Scott know the detectives were waiting. "I hate to leave you like this, but I really need to get going."

"Not a problem."

Scott came out a few minutes later, and then he, Mac, and Dana spent the next forty minutes talking to his partners in the boardroom. Scott, who seemed to have eased off the attorney ultimatum from the last time they'd talked, had already spoken to his partners, and they shared the details of how Owen Sinnott came to be working on one of their projects. The men, both Scott's age, looked Ivy League, with dress shirts and ties. Except for the varying shades of hair and eyes, they looked like they'd been cast out of the same mold.

Patrick Simmons and Donovan Keller recognized Sinnott as one of the men the contractor on the last job had hired. "What a fiasco that was," Donovan said. "We ended up firing the contractor and letting a bunch of his guys go. He wasn't very careful about who he hired."

Scott nodded. "We weren't careful enough about checking him out."

Patrick wove a black drawing pencil through his fingers. "That's right. The contractor ended up skipping town without paying his workers. We don't have anything to do with hiring or firing or paying anyone on the payroll except for the contractor. We had several of the men calling and wanting their money, and we couldn't pay it."

"Was Sinnott one of those men, and do any of you remember talking to him?"

"Patrick and I did," Scott said. "I don't know in what order. We both told him he'd have to go to the contractor."

Mac glanced at his partner. Maybe Owen Sinnott had motive after all. "Did he seem angry, or did he threaten you in any way?"

"They were all angry, and I don't blame them, but . . ." Scott stopped. "Do you think he retaliated against us—me—by killing Sara?"

"That is a possibility."

Scott stared out the window, tears gathering in his eyes. He pinched the bridge of his nose. "If I'd had any idea, I would have written him a check."

Patrick clasped Scott's shoulder. "We couldn't have known he'd retaliate."

Donovan splayed his hands. "I had no idea—I mean, we thought the contractor was in big trouble, not us."

MAC AND DANA HIT RUSH-HOUR TRAFFIC and didn't make it back to the office until nearly six. On the way, they filled Kevin in on their discussion with Scott and his partners.

"Good job. Are you satisfied with the findings?"

"Not really," Dana said. "I'd still like to see Grant Stokely behind bars."

Mac still struggled with the feeling that they were missing something. "I still don't know what to make of the Native American tie-in," Mac said. "Maybe Sinnott knew about the clash between the senator and the Confederated Tribes and used it to throw us off."

"That sounds plausible to me."

"I suppose."

"Go home and sleep on it. You can tackle your reports in the morning."

"Good plan. See you in the morning." Mac signed off. "Want to catch something to eat before we head home?"

Dana yawned. "I don't think so, but thanks anyway. I have a date with Jonathan if I get home at a decent hour, but I may even skip that and go to bed right after dinner. I'm beat."

"Did that pervert call you again last night?" Mac asked.

"No, he didn't, but the whole police force must have been hanging around there last night. Did you call them?"

"I did. Hope you don't mind."

"I don't. Thanks."

"Are you seeing Kristen tonight?" Dana asked when they pulled into the lot.

"I was thinking about calling her." And after saying good-bye to Dana, he did just that.

THIRTY-THREE

Claire read the cryptic e-mail from Scott's office in a panic. *Meet me at the Washington Park Zoo at the trailhead to the Japanese Gardens at five. It's urgent. We need to talk. Scott*

Why the Japanese Gardens? Why couldn't he talk to her here at home? Unless . . . Could the police be pressing him again? How could they suspect Scott? Couldn't they see that he was innocent? Apparently her call to put the spotlight on Grant had failed.

Claire felt bad about that. All those years ago, when Sara had come home from her date in a bad mood, she'd never said anything about Grant doing anything wrong. For all Claire knew, they had a personality clash.

She'd been grasping at straws and going mad with worry over Scott. She and Scott had finally acknowledged their love for one another. Maybe he wanted to surprise her with dinner out or something. Claire looked over at the sleeping child. Should she take Chloe and Allysa or get a sitter? A sitter, she decided. She called the next-door neighbor, who had sat for them before, and made the arrangements.

Claire's excitement grew, along with a sense of foreboding and fear. Anxiety. *What if Scott did hire Owen Sinnott to kill Sara? What if you're next?* The thought came unbidden and she pushed it aside. *Not possible.* She'd seen Scott's grief, his hopelessness and his tenderness with Chloe and Allysa and with her. Claire felt guilty for entertaining an idea too ridiculous for words.

Is it really all that bizarre? The night before, when they'd talked about their relationship, Scott admitted to having a brief affair with Jackie before Sara found out she was pregnant. He said he felt he needed to tell her. He seemed genuinely tormented by his indiscretion. "It happened on a weekend," he'd told her. "We'd gone on a business trip, and I needed Jackie there to handle the paperwork. We'd had too much to drink, and when I woke up the next morning, she was there."

"Did Sara know?" Claire asked.

"No. I should have told her, but I couldn't. When I got home from that trip, Sara told me she was pregnant. I couldn't tell her I'd just had sex with my secretary."

Claire understood that. Scott had told her there was nothing between him and Jackie now. They both realized it had been a mistake. It bothered her that Jackie was still working for him, but Claire trusted Scott and couldn't let suspicions cloud her mind. He had truly loved Sara. "And he loves me. That much I'm sure of."

Claire arrived at the giant commuter parking lot five minutes early and drove to the parking area Scott had designated. There were several other cars in the lot when she pulled in, but she didn't recognize Scott's. She drove out of the primary lot to the secluded trailhead lot for the Japanese Gardens. When the paved road turned to gravel, she spotted a single car in the trailhead parking area. No one was in the vehicle, and she suspected the occupants had gone for a walk on the rustic three-mile trail, which was a secondary route into the expansive park's beautiful Japanese Gardens.

Claire wished Scott had picked another meeting place. This one gave her the creeps. It was too close to the woods. Not long ago, a woman had been dragged off the trail and raped. She reached over to lock the doors. Before she had a chance, the passenger door opened. A hooded figure slipped into the seat, but Claire didn't see the face. All she noticed was the gun.

THIRTY-FOUR

"Mac! I'm glad you called." Kristen sounded like her old self.

"Are you home or . . ." He left the question hanging.

"I am."

"Um—have you eaten yet?"

"No, but dinner's on, and there's an extra chair. How does pot roast, mashed potatoes, gravy and fresh green beans sound?"

"Perfect. I'm on my way."

Not only was Kristen back home, but she seemed eager to see him. Mac's spirits took flight. She sounded like her old self. He parked in front of her house, behind her silver Volvo, and was halfway up the steps when Andrew hit the door running and acting as if he hadn't seen Mac in months.

Mac caught him on the fly, hugging the little guy before tossing him up on his shoulders. Kristen was waiting at the door, wearing a white apron over a black dress. Her hair, as always, was different. Tonight it was a blood red and stood up in spikes. Just as he was wondering if he'd ever get used to her wild hair, she planted a kiss on his mouth that left him wanting more.

His gaze settled on hers, searching for answers to questions he still had. *Where are we now? Do we go back to the way we were?*

She smiled and moved away. "You're just in time. Dinner is ready; all I have to do is plate it." To Andrew, she said, "Show Mac where to sit, sweetie."

He set Andrew down and allowed the boy wonder to pull him to the table. He almost lost it when he saw the small piece of yellow construction paper with his name and a stick figure on it."

"You sit here," Andrew patted the chair at the head of the table. "See, I maded you a name tag. It has your picture on it."

"Wow. Looks just like me. I didn't know you could write and draw that well."

He placed his hands on his hips. "I been practicing." Andrew climbed into the chair to Mac's left. "Mommy is sitting over there. I made her a name tag too."

Mac held back a chuckle as he noted the stick figure with red hair sticking out at all angles. "You captured her, Andrew."

Kristen set a plate in front of him, then Andrew. She chuckled. "He did, didn't he?"

She was back in less than a minute with her own plate. Sitting down, she clasped his hand. "Would you say grace for us, Mac?"

He took Andrew's hand. The prayer was sincere, and Mac's heart felt more complete than it had in a long time. This was what he wanted—to come home every night to a little boy and his mom. But did Kristen want the same thing? Maybe he'd find out after dinner.

Unfortunately, life had other plans. They'd eaten dinner and done the dishes and were putting Andrew to bed when he got the call.

"Detective McAllister, this is Scott Watson." There was a break in his voice. "Can you come over right away? Claire is missing."

A FEELING OF DÉJÀ VU settled over Mac as he pulled into Scott Watson's driveway. Dana would be meeting him there. Her attorney friend was to drop her off, and Mac would take her home. His mind had been a flurry of disjointed thoughts as he raced over to the northwest side of town. Sinnott must have had an accomplice after all. Maybe Sinnott had been working with some of the other members of the construction crew. But why take Claire? Could it be that Senator Wilde was the target after all?

Dana pulled in right behind him. She leaned over to give her friend a kiss before exiting the car. Mac remembered seeing him before at the courthouse. He gave a quick wave as the guy drove off and then waited for Dana to join him at the entry. "You look nice." She was dressed in a knee-length black dress and heels with a light-weight iridescent green shawl. She'd pulled her hair up into a chignon and curled the tendrils that framed her face.

"Thanks, I think. I feel funny working in this outfit, but I didn't think I should go all the way home. What's going on?"

"Claire left the kids with a sitter who was here when Scott came home. Apparently, she told the sitter she was meeting Scott and didn't know when she'd be home. Trouble is, Scott came home right after work and claims he doesn't know anything about the meeting."

"That's odd."

Mac reached for the doorbell. "I put out an APB on her and her car."

Scott opened the door. "Thanks for coming. I didn't know who else to call. You guys have been working the case and . . ." He hesitated. "I don't know if there's a connection. The sitter could have heard wrong, but this isn't like Claire."

"You were right to call us," Mac assured him.

Scott turned and introduced them to his neighbor, Mrs. Thompson. After shaking hands, they asked her to tell them what had transpired with Claire.

"She told me she was meeting Scott. She seemed excited." Mrs. Thompson paused. "Maybe a little hesitant, now that I think about it. She left at four thirty and said she was supposed to meet him at five."

"Did she say where?"

"No. She thought maybe he was going to surprise her with dinner or something." She pressed a hand to her chest. "That's all I know. Then when Scott came home—you can imagine my surprise. He didn't know anything about meeting her."

"Where are Chloe and Allysa?" Mac asked.

"In Chloe's room." Scott said. "Allysa is reading to her."

Mac glanced around the kitchen and family room area. "Do you have caller ID? That might give a clue to who she might be meeting."

"I checked. Only one caller all day except for Mrs. Thompson, and that was Claire's mom—she called this morning."

Dana glanced toward the stairs. "I seem to remember Claire saying she was staying in the guest room. Would she have an appointment book—and what about a computer?"

"She uses a laptop," Scott said.

"Do you mind if we check her e-mail?"

"Go ahead. I should have thought about that."

Mrs. Thompson excused herself to look in on the children as Scott led the detectives into the guest room. Claire's laptop was on, and Dana clicked the mailbox. The message from Scott's office flashed on the screen. "Here's the note. It was sent at three fifteen this afternoon. And it has your name on it, Scott."

Mac read the note over her shoulder. "The meeting was at Washington Park near the trailhead for the Japanese Gardens. That's way over by the zoo parking lot."

"I didn't write that." Scott had a white-knuckled grip on the back of the chair. "It's the business address. We each have our own private one. If I were going to e-mail Claire, I'd have used my private account."

"Do you have any idea who might have sent this?"

He shook his head. "Donovan and Patrick left before I did. They were going to a dinner meeting with a client. Jackie left work early for a doctor's appointment. We have office temps once in a while, and a bookkeeper who works out of her home. Maybe someone broke in."

Mac's cell phone vibrated. He excused himself and moved into the hall, away from the others. "Mac here."

"Yeah, it's Kevin. I got your message."

Mac apprised him of the situation and told him about the note. "Better get some uniforms out there."

"I'm on it. By the way, I got the rest of the file from the feds. They cleared Aaron and Denise Galbraith. I also have a list of people whose prints were on the inside of that curio cabinet of Sara's—Sara, Claire, and Jackie Palmer."

"You're sure?"

"Yep—the feds got elimination prints and DNA from all the parties involved."

"OK, thanks." Mac closed the phone and joined the others. "Scott, can you tell me why your secretary's prints are on the inside of the cabinet where Sara kept her Native American collection?"

"No. What does that have to do with anything?" He lowered himself to the bed.

Mac thought it might be time to tell him about the small pouch and rock that had been found in Sara's mouth when they exhumed the body.

Scott stared straight ahead. "You suspect Jackie?"

"Do you?"

"Of course not. I'm sure if her prints were there, she was just looking at the collection. Sara showed that stuff to everybody who took an interest."

"Did Jackie have any reason to want Sara dead? Any reason to harm Claire?"

Scott's silence hung over the room.

Mac kicked himself. They should have spent more time on Scott's relationships—on the women in his life.

Dana turned around in her chair. "Were you having an affair with Jackie?"

He sighed. "A long time ago—it was a one-night thing. I'm sorry it ever happened."

"And she's still working for you? How did Sara feel about that?"

"She never knew. Jackie and I both realized it was a mistake." He stood up and began to pace. "I—I think I've made a terrible mistake."

"What do you mean?"

"Today, Jackie talked about wanting to get back together. I told her that wasn't going to happen. Claire and I—please don't take this the wrong way, but we've fallen in love. I told Jackie I intended to marry Claire. Now Claire's missing."

Another call came in on Mac's cell. "Yeah, Sarge."

"We found an empty vehicle parked near the entrance to the trailhead. It's registered to Jackie Palmer."

"Any sign of Claire?"

"None."

"Great." Mac told Kevin about the affair. "How could we have missed this?"

"Don't beat yourself up about it, Mac. You and Dana took the logical approach. You got Sinnott, and you kept looking. That's what counts."

"Tell that to Scott and Claire."

"Hang on a sec, Mac."

While he waited, Mac tried to clear his head. Jackie had apparently met up with Claire, and he doubted it was to get better acquainted. Jackie's behavior, her apparent closeness to the family, and her wanting to protect Scott made sense now. She'd been dumped once when Scott chose his wife over her. Now she was being passed over again.

"Mac?" Kevin said.

"I'm here."

"Just got a report from an officer who checked Jackie's apartment. She isn't at home."

"All right. Maybe Scott has an idea of where they might be."
Mac had an idea. It was a long shot but worth a try.

"Scott, does Jackie have a cell phone?"

"Yeah, why?"

"I want you to call her."

"I can't." He dropped down on the bed again and pulled the cell
phone out of his pocket.

"What's going on, Mac?" Dana asked.

"Our guys found Jackie's car in Washington Park, where Scott
was supposedly going to meet Claire. There was no sign of Claire or
Jackie. Our uniforms and the city police will do a foot search of the
area. We need to find Jackie, and I'm thinking Scott can help us do
that." Turning to Scott, he added, "I want you to call her. Tell her
you made a mistake, that you want her, not Claire."

"I don't see how that can help."

"There's a chance Claire may still be alive. I want you to make
the call while I listen in. Can you do that?"

He nodded. "I'll try. I still don't understand. How could she do
something like this?"

"Maybe your rejection today sent her over the edge," Dana said,
accepting the phone recorder from Mac and helping Scott place the
tiny receiver piece in his ear without asking his permission. His
cooperation was not an option at this point.

Scott dialed the number, and it rang for a long time. "She isn't
answering, and her voice mail isn't picking up." He stopped when she
finally answered. "Hello." The voice sounded thin and frightened.

"Jackie, it's me, Scott." He looked at Mac as if needing support.

"Why are you calling me?"

"Jackie, I know you set up a meeting with Claire. Please tell me
you didn't do anything stupid."

His comment was met by ragged breathing, then, "How did you
know?"

"I saw your note on the computer. Listen, about what I said today. I'm sorry. I've been giving it a lot of thought and . . . well, you're right. I am making a mistake. You've always been there for me, and . . ." He glanced at Mac as if needing courage.

Mac nodded and mouthed, *"Keep going."*

"I love you. Please tell me you haven't done anything to hurt Claire."

Silence. "You think I'm stupid or something? You're just saying that so I won't hurt Claire."

"No, that's not true. I do love you, Jackie. I need to talk to you."

She sniffed. "You love me?"

"Of course. Are you OK? You sound like you're crying."

"I was. But I . . . I don't know what to do!"

"Just talk to me, Jackie. Can you come over here?"

"N-no. You come here. To your office." The voice seemed stronger now.

"Is Claire with you?"

"Why does that matter?"

"It does. If you and I have any hope of a future together, you mustn't harm Claire." He hesitated. "Jackie?"

"I won't hurt her."

Scott closed his eyes. "Let me talk to her, OK. I want to tell her it's over between us."

"You don't need to, Scott. I'll tell her myself." Jackie's tone had changed from whimpering to haughty. Mac hoped that was a good sign.

"OK. I'll be there in ten minutes max."

Mac remembered to breathe as he turned off the recorder.

"Was that OK?" Scott lowered the phone and handed Mac the earpiece.

"You did fine, Scott."

"I told her ten minutes. I assume you're coming with me."

"You won't be going." Mac read the determination in his brown eyes.

"Please. If you show up instead of me, there's no telling what she'll do."

"It's too dangerous."

"At least let me come. If you need me to talk to her, I can be there." Scott seemed determined, and Mac had a hunch if they didn't bring him along, he'd follow them.

"All right, but you need to let us handle it."

He nodded. "I will."

Mac put in a call to Kevin on the way. Russ and Kevin would meet them there as well as the SWAT team if they were needed, although their ramp-up time would probably delay them for at least an hour.

Mac and Dana were waiting for backup when Scott bolted from the car and ran toward the building. "What the . . ." Mac took out after him, drawing his weapon. "Stop!"

"Scott, stop! We don't want to have to shoot you." Mac still didn't know how involved Scott was in his wife's death. This whole thing could have been a setup to destroy evidence inside the business.

Mac wasn't sure how Scott had done it, but he'd managed to slip into the building and lock the outer door. "I knew I shouldn't have trusted him." Mac stepped back and pumped two bullets into the heavy glass door.

Dana had kicked off her heels and was now screaming into the radio for backup. She gave their positions while waiting for Mac to kick out the shattered glass and unlock the door. "This way." Mac bypassed the elevator, which was moving toward the third floor, and headed for the stairs. Guns drawn, they raced up the stairs. The lobby was empty when they pushed through the door. Watching their backs, they made their way down the wide hall. At Scott's office suite, they stopped at the open door.

The receptionist's office was empty, and the door to Scott's office was slightly ajar.

"You have to believe me, Jackie," Scott pleaded.

Mac and Dana made their way to the office door, one on either side.

"Why, so you can lie to me again? I can't believe I actually thought having Sara killed would make a difference. I should have shot you instead."

"Then shoot me and let Claire go."

"Not a chance. Do you really think I could let either one of you live? I'm thinking a murder-suicide might make a great story for tomorrow's paper."

Mac signaled Dana, fear rising in his chest. They had to move fast and hope none of them would end up dead.

Mac took the lead, opening the door and bursting into the room. "Police! Put the gun down. Now!"

Dana shouted the same warning. She stood to his right, both hands holding her weapon straight out.

Jackie turned and took aim at Scott.

"Get down." Dana's feet left the ground, tackling Scott to the floor seconds before Jackie's gun went off. At the same moment, Mac fired and got a hit, but not before she fired a second time. He felt and heard the bullet zing past his ear.

Mac's stomach felt like it had been turned inside out. By the time their reinforcements arrived, he had called the paramedics. Scott had taken a bullet in the shoulder, and Jackie had taken one in the chest. Claire was still alive, bound with duct tape and lying on the floor in the corner.

Dana removed the restraints, and Claire crawled over to where Scott lay.

"Jackie hired that guy to kill Sara." Claire seemed surprisingly calm as she knelt beside Scott, holding pressure on his wound like Dana had showed her. "She wanted Scott and was willing to do whatever it took to get him. She's crazy. I just don't know why I never noticed before."

Mac wasn't sure he'd call Jackie insane. Cunning, maybe. Scheming, dangerous, evil. Even now, lying on the stretcher, her eyes held contempt.

He felt a hand on his shoulder. "You did good, partner," Kevin said. "You, too, Dana. I'm proud of you both."

The ordeal was over. "I just wish we'd had the information about Jackie's print being in that cabinet earlier. We might have taken a closer look. We might have kept her from abducting Claire." Mac was going through the typical what-if scenarios all cops process after a deadly physical force incident. He would take his place alongside Philly on administrative leave until the case was investigated and the shooting was cleared by a grand jury. He handed his gun and magazines to Kevin and headed for the elevator. Dana put her hand on his shoulder. He had been there for her; now she would do the same. The two friends rode the elevator down without a word.

Dana, Kevin, Russ, and Mac met at a twenty-four-hour restaurant near the office and talked until after midnight. It had taken that long for their adrenaline rush and caffeine high to settle. He smiled at the easy camaraderie they'd had while enjoying their late-night desserts and coffee. During their debriefing, Russ filled them in on Philly's progress. The big guy had checked himself into an inpatient rehab program, where he'd spend the next six weeks getting his life back together again.

At around one, Mac took Dana home. A Vancouver police car reminded them of the stalker who'd been tormenting Dana. "They'll get him," Mac said.

Dana nodded. "I hope so."

MAC AND THE OTHERS WERE BACK TO WORK by eight. He would be grounded in administrative work until his shooting was cleared. He spent most of the day tying up loose ends in the Sara Watson case. Besides the paperwork, Mac had interviews with Internal Affairs and had his blood drawn to prove he wasn't under the influence of any intoxicants during the shooting. He felt bad about having to shoot Jackie, but he was relieved that she had lived through it and would be facing charges. She'd procured an attorney and wasn't telling them anything.

The investigation was over, and the D.A. would have no trouble proving their case against Jackie. They had testimony from Claire and Scott, and they'd even managed to dig up a witness who had seen Jackie talking to Sinnott at the construction site.

Though she hadn't confessed, they'd managed to put the pieces together. Jackie had used the Native American connection with the senator to her advantage, making the murder look like the Confederated Tribes were involved. She likely had given Sara's beaded pouch and stone to Sinnott and instructed him to stuff them in Sara's mouth and then bury her near the reservation. In a search of Jackie's apartment, they'd found articles about the casino dispute as well as a stamp bearing the Tsagagalal insignia, which clearly tied her to the second set of letters.

That night, after a grueling day, Mac steered his car toward Kristen's warm and comfortable home. Dinner the night before had been amazing. After the shooting episode last night, he was in great need of good food and comfort.

Mac felt like things were coming together for him all the way around. He could hardly wait to talk to Kristen about her trip to Florida. He wanted to know where he stood with her, but he wouldn't press it. He wasn't ready to commit to anyone just now anyway. The last thing he wanted to do was leave behind a widow, like Daniel had. And last night had proven once again just how tenuous life for a cop could be.

There was no little torpedo to greet him as he made his way up the walk to Kristen's front door, but then he knew there wouldn't be. Mac missed the little guy already, and it was just for the evening. Kristen had told him that Andrew would be staying with his grandmother so the two of them would have the evening to themselves. On one hand, he was looking forward to it; on the other, he felt like he was walking into a trap.

Kristen met him at the door. Her arms went around his waist as he pulled her close for a kiss.

"I take it we're back to seeing each other." He could already feel the tension draining out of his shoulders.

She nodded. "If you think you can put up with a flake like me."

"What about Brian?"

She stepped back. Head down she closed her eyes. "He died, Mac."

"I'm sorry."

She looked up at him, eyes shiny with tears. "Even if he hadn't, I wouldn't have gone back to him. While I was gone, I did a lot of thinking. I like the way I feel around you. I like the way you care about Andrew."

Mac swallowed hard. "So you want to get married?" He hadn't meant to say that.

She raised an eyebrow and smiled. "No. At least not for a while. We have something special, Mac." She leaned into him, driving his desire off the scale. "I still think we should take it slow."

"OK." Mac didn't want to take it slow. His earlier resolve not to make a commitment melted. Life was too short for slow. But he'd go along with her for now. "How slow?"

"Have you thought any more about your feelings for Dana?" she asked.

"Dana?"

"Your partner." Kristen laughed.

"Not when I'm with you." That much was true. Standing there kissing Kristen, Dana Bennett had been the furthest thing from his mind.

Taking his hand, she led him to the table, which she'd set and decorated with candles, flowers, cloth napkins, and everything they needed for a romantic dinner. A fire glowed in the living room fireplace. Kristen brought out seafood pasta with a lemon pepper cream sauce. She slipped into the chair beside him and took his hand, offering a prayer. After the amen, she placed a napkin on her lap. "Now tell me about the Sara Watson case, and don't leave anything out."

They talked for three hours between kissing sessions, and Mac couldn't remember ever enjoying an evening quite so much. Nana had told him to follow his heart, and it looked like that advice had led him straight to Kristen and Andrew.

Open up the first of The McAllister Files

With his newly minted detective badge firmly in place, "Mac" McAllister reports for his first assignment with the Oregon State Police Department: a particularly gruesome homicide. It's a headline case, as the victim—Megan Tyson—was brutally murdered mere weeks before her wedding.

The investigation and autopsy turn up far too many suspects, and too little hard evidence. Why would the beautiful Megan, engaged to a wealthy businessman, be involved with the seedy lineup of characters who seem connected to her? With more questions than answers, Mac and his partner try to uncover the secrets Megan took to her grave and sort through the lies and alibis before Megan's murderer strikes again.

Not sure that he can trust his instincts, Mac depends heavily on the advice of his partner—a seasoned detective with a strong faith in God. A faith Mac has no use for until he must come to terms with his own past and the secrets that haunt him.

Fiction that reflects the grittiness of real life . . . and the reality of faith.

AVAILABLE WHEREVER BOOKS ARE SOLD
ISBN 1-59145-081-0

Mac Is Back!

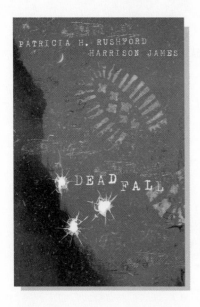

It's been just three months since Detective "Mac" McAllister solved his first homicide case with the Oregon State Police. Now he's working the search for a ski instructor who has mysteriously disappeared. The man's parents claim their son wouldn't have committed suicide, but they suspect his girlfriend of something sinister.

The case gets more complicated when Mac and his partner, Kevin, are called to investigate a gruesome homicide nearby that may or may not be related. A few days later a body turns up in the Columbia River, and the autopsy reveals surprising information about the victim's suspicious death.

When their investigation seems at a dead end, Mac is determined not to let the crimes go unsolved—even if it means putting his life on the line to catch the killer.

Fiction that reflects the grittiness of real life . . . and the reality of faith.

Two dead bodies.
A web of conspiracies
and cover-ups.
A young detective,
searching for answers to the
case . . . and to his heart.

The body of a retired, wheelchair-bound rail yard worker has been discovered on the tracks near his home. A tragic accident—or murder?

Detective Antonio "Mac" McAllister and his new partner, attractive rookie Dana Bennett, suspect the worst. And their suspicions are confirmed when they encounter the complicated web of conspiracies and cover-ups that surround the case, including burglary, arson and yet another murder. Now Mac and Dana need to find the killer before he can destroy any more evidence—or take anyone else's life.

Fiction that reflects the grittiness of
real life . . . and the reality of faith.

BOOKS BY PATRICIA RUSHFORD

THE MCALLISTER FILES
Secrets, Lies & Alibis
Deadfall
Terminal 9
She Who Watches

THE ANGEL DELANEY MYSTERIES
Deadly Aim
Dying to Kill

THE HELEN BRADLEY MYSTERIES
Now I Lay Me Down to Sleep
Red Sky in Mourning
A Haunting Refrain
When Shadows Fall

THE JENNIE MCGRADY MYSTERIES

NON-FICTION
Have You Hugged Your Teenager Today?
What Kids Need Most in a Mom
It Shouldn't Hurt to Be a Kid

For more information, visit Patricia's Web site at
www.patriciarushford.com.

BOOKS BY HARRISON JAMES
THE MCALLISTER FILES
Secrets, Lies & Alibis
Deadfall
Terminal 9
She Who Watches